BECOMING AMERICAN

Callie J. Trautmiller

Praise for *Becoming American*

"Indeed, the smear of injustice forced upon Americans of Japanese descent during World War II was and remains a dark time in United States history. Amazingly, the victims chose honor and immeasurable sacrifice over revenge in their quest to prove their loyalty to the USA. Callie Trautmiller's *Becoming American* is an engaging and important addition to the literature preserving this difficult—and inspiring—time in our history. Highly recommended!"

—Graham Salisbury, Author of multiple award-winning *Under the Blood-Red Sun,* including the Scott O'Dell Award for Historical Fiction

"*Becoming American* is a warmhearted, thought-provoking, and well-researched tale about a chapter in American history that has recently become all too relevant again: the incarceration of Japanese Americans in internment camps during World War II. Readers of all ages will root for young Allu Noguchi and her family as they struggle to survive, while never giving up hope, as prisoners in their own homeland."

—Elizabeth Ridley, Author of five novels and four co-written memoirs, including *Saving Sadie: How a Dog That No One Wanted Inspired the World* (with Joal Derse Dauer), and *Incredibull Stella: How the Love of a Pit Bull Rescued a Family* (with Marika Meeks)

"For those who weren't alive when the Japanese attacked Pearl Harbor in 1941, *Becoming American* makes it real, from the bombs and bullets, death and destruction, and the insane paranoia that followed. Trautmiller brings home the ugly persecution and forced internment endured by Japanese American citizens following the attack."

—Charles M. DuPuy, Author of the E.Z. Kelly mystery series

"Callie Trautmiller skillfully presents a you-are-there description of the attack on Pearl Harbor and the panic of WWII as seen through the eyes of Japanese American teenagers. A must read for those too young to remember."

—C. C. Harrison, Award-winning author of *Death By G-String,* a Coyote Canyon Ladies Ukulele Club mystery

"*Becoming American* tugs at your heart strings and brings tears to your eyes. The story of a Japanese American family during WWII comes to life in this compelling story by Callie Trautmiller. The author carries you back to a not so proud time in American History. It is a story that must be told so we do not forget and will not repeat."

—Flo Parfitt, Author of *Sara's Sacrifice* and other historical fiction

BECOMING AMERICAN

A World War II Young Adult Novel

Callie J. Trautmiller

Written Dreams Publishing

Green Bay, WI 54311

Publishing Editor: Brittiany Koren

Editor: A.L. Mundt

Cover Art Designer: Sunny Fassbender

Interior Layout Designer: Katy Brunette

Category: Young Adult World War II Historical Fiction

Description: *Siblings are sent to a Japanese American internment camp during World War II and find different ways of coping with their circumstances.*

Hardcover ISBN: 978-1-951375-15-7

Paperback ISBN: 978-1-951375-10-2

Ebook ISBN: 978-1-951375-11-9

LOC Catalogue Data: Applied for.

First Edition published by Written Dreams Publishing in October, 2019.

Green Bay, WI 54311

This book is dedicated with love to Freddy, Jada, Jaelyn, and Sterling and with the utmost respect to those courageous men and women who served and continue to serve our country in the United States military—most notably the 100th Infantry and 442nd Infantry Regiment from whom this book was inspired, and the thousands of Japanese Americans whose lives were disrupted by Executive Order 9066.

Prologue

"Allu-chan!"

Cold fingers clutched her arm, followed by the thud of feet hitting the floorboards. As far as Allu Noguchi could tell, it was still dark outside. She rubbed her eyes wearily as her mother pulled her from the bed.

"Get up!" Mama cried. "It's time!"

Allu forced her eyes open as the words hit her full force and her fear lurched to her stomach. She'd known this day was coming, but now that it was here, a sheer panic settled in, squeezing her heart tight, threatening to choke out any air from her throat or hope that remained.

"Where's Robbie?" Allu asked.

"Downstairs," Mama said. "Hurry. Grab your bag!"

She dressed quickly, taking one last look around her room. Her beautiful bedroom with sunny walls that had been painted yellow the summer before and floral curtains she had begged Mama to make. Stripped down, it could have been any girl's room, and Allu imagined important men in suits walking through it, saying to themselves, "This was a mistake. This girl is just like mine. She can't be the enemy. Look, she likes to paint. She even made her bed."

And how silly it was, that she had made her bed as if she would return after some vacation. A beach vacation, perhaps—

"Allu!" Mama's voice cut through her thoughts.

Without another glance, she flicked off the lights and hurried to where her family waited.

Chapter One

Santa Ana, California

November, 1941

Allu Noguchi turned the seashells over in her hand, blowing remnants of stubborn sand from the hollows as she traced the rigid markings the ocean had left upon their surface. It was the point of the morning when the sun met the sky with an orange glow—hard to imagine there was a war happening on the other side of the world.

"They're beauties," Mama said as she dumped the seashells on the weathered floorboards.

Built several years ago from leftover wood Papa had collected from the hardware store's scrap pile, the porch, at one time, had been constructed better than a tree fort. It was Allu's favorite part of the house, and her primary sleeping place on summer nights when Mama draped cotton sheets from the rafters, transforming it into the mast of a large ship. Under a blanket of stars, she'd sail the oceans in search of new lands and faces forgotten by time.

But that had been back when she was a kid, and the railings had still been white. Before the wood had yellowed into a dirty cream, peeling away from the boards from years of neglect, as if the house were shedding a layer of skin.

Allu was much too old for make-believe now. But still, every so often she'd take the memory out and play it in her mind, as if it had been magically bottled and carefully labeled as an important piece of her past.

"Mind your manners now, understand?" Mama said as she threw a warning glance Allu's way. She pushed her large body through the screen door, balancing a load of laundry on her hip as she made her way to the clothesline. Her brown eyes darted to the black dust peppered across Allu's skirt. She shook her head but said nothing. "Make yourself useful and feed the chickens before you go."

Allu wanted to remind her it wasn't her turn, but Mama was already halfway across the yard, and she knew it was a losing battle. Mama was not a woman to be crossed.

"Robbie!" Allu yelled, cupping her hands around her mouth.

She heard a hard crack from somewhere behind the shed. It was just like Robbie to avoid responsibility and find something better to do. Not just something better, but *baseball*. Baseball made it alright. At least according to their parents. Maybe because it made them blend in more with their neighbors. Or maybe because her father wished he'd had the chance to play sports. Either way, somehow baseball trumped everything in their parents' eyes and Robbie knew it.

He flashed a grin when he noticed her stomping over, his dark brown eyes full of mischief. At seventeen, Robbie towered a few inches over Papa. "Ma, you've shrunk," he said sarcastically and smirked, hitting another ball.

The sun had been good to him and his cheeks flushed just enough color against his tan face to show the hours of practice in the sun.

"Your turn to feed the chickens," Allu said, shoving a bucket of seed toward him. "And I need a ride home from school today."

He raised his eyebrows and ran a hand through his dark hair. "Where are your manners, little sister? You mean, please. *Please, dear Robbie, give me a ride home from school today,*" he said, clasping his hands to his heart in mock admiration.

He'd refused the seed, so Allu set it down at his feet, then clenched her fists, her face getting hot.

"*Or,*" he continued with a shrug, "you could drive yourself." He tossed the ball to her. "*On your bike.*"

Allu caught the ball, then sucked in a breath. She wanted to wipe the grin off his face, if only she could reach it. She pulled her fist back and went for his arm instead.

"Nice one," he nodded, toeing the bat on the ground and lifting it to his hand. "That'll be sure to make you popular with the fellas someday."

Mama would disapprove, but she didn't care. He had it coming, and Mama wasn't watching. Neither were any boys from school. Robbie was a lot of things, but one thing he wasn't, was a snitch.

"Bus!" their mother's voice called from the other side of the shed. With his other hand, Robbie grabbed the pail of seed.

"Three-thirty, Robbie. Front of school. Got it?" Allu asked.

"Yeah, yeah," he said. "Three-thirty. But you get the back seat, okay?

I don't need you cramping my style."

She nodded in agreement and turned toward the house. What was it all the girls saw in him? He could be a real jerk. Nonetheless, she could hear the clanking of the bucket as Robbie made his way to the shed behind her. At least the chickens would get fed.

Chapter Two

Allu found her best friend, Lucille, perched in her usual spot on the cement slab outside of the school, surrounded by a small group of girls, hanging on her every word. By the exaggerated looks on their faces, they were deep in conversation. One thing about Lucille—she never had a shortage of friends. Allu often wondered if it was because she came from an upstanding family, or if it was because she always had an opinion on something. Surely, it didn't hurt that her father was on the board for almost every school function and was an insurance salesman, by trade. She always wore the latest styles, buying her popularity.

Not that Allu was jealous—it just seemed to be discrimination—for some kids to be born to parents who happened to know the right people or *be* one of the right people, while other kids were left to follow or try their best to go unnoticed in the crowd.

Allu saw *those people* all the time—serving on the baseball boards, school boards, belonging to supper clubs. And at one time, she was even foolish enough to believe her family could become *those* people, too, and went so far as to ask her mother if she wanted to be on any committees at school.

Her mother's eyes had widened. "Oh, no," she said, adamantly shaking her head. "You didn't write our names down, did you?"

"No, Mama."

Her mother's shoulders had dropped in relief when she realized she hadn't. "No time for that, Allu," she'd muttered as if it was an after-thought.

Allu suspected it ran much deeper than not having enough time.

"Allu!" Lucille waved her over and within seconds, six faces were watching her. One of the older blondes whose name Allu had forgotten, scanned her pink dress and whispered something to the girl next to her, who broke out in giggles.

Allu's heart beat faster. Her mother had made the dress, insisting on the white polka dots. She begged for the one in the store window, but Mama had said she could make the same thing for less. Mama would never understand. Sometimes she felt they were raised worlds apart.

What would Robbie do?

Allu forced a smile and pulled her shoulders back as she approached the group. If Lucille noticed her dress, she mentioned nothing of it, but instead motioned for Allu to sit beside her.

"We were deciding whether or not Miss Rose colored her hair. It seems different. What do you think?" Lucille asked.

The blonde narrowed her eyes, smacking her gum.

"Definitely," Allu said, agreeing. She smoothed her dress and took a seat beside her friend.

There was a slight pause, the weight of decision resting on Lucille's reaction.

"Yes!" Lucille clasped her hands together. "That's what we were thinking."

If the other girls disagreed, they said nothing.

"Anyway," Lucille said, lowering her voice, "yesterday, she was talking about the war and burst out crying. I heard she has a British sweetheart overseas fighting the Nazis. Father says it's just a matter of time before we're all at war…"

Miss Rose had cried in Allu's class as well. Allu wondered if maybe she should start teaching something other than world events. Like math. No one ever cried over math. Crying aside, Miss Rose was by far Allu's favorite teacher. Not because she was beautiful and changed her hair often, but because she liked to give hugs *and* let kids chew gum in class. She didn't care what you looked like or who your father was. She gave everyone gum. Or hugs.

"*Just ask her,*" one of the other girls said.

Allu realized all eyes were on her. Again. *Were they still talking about Miss Rose? Nazis? Miss Rose surely wasn't a Nazi.*

"What do you think about all the *Japanese* workers taking over jobs in California?" It was the same blonde. She waited with expectant eyes for Allu's answer.

But the words were a slap in her face. Allu tugged at her dark hair. "I guess I don't know."

"Well, you *are* Japanese, aren't you?" another girl asked.

Allu's cheeks burned. She'd never been asked that before. Ever. Her grandparents were from Japan, but she knew nothing of the place other than some of the songs Father sang when they picked fruit in the orchard. Sometimes, Mama spoke Japanese when she was angry, but Allu had no idea what she was saying, though she suspected they were not words for her ears.

"She's American," Lucille's voice cut in, to her relief.

"Right, Allu?" Lucille faced her. "You live in America, so that makes you *American,* doesn't it?"

Allu quickly nodded, suddenly grateful for Lucille's loud opinions, so long as she fell on the right side of them. "Yes," she stammered. "I'm American."

But this time, she suspected not even Lucille could sway the others.

***

All day long, Allu felt as though there were some rumor about her going around. Something she didn't know but should. Like maybe her name was written in the bathroom, or something. Miss Rose was the only one who didn't look at her with suspicion, but then again, she was too busy crying. Poor woman.

Allu slipped into Robbie's car after school. It didn't even bother her that he was five minutes late or that he parked close enough for the other kids to see the rust on the side of the door.

"Rough day?" Robbie asked, peeling out of the parking lot. He gave her a look of concern.

"It's just the war," she lied, giving a shrug.

"I know what you mean. It's on everyone's minds these days." He focused on the road. "I know some guys who are enlisting."

"What?" Allu asked, shocked. The war was happening so far away and seemed removed from their part of the world.

"Why not? I mean, why wouldn't you help your country?"

But was it *their* country? It sure didn't feel like it lately, not to her. Allu's mind swirled with confusion as they pulled in next to Mr. Benson's hardware store.

"Five minutes, okay?" Robbie's voice was distant in her ears.

Old Mr. Benson looked at her funny with his beady eyes as she pushed her way through the heavy glass door. He was tall, with thin wisps of white hair, combed to the side of a balding head. He wore small spectacles that balanced a little imperfectly on the edge of his sharp nose. Allu could never see through the smudged lenses fully enough to see the color of his eyes, not that she'd want to.

Now, he scrutinized her with pursed lips. Did he ever smile? She felt his eyes on her and quickened her pace to the birdseed aisle. Why *was* he watching her? Five years she'd been coming here and she'd never noticed him watching her so closely.

Allu glanced over her shoulder, but now Mr. Benson was busy stocking cans on a shelf in another aisle.

Do it for the birds, she reminded herself. The birds in her backyard were the closest things she had as a pet, besides the noisy chickens. Like Papa, she had become familiar with California clapper rails, orioles of all variations, and her favorite, the lazuli bunting, a blue-headed beauty with an orange breast to alert the world it belonged here.

On quiet evenings, she'd often go bird-watching with Papa. They'd walk down the rows of green beans and sugar snap peas, admiring the delicate pink blossoms that popped open after tender days of rain, then suck the juices from the rinds of small oranges Mama had packed for them. They'd make their way to their sitting tree, where Papa would whistle melodies that had been passed down from the older generations of family who had lived in Japan, and there, he'd rest against the trunk with his hat pulled down over his eyes.

"Looks good, Allu-chan," he said, stealing a glance at her sketchbook as she sat cross-legged next to the tree, her plaid dress smoothed beneath a bird book. "You're going to make a fine artist one day. How about if you add a streak here?"

"Oh, Papa…"

Allu filed away the memory and pulled the bag of sunflower seed from the store shelf, propping it on her shoulder as she had often seen Papa do. She wanted the day to be over. To be in her bed, with Mama's quilt tucked under her chin. To be safe in a place where it didn't matter what she looked like or who she was. Or if she wore polka-dots or flowers.

Mr. Benson pecked his bony fingers noisily on the register as she dropped the bag on the counter. "Two fifty," he said.

She handed him the money she'd saved from helping Papa. He dropped the coins in his drawer.

"Your father going to be at the market Saturday?" His voice was stern as he peered at her through dusty glasses.

"Yes, sir," Allu said hesitantly, fixing her gaze on the counter. She wanted to run out, but Mama's consequences for being rude were much greater than any look Mr. Benson could give her. Besides, Robbie would tease her for being paranoid.

"Good," he said, ripping the receipt off the reel. "I need vegetables and there's no one who can grow them better than him."

Chapter Three

Santa Ana, California

From where the ball field was situated, Robbie could smell the saltiness of the ocean as it lingered in the air. It gave a sort of freshness to the day, as if anything were possible. *Who knew?* Maybe he'd get a home run this game.

He stood near the batting cage and practiced his swing, pausing long enough to wink at a group of girls whispering amongst themselves in the stands, sending them into a fit of giggles. He still had it, but only one girl piqued his interest. He raised his arms back until he could feel the weight of the bat shift behind his head and extended his arms out, coming down into a full swing. Yes, it was a good day for home runs.

"I hear there's a few scouts in the crowd today," boomed a loud voice.

"Good," Robbie called back to his best friend, Jimmy. "Hope they're ready for a show."

"Yeah, well, Jack's old man called them, so you'll have to make sure you get that home run to get their attention off of the *golden child.*"

One thing about Jimmy was he didn't sugar-coat things. Not usually, anyway. Jack was an okay guy, and an even more average player, but he thought he had the cat by the tail being the banker's son. His old man didn't look like he'd run a day in his life, but he was an expert on baseball if you'd ask him—though no one ever did.

"Well, UCLA doesn't take anyone." Jimmy spit sunflower seed shells into the dirt. "You can't just have talent; you gotta have the smarts, too."

Robbie pulled his bat back once again. "Looks like that excludes you then, doesn't it?"

His friend laughed. "Have to have money, too, which of course, excludes you."

Now they both laughed. Neither of their families had any money. Jimmy's old man was a mechanic and a drunk. A drunk first. And he'd never approve of Jimmy hanging around with Robbie, but then again, he was never around to notice. Truth be told, he didn't know much about his son other than the fact he had cropped brown hair, with matching eyes and a somewhat large nose. Hell, his old man probably gave him the large nose.

Both Robbie and Jimmy were hell of ball players, though. The thing about not having a silver spoon shoved in your mouth was that you had to work for what you wanted—they had that in common.

"Batter up!" called the umpire.

Robbie flashed his buddy a grin before stepping to the plate.

A loud crack filled the air.

The crowd jumped to its feet as they watched the ball fly deep into left field, the bleachers a mixture of clapping and hooting.

Robbie pushed forward as the left-fielder frantically chased after the ball to the outskirts of the field. By the time the ball was in the player's hand, Robbie was already rounding second base and not slowing down.

Sliding into third, he stood up with a smile and glanced toward the bleachers to make sure *she* was watching.

With lips the color of cherries, Daisy Hammon was a force to be reckoned with, and unlike any other girls at S.A. High. She blew him a kiss, and for a second, Robbie forgot he still had to make it to home plate.

***

"Oh, come on, Robbie," Jimmy pleaded after the game, tossing a ball casually at Robbie's chest. "I'm dying for a burger. Plus, there might be some gals there."

"I don't think today works," Robbie said, giving a quick glance toward the bleachers before returning his focus to his bat bag. Susie had left, leaving Daisy and Dee, who were taking turns passing a hand mirror back and forth as they touched up their faces.

Jimmy eyed him suspiciously, then craned his neck around the wall of the dugout to see what had robbed him of Robbie's commitment. "Oh, I see," he said with a smirk. "I'm competing with Daisy Hammon."

Robbie felt his cheeks burn.

"I knew it! That's it, isn't it?" Jimmy socked him in the arm. "Dee's spoken for, and Daisy's the only other gal up there. *Unless...*" He paused, tilting his head mockingly. "There's a chance you're sweet on

Mr. Perkins."

As if overhearing their conversation, the older man stopped sweeping the bleachers and tipped his hat to them.

Robbie slugged Jimmy in the arm. "Odds would be better with Mr. Perkins," he said, zipping up his bag.

"Say it ain't so!" Jimmy dropped to his knees, throwing his hands to his chest. "Robbie's in love? Either that, or he has a death wish."

"You're a real treat, Jimmy. A real treat." Robbie slung his bag over his shoulder, wincing slightly at the ache in his right arm. He wondered briefly how many throws he had left in it.

"Look, just go talk to her. If she didn't want to talk to you, she would have freshened up in the car or ladies' room. Besides, I don't see Calvin or the ugly crew."

"Think so?"

"Look, you know baseball and I know girls. We can't all be as talented as you." He shrugged. "I make up for it in other places."

"Like with your sisters?" Robbie laughed, shielding his chest from Jimmy's swing.

Having three older sisters, women didn't intimidate Jimmy the way they did other guys. Hell, there wasn't even much that scared him. He'd seen it all, but based on what he said, Robbie thought there were quite a few reasons to fear them. But that didn't stop Jimmy. It was the rare occasion he lacked the company of at least one pretty face. This week, it just so happened the pretty face belonged to Dee. And Dee was best friends with Daisy Hammon, the prettiest girl in school—who, until recently, had been dating Calvin Jensen.

"I'll tell you what," Jimmy said. "You can follow my lead."

"Jimmy, I…"

Too late. He was already jogging across the field.

Robbie watched the girls erupt into giggles. What the hell was he saying? He wasn't even that funny. Robbie unzipped his bat bag and reassembled its contents.

"Robbie!" Jimmy's voice called out as he waved him over.

He grabbed a mint from his pocket, hastily shoving it in his mouth. He could feel Daisy's eyes watching him as he made his way across the field. Robbie hoped he didn't smell too sweaty. He didn't know whether to hit Jimmy or hug him.

"The girls here were wondering if we'd want to catch a movie at the drive-in." Jimmy raised his eyebrows, clearly proud of his efforts. "I told them we'd have to turn down a few other gals first."

"I seem to remember *you* asking *us*," Dee said, slapping him gently on the arm.

"Only reading your mind," Jimmy said with a wink. "Thought I'd save you the uncomfortable risk of being rejected."

"Oh, thank you." Dee put her hand up to her cheek and batted her dark lashes in exaggeration.

She was pretty in her own way, with soft brown curls and innocent doe-like eyes. Definitely Jimmy's type.

"How could we *ever* repay you for being so generous as to be seen with a couple of girls as pitiful as us?" Dee asked.

"Oh, I can think of ways." Jimmy smirked.

Robbie waited for her slap across his face, but she swatted at his friend affectionately instead. *Only Jimmy.*

"So," Robbie said, turning his attention to Daisy. What should he say? He was fairly sure Jimmy's slick lines wouldn't work with her. But then again, she *had* dated Calvin.

She blinked at him. "So?"

He realized he'd never been this close to her before. Hell, the closest he'd ever gotten was in sixth grade when he had been paired with her for science. He wished his tongue wasn't so tied.

"So, Jimmy asked us out, but he doesn't seem too interested in *me*," Daisy said, raising her eyebrows as she watched him carefully. Her eyes had a mysterious depth in them that reminded Robbie of swimming in the ocean—a shade of blue shallow waters that flirted with dangerous depths.

"I suppose we could make it a double." Robbie tried to sound casual, smiling just enough to expose his dimples, which he'd been told by a few gals were his greatest asset. Jimmy and Dee were laughing, probably involved in some ridiculous hand-swatting battle or something.

"I suppose we could," Daisy said matter-of-factly. She gently brushed her hand along his cheek and instantly, a rush of excitement swept through his body, threatening to explode him into a million pieces. "You, by the way, look absolutely darling in red." *Swell.* Was he blushing?

And all the while, her lips of red taunted him to lean in right there, right now and kiss her. Even as her cat-like eyes flashed warnings.

"Pick you up at seven?" he asked, trying to play it cool.

A slow smile played across her lips. "I'll be waiting."

***

"Which girl is it tonight, Robbie?" Allu taunted, taking a sip of lemonade as he checked his watch for the third time that evening.

Robbie glared at her. "And why would you think I'm waiting on a girl? What do you know about dating?"

She shrugged. "Enough to know you put beeswax in your hair. *And* you're wearing church clothes."

He looked down at his tan khaki pants and polo shirt, suddenly wondering if he was overdressed.

"Don't get too overinflated, but you look like a regular handsome chap." Allu took another sip of lemonade, settling into Mama's rocking chair on the front porch. "I hardly recognized you."

"Is that so?" He jumped across the porch and wrapped his arm around her neck.

"Robbie!" she squealed. "Stop. I take it back!"

He let her go, a smirk on his lips. "You're not too bad, sis. I've seen worse."

Allu smiled, knowing it was his way of giving her a compliment.

***

The drive-in was busy, even for a Saturday night. Rows and rows of Chevys and Fords lined up, tops down as girls laughed with their girlfriends and young men hung over lifted hoods, inspecting each other's engines.

"Geez, Jimmy," Robbie said. "Do you think you could drive any slower?" His Chrysler New Yorker was a real beauty, but still.

"This gravel is hell on a paint job," Jimmy replied. "They ought to pave this whole damn thing." He had saved three years for the car, working mostly odd jobs. The steadiest thing he'd ever had in his life was detention after school. It was amazing he had a social life outside of it. But apparently, he was attracted to shiny blue things enough to save his money. It was an assumed fact that he'd do all the driving after that as long as Robbie kicked him a few bucks here and there for gasoline. They agreed it was better than being seen in the old thing Robbie's family owned.

After what seemed like endless minutes of slow-paced rolling along, Jimmy chose a spot at the edge of the lot, away from the other vehicles.

"Gee, Jimmy." Dee poked his side. "Do you think we're too close? I wouldn't want to hurt my eyes and land myself with glasses."

"I think you'd look mighty fine with glasses," Jimmy teased, putting the car in park. "In fact, I kind of like a girl with glasses. Lends a certain kind of sophistication, you know?"

"Or maybe they're just embarrassed to be seen with us." Daisy shifted her eyes to watch Robbie's reaction.

"Why are we parked so far away anyway? Worried someone might look at your car the wrong way?" he asked, leaning over the front seat.

"Look," Jimmy said, pulling a soft cloth out of the glovebox. He began to wipe the gravel dust from the dash. "Get off my case or next time, *you* can drive."

The girls giggled.

"I'm sorry, Dee," Robbie said, slipping his arm around Daisy, who he pulled in closer. "I should've warned you that you'd be competing with the car tonight for Jimmy's attention."

Finding his courage, he turned to Daisy. "Why don't we give Dee a fighting chance and get some popcorn?"

Daisy bobbed her head in agreement and they quickly exited the car.

"Oh, dear God! I thought we'd never get away from them," Daisy exclaimed once they were out of earshot. She slid her arm through Robbie's, and a twinge of excitement ran along his spine. "Jimmy's all she ever talks about. It's Jimmy this, and Jimmy that! '*Jimmy wore a hat today, isn't it cute? Jimmy likes pepperoni pizza, isn't he dapper?*'"

Robbie laughed, knowing there was someone else out there who found his friend's tactics just as annoying as he did. But then again, he did owe Jimmy one. If it had been left up to him, he'd be with the chickens right now. He felt Daisy's hand tighten on his arm.

"I'm not hungry after all," she said.

"Really?" he glanced at her, but she was looking ahead, her face serious. He followed her gaze but didn't notice anything unusual. Just a line for concessions. "Daisy, what is it?"

She dropped her hand from his arm and turned away. "It's nothing," she said, trying to sound casual. "I just want to go back to the car is all."

Robbie didn't know what else to do. "Alright, if you're sure."

They walked in silence as he tried to figure out what had happened. Was it him? He'd always been smooth with the gals. He replayed their conversation and decided she was too important not to know.

"Say, Daisy—" He stopped when he saw Jimmy and Dee standing near the car, the looks on their shocked faces astounding as they studied the car.

"Jimmy, what's going on?" Robbie asked, rushing to his friend's side.

"*What's* going on?" Jimmy's twisted face was the only visible part of him as he squatted on the passenger side, scrubbing frantically.

Dee hesitated. "Someone keyed his car."

"What? When?" Robbie asked. When they'd left, Jimmy and Dee were still in the car.

"We just stepped away for a minute. Dumb luck, I guess," Jimmy said.

Robbie took a closer look, his adrenaline pumping at the thought of a good fight. That car meant everything to Jimmy. When he found out who did this, he was going to knock him into next week.

Jimmy stood up in front of him and put a hand on Robbie's chest, stopping him in his tracks. There was a look on Jimmy's face that he couldn't quite figure out. He was hiding something.

"What is it?" he asked, trying to sidestep him.

"Let's go," Jimmy said.

"Look, Jimmy, you're not making any sense. It can't be that bad. Nothing your old man can't buffer out."

"I'm telling you, it's no big deal. Let's take a walk."

Robbie wouldn't back down. The hell if his best friend was going to stop him from seeing what was going on. It was probably a rival ball player, carving their emblem on the car or something stupid from a fellow kid in detention.

"You're overreacting," Robbie said, shoving past his friend as Dee and Daisy whispered amongst themselves. What could possibly be so terrible about a keyed car door that would leave Jimmy so rattled?

And then he saw it.

For a minute, he couldn't say anything. They stood in silence, watching him for his reaction.

Daisy put a hand on his shoulder. "Robbie?" she asked, her voice wavering. "Are you alright?"

He could feel the burning knot in his stomach moving to his face. He wanted to lash out. To fight. *Who did this?* That's what he needed to know. *Who the hell did this?*

Go back to Japan was scrawled in ugly scratches across the door.

***

"I should've known," Daisy said. "It was Calvin. I know it. Who else would do that?"

The moon was set high in the dark night and the evening air had a chill coming off the ocean. Robbie's shock had calmed into something deeper and more resonating. Something buried within his soul that didn't belong there but was there just the same.

"I saw his car," she said quietly. "Calvin's."

Robbie turned to face her. Even in the darkness, her eyes sparkled. "Where?"

She sighed. "By the concession stand. I knew it right away. I should've said something, but I didn't want any trouble. He can be…well, you know how he can be."

Yes, Robbie knew how Calvin Jensen could be. Everyone did. The fist fights behind the school in evenings usually involved him. Break-ins around town or smashed windows usually came with rumors swirling about Calvin and his gang.

"Anyway, this place is pretty," she said.

"It is," he said, looking around. Several gardens and pathways separated the water from the playgrounds and ball fields. He never remembered anything from the park besides the ball fields he played on as a kid. Still, there was Calvin. He couldn't take his mind off of what happened. How could he and Jimmy ever stand a chance?

But something had to be done. He'd vandalized his buddy's car and it had nothing to do with him. No, this was personal.

Robbie glanced over his shoulder.

"Oh, they're fine," Daisy said, her voice soft, low.

He shook off his paranoia. Surely Calvin hadn't followed them.

She locked eyes with him. "It's not your fault, you know."

Robbie's jaw began to pulsate. He was angry. "Like I said," she said, smiling, trying to dispel his mood, "you look great in red."

She leaned in, pressing her body close to his. She was inches away from him, waiting and watching with eyes that could hurt. Eyes that could taunt him and twist him into a wasted nothingness before discarding him into the depths. Everyone knew it. Everyone knew that associating with Daisy came with consequences.

And yet, he had waited for this. Imagined it. The night was already messed up enough. Why not mess it up more and dive in all the way to proclaim to the world he could be as reckless as he wanted? He could play in the water without getting hurt.

He tilted her chin up and without hesitation, pressed his lips gently to hers.

Chapter Four

Oahu, Hawaii

December 7, 1941

Circling high above, the island was in plain view, a diamond-shaped mass of emerald green surrounded by clear teal waters of varying shades.

He'd anticipated this moment and now it was finally here.

He lowered the lever as he approached the island, careful to clear the Waianae Mountain Range that lay ahead on the west side of the island. The range had several ridges extended from its spine as it sloped downward into a plateau that stretched across the island before giving way to the Koolau Range on the east. The valleys created by these ridges were stunning, the precipitous cliffs ideal for lookouts on the ocean. Nestled between the two ranges was an expanse of civilization, of natives and army and navy bases. It was a nest protected by nature's natural fortress of the four million-year-old mountains.

He knew the island well. He'd studied the pictures, memorized the maps. But to see it with his own eyes gave more significance to its value. It was beautiful, yes, but beauty wasn't what made it important—important enough to risk everything.

Wheeler Field lay stretched before him, along with the Schofield Army Barracks. Pearl Harbor was approximately ten miles away.

He sucked in a slow calming breath before pointing the nose of his plane downward.

The small rectangular shapes of the barracks slowly grew in size, larger and larger until he flew low enough to see their windows and the shadow of his own wings spreading across the buildings like a predatory bird.

Close to two hundred American planes stood in the field before him, their silver bodies shining in the early morning sun. The island was still asleep.

He glanced to his right, then to his left. Japanese fighter planes and torpedo bombers flew behind him, ready and waiting.

***

Santa Ana, California

December 7, 1941

The yelling grew louder and she didn't recognize the voices. Allu set down her paintbrush. Something was wrong. *Very wrong.* A feeling took hold of her, deep in her gut. *Please, not Papa.*

She prayed it wasn't the crop machines. The feeling in her gut grew. Especially the combine. Just last year, she'd heard a story of a farmer whose sleeve got caught in the combine. His poor wife had tried to pull him free but was no match for the sharp teeth of a hungry machine.

Allu ran down the stairs, her feet heavy.

Mama sat at the table with her hand over her mouth, Papa beside her. The relief lasted only momentarily—their silence magnified by faces twisted in fear.

"What is it?" she asked, her voice cracking. "Mama, what is it?"

Mama's eyes hid a thousand words. Papa put a hand on Allu's shoulder, and she realized the erratic voice was coming from the radio, slicing through the thickness in the room with sharp, angry words.

What were they talking about? What did it mean? She heard the word *bomb* and started to panic.

"Allu-chan, go help Robbie with the chickens," Papa said, his voice insistent and steady, his eyes fixated on the silver radio.

"But—"

"Allu-chan," Mama snapped. "Now."

Without a backwards glance, Allu moved.

Opening the large seed bag, she scooped a hefty handful into the bucket before finding the chickens. *Where was Robbie? What was going on?* No one ever acknowledged she was almost a teenager.

She watched as the feathered creatures noisily squabbled over each other to reach the seed she had scattered around the coop and wondered if they could ever survive on their own.

She was still throwing seed at the ground when she noticed Robbie pacing the side of the house, stopping every once and a while to cock his head to the open kitchen window. His face had a look of concern as he frantically ran his fingers through his hair.

He caught sight of her and placed his finger over his mouth to silence her.

"It's not respectful to eavesdrop," she whispered, approaching him.

He narrowed his eyes at her.

"What's going on?" Allu asked, and stretched herself up on her tiptoes so she could peer inside the window.

"Quiet!"

"Robbie?" she whispered louder.

"We're under attack," he snapped, running his fingers through his hair again. "There. Happy now?" He seemed to regret the words as soon as they came out of his mouth.

Allu tried to bridge the gap between what he said and what she felt. "Under *attack*?"

She waited for him to start laughing or mess her hair up like he did after one of his pranks. Instead, he turned his attention to the window.

"Robbie?"

"What?" he asked, irritated.

"Papa wanted us to feed the chickens," she said quietly. Dumb, yes, but it was all she could think of. The only normalcy about that morning.

A blank look crossed his face.

"*Feed the chickens?*" he erupted. "I don't give a *flying shit* about the chickens! Have you even heard of Pearl Harbor?"

Pearl Harbor. She'd heard about it. Wasn't that where Papa fished? No, that was a different harbor. "Of course, I have," she lied.

"Right," he said incredulously. "But, do you even know *where* Pearl Harbor is?"

Allu shook her head.

"*Hawaii,* Allu. Pearl Harbor is in Hawaii. And where do we live?" He accentuated every word, as if she couldn't possibly understand. He interrogated her with his eyes. "California. *We* live in California. Have you heard of the things the Imperial Japanese Army does to people? What they did in China? I have to get ahold of Jimmy."

Allu opened her mouth, but nothing came out. What questions should she ask? *How far was Hawaii from here? What did it all mean?*

Robbie's next words shook her the most.

"Allu-chan, be careful… We may be next."

Chapter Five

Pearl Harbor, Oahu, Hawaii

December 7, 1941

Japanese torpedo bombers covered the sky, blocking the sun. The second wave of the Imperial Navy was here. Twenty-four-year-old Private Yukio Takahashi ran hard, praying he could avoid the bombs and torpedoes that blasted all around him.

He looked up, and for a brief moment, locked eyes with a Japanese pilot. Within seconds, dirt sprayed his face and a flash of heat engulfed his body as an explosion filled his ears and lit fire to his right.

A surge of panic filled his body. *Battleship Row.* He had to make it to Battleship Row. How far away was he? Two miles? Three?

Something hit his leg and he cried out in pain. *Shrapnel?*

Searching frantically, he spotted something left of a cement military storage building about twenty yards out. He needed cover from the rain of bullets and explosives.

Yukio glanced quickly to the sky, weighing his odds, but there was no time to think. Act now. Pray. Think later.

He ran through the smoke for the building, diverting debris he couldn't see until it was right in front of him, keeping one hand on his gun.

The loud humming of Japanese fighter planes sounded above him, their ominous shadows covering his beloved island. The first wave had sounded sirens just after sunup. It was Sunday morning. The sirens could only signal an attack.

When he reached the building, it was dark inside. Piles of rubble covered the floor. The gunshots, explosions, and yelling of men were more prevalent as they weren't drowned out by the closer threat of staying alive.

Quickly, he rolled up the leg of his pants, a red, wet line trickling down his shin.

Something had sliced through his skin, but not shrapnel. Shrapnel wouldn't have allowed him to put weight on it. Yukio ripped a piece of cloth from his shirt and wrapped it tight around his leg.

Thoughts filled his mind in fragmented splinters. How could this be happening? Wheeler Field was on fire. Hundreds of unprotected American aircrafts were in flames. He thought of a few buddies who were pilots, and prayed they were safe.

The war alert had just been lifted. Pearl Harbor was one of the strongest fortresses in the world. Japan *couldn't* win. They'd destroy the United States.

Gut-wrenching fear punched him in the stomach. The Imperial Army didn't go easy on their victims. He'd read what their soldiers had done to innocent families in conquered Chinese towns. How could they be *here*?

Mother? Father? Grandfather? Oh God, please be safe. Grandfather had been through so much already, working the sugar plantations like most other Japanese immigrants.

Gaman. Quiet endurance, Yukio reminded himself. "Be patient in the little things," he'd say. "Learn to bear the everyday trials and annoyances of life quietly and calmly, and then when unforeseen trouble or calamity comes, your strength will not forsake you." Grandfather was a survivor. Surely, he was fine.

Battleship Row. He checked his gun and exhaled sharply as he crouched low and exited the building.

Smoke instantly filled his lungs and burned his eyes. He couldn't see. Something exploded within a few feet of him. *Where?*

He ran through the smoke, under the shadows of the Japanese dive bombers, torpedo bombers, and fighter planes, their ominous red circle symbols visible between belches of smoke. Yukio could hardly see where the machine gun noise was coming from, or where the bombing was hitting or just how close it was to him.

But he knew the island.

He had been born here and served the Hawaiian National Guard well. One year left. One year, and he was out.

The explosions were getting louder and more frequent as he got closer to the harbor. Dive bombers shrieked through the air in front of him, low enough to skirt the tops of buildings and easily target him. But it wasn't him they were after. It was the many ships that sat in the harbor. Ships full of men. American sailors, of the U.S. Navy and Marines. His friends.

31

A thunderous crack sliced through the sky. Billows of black smoke poured out from the waters ahead of him. The smell of burning oil filled his senses and his skin burned from the heat of the flames surrounding him.

Civilians were frantically driving their cars off the streets and away from the chaos as military police in jeeps shouted orders of evacuation. "To the sugarcane fields!" a soldier ordered over the noise. "Hide in the fields!"

The cars were diverted to the northern part of the island, away from the attack.

A loud noise shrieked before him, drowning out the bomber planes and causing him to instinctively drop to his knees. Tears stung his eyes. There was a blinding flash of light, followed by the booming noise of explosions.

"The Arizona!" someone yelled. "It's on fire!"

Yukio glanced in the man's direction. *Couldn't be.* The *U.S.S. Arizona* was indestructible. Everyone knew that.

Crowds of civilians fled past him, away from the harbor as he ran toward it. It was hard to tell where the land stopped and the water began. Ford Island, the harbor of ships and water alike, were covered in flames and smoke. He gasped in disbelief.

The *Arizona*, engulfed in flames, was sinking. Ten-thousand pounds of steel lit on fire, was sinking. And the men. God, the men! Hundreds of men must've been inside the ship asleep when it was hit.

The deck of the nearby *Oklahoma* was a frenzy of sailors manning their stations. Anti-aircraft guns were being fired at the Japanese bomber planes, sending a volley of fire, but there were too many and they were too high above in the sky. And all the while, the sailors were being hit by a shower of bullets.

Men shouted. A uniformed officer jumped from the flames of the ship into a flaming pool of oil-filled water below.

Private Yukio watched in horror as nausea overwhelmed him.

For a moment, all seemed lost. Japan was taking over the world.

He heard a scream coming from the water as a wounded sailor struggled to swim to shore.

Without hesitation, Yukio tossed his gun to the ground and jumped into the debris-filled water. He swam hard, pushing past floating bodies, trying not to look at the burned faces of the dead. The water sent chills throughout his body and added weight to his uniform, making it more difficult to swim as the cloth clung to his legs and arms.

He'd reached Battleship Row. His orders were to save who was left of the living.

But first he'd have to find them among the dead.

The scream cut through the noise, this time louder and closer than before. He sucked in another breath and pushed forward.

Chapter Six

December 8, 1941

Allu climbed into the school bus, wondering if Lucille had heard what happened. It was unusually quiet as the other kids whispered to themselves, probably about the bombing. She grabbed the first open seat and peered out the window. There were three stops before Lucille's.

Lucille's house had big blue shutters and white siding, with three rows of windows going down and two going across. Allu had never been inside but had memorized every detail of what she could see. Beautiful curtains hung on both sides of the windowpanes—she imagined they were silk—and Lucille's yard was perfectly manicured, as her father made Sundays and Fridays his days to groom it. There was a tea patio in the back for entertaining, which Allu could never quite see from the bus, no matter how much she stretched her neck. Once she'd begged Mama to drive past to get a better look, but Mama had quietly told her that she didn't feel "at place" in this neighborhood. Oh, how she wished she could see inside the house.

Stops one and two seemed to take forever before the bus finally lurched to a stop in front of Lucille's. Allu glanced out the window, but Lucille wasn't waiting in her usual spot by the road.

She felt a pang of disappointment. Surely Lucille had opinions about Pearl Harbor and could fill her in on the details her own parents wouldn't speak of. And what about her perfect attendance? Lucille looked forward to that award every year. What about her group at school? Who would lead it without her? She started and kept every conversation going. Would they even include Allu? No, she thought, probably not. Especially if it were up to the older blonde who seemed to dislike her without reason. The more she thought about it, the more anxious she became.

And then, the door of the house was opened, and Allu could see a slice of *navy blue.* Sophisticated navy blue walls. Lucille was running late!

She scolded herself for being so sensitive.

Lucille's mother stepped out in a sunny yellow dress and matching white gloves. Her posture and heels made her appear much taller than she really was. Lucille had the same shade of blonde ringlets and the same air of confidence as her mother, who now led her daughter out to the bus.

Allu knocked on the window, waving to Lucille.

Lucille raised her eyes momentarily before lifting her fingers in a weak wave then quickly looking away.

Why wasn't she talking? My God, the girl never stops talking.

Allu slid over to make room for her friend and was nearly knocked over as the bus pulled away. Why wasn't she getting on the bus? She watched as Lucille and her mother got into the family car.

That day in class, Miss Rose talked about the attack. Normally, this would be cause for commotion and excitement, but today, the boys who usually caused trouble and shot paper airplanes in the back of the room were silent.

The United States had declared war on Japan.

Rumors were that over twenty-one ships, along with nearly two hundred planes, were destroyed or severely damaged in the Pearl Harbor Naval Base. The *U.S.S. Arizona* had exploded and sunk after the ammunition storage room was hit, killing twelve-hundred crewmembers. The ship had sunk within nine minutes of the attack, and the ripple effect had been felt by the entire nation, leaving California citizens watching the skies in fear they may be next. Of course, radio broadcasts didn't mention too many of the details in fear Japan may be listening.

The class held a discussion about Japan's alliance to Adolf Hitler and the regime, which according to Miss Rose, was a force of evil building. She wiped her hands on her dress as she spoke. For once, she wasn't crying, but looked completely terrified. It felt like the world was coming to an end, starting on the West Coast.

Things at school shifted by the hour. Lunch ladies no longer smiled when dishing food on plates. Teachers talked amongst themselves in small clusters in the corners of the hallway or behind shut doors. Kids whispered and divulged whatever information they had acquired from eavesdropped conversations at home. And everyone around Allu seemed to be watching—watching the skies, watching her.

She fumbled with the lunch Mama had packed, sitting at her usual corner table. She chewed slowly, counting the number of bites it took to finish her sandwich. The day had been endless and lonely, and she

35

couldn't wait to get home.

She breathed a sigh of relief when she saw Lucille enter the lunchroom. Everything would be okay. How silly she had been to feel so detached.

Allu threw her hand up and waved her over, wondering what kind of things Lucille had to say about the war. She'd be lucky to get a word in besides, but she didn't care. Lucille, and her constant opinions. It felt like ages since they'd last spoke, and despite herself, Allu was overjoyed to see her best friend.

"Lucille," a voice called out from behind Allu as she slid her lunch bag over to make room.

Lucille hesitated, glancing momentarily over at her. But something was different. *She* was different. Allu couldn't just feel it—she could see it in Lucille.

It was in the way her mouth drew tightly shut, as if to keep words from spilling out. The way her eyebrows came together into a serious look Allu had never seen before on Lucille. And her eyes usually full of spark and opinions and laughter, now looked at her, questioning and uncertain. Deep sadness brewed within their depths. Maybe not quite sadness, but a shade of it.

And then it hit her.

Pity.

The word stung at Allu's heart, and she knew that was it. Lucille looked at her in pity.

And then, just like that, Lucille looked beyond her.

She passed their usual table without a second glance and sat two feet behind Allu. The buzz of the lunchroom filled Allu's ears with ringing. The animated lunch with Lucille she had imagined had been replaced by a deafening silence that sliced through her and slashed at her soul. Lucille's opinions were loud, even in their silence.

Allu counted the seconds until the bell dismissed them, shielding her face with her hands so she wouldn't have to see her classmates' whispers.

And they couldn't see her shame.

After the last bell finally dismissed school, she didn't make room for Lucille on the bus, but piled her books beside her instead, occupying the entire seat. She didn't want to sit by her, or by anyone. She needed to get to her sitting tree to think, to cry, to scream. Scream at the birds or whoever would listen. *What had she done?* She loved California just as much as anyone. It was the only home she had ever known.

Tears threatened her eyes, and Allu tried to get her mind off Lucille's actions. No one would see her cry. At least not on that bus. She wouldn't let her family down. She had pride.

To keep her mind occupied, she listed off the different types of birds in her head.

The California thrasher, the song sparrow, the starling—the chestnut-tailed starling was her favorite... The bus grew louder and she tried to concentrate.

Rosefinches...

A paper ball hit her in the back of the head. Why hadn't she asked Robbie for a ride? The bus was full of loud misfits, although that usually didn't bother her. Usually, Lucille would have walked over and given those boys a lesson on etiquette and maturity and all that.

But Lucille wasn't on the bus. And she wasn't sure whether Lucille was even her friend anymore.

California scrub jay, California thrasher, rosefinch.

The noise of the bus became hoots and hollers in a unified voice, and right then, most of the kids came to Allu's side of the bus, peering out the windows. A fifth grader leaned against her, his shoulder blocking her face as he looked beyond her as if she were invisible.

She turned to see what they were all looking at to be shouting like a bunch of...

It was just Olsen's Hardware Store. Where she and Papa bought their birdseed. Only it didn't look like Olsen's anymore. None of the stores did. They had all changed during school that day, as quickly as the people around her.

Allu felt the faces on the bus look at her for her reaction. Under Olsen's sign and most of the signs in town, were handmade signs, most of them reading the same thing: *No Japs Allowed.*

Chapter Seven

"It's been building for a while," Mama said one night, her voice low and quiet. It had been a couple of weeks since Pearl Harbor had been bombed and it consumed everyone's conversations. Her parents seemed not to take notice as she washed the dishes after supper, but Allu could hear their hushed voices from the living room.

"You see the way many of the *hakujin* farmers look at us in the market."

There was a pause.

"They feel their jobs have been taken by immigrants," Papa said. "The bombing was fuel to the fire and very unsportsmanlike of Japan. Give them time."

"Yes, but you were born here. I've been here since I was a kid," Mama said. "We're hardly immigrants. You've *served* this country. It's a land-grab and you know it."

Another long silence. Did they know she was listening? She rattled the silverware around the water, hitting the sides of the sink in a clanking noise.

"Yo-chan, you mustn't say such things." Papa was always respectful, but his voice wavered. "*Shikataganai*," he said. *It cannot be helped.*

"I can't bear to bring the children out in public," Mama went on, her voice soft. "The town looks at us with disgust. And what if the kids read the newspaper headlines?"

Allu *had* read the headlines. Felt the hate. Racist comments from a few generals and politicians were prime headline material, making "Jap" a term prevalent in most conversations.

It had been used not only to describe the enemy, but also to refer to almost anyone in the United States with slanted eyes and dark hair, *regardless* of their ancestry. Just that morning, the news cover had showed a big picture of Chinese-Americans wearing badges proclaiming, *"I'm Chinese, not Jap!"* The newspapers were all there to read in her school library.

"As much as I want to, we can't shelter the kids from this. There's no way around it." Papa's voice was weary and distant.

Mama sighed. "I don't know what's going to happen." She paused. "There's been a lot of talk."

"Never mind that. We'll take it one day at a time."

Allu heard Papa get up from the chair and approach the kitchen. She bent her head down over the sink and scrubbed at a pan as Papa eyed her suspiciously.

"You don't have many dishes done, Allu-chan," he said with a wry smile. "I also noticed you didn't eat much at dinner." His observations never slipped past anyone. He began drying the dishes, neatly stacking them beside the sink.

"Papa?" She hesitated. "Are we…American?"

He stopped wiping for a moment, as if trying to decide how to answer. "Yes, Allu-chan, we're Americans."

She let out a deep breath she hadn't realized she'd been holding. Papa's face was lost in thought as he slowly wiped the cloth over the plate.

"Why don't people see us that way?" she asked.

He set the plate down. "Oh, my sweet Allu-chan." He beckoned her to the table. "Come sit with me for a moment. He pulled a chair out, looking tired and somewhat distant as if wondering how to answer her question. "How often do I tell you that you could become the best illustrator one day?"

She shrugged. "Too many to count."

"Yes. The best illustrator to be seen." He tucked a strand of loose hair behind her ear. "You have more talent in your pinky than courage for change in most men. It takes courage to face change, and for most people, change is uncertain. Fear feeds on uncertainty. It is difficult. People fear the war and the change that will come with it. Our ancestry reminds them of the changes and uncertainty they face."

Her father sighed, his shoulders dropping. "When your grandfather left Japan for Hawaii, he faced much uncertainty. He worked hard and made his family proud. He built a reputation as a farmer in a new place for little pay, even if he wasn't allowed to be a citizen."

Listening to his wisdom, she considered this. "Were *you* scared? When you joined the war?" Papa never talked about his time serving and she was surprised when he answered.

"Yes," he said, shaking his head. "But I wanted to bring my family honor. When they allowed Hawaiian Japanese Nisei to serve in World War I, I knew I must. I was a second-generation immigrant, but American in heart. Now, here you are, sansei, third-generation, with even more choices than I had. That makes it worth it."

She thought of many of the kids at school who didn't have to try very hard to fit in and wondered if it would ever be that easy for her someday, too.

"Papa?"

"Yes?"

"Do you think I could still become an illustrator? I mean, even after the war?"

"Allu-chan, you can become anything you want as long as you use the uncertainty as a catalyst for courage and faith. Besides…" He stood up and piled the stack of bowls into the cupboard. Although Mama had entered the room, she didn't scold him for helping. "I don't believe God would give all the talent and inspiration to white men only. Do you think?"

Finished, he rested his hand on Allu's shoulder. "Never fear change, Allu-chan," he said softly, reading her eyes. "Or the positive results that come with the turmoil of the process. Sometimes change cannot happen without discomfort, but that discomfort will create an ultimate greater good in the end."

"Thank you, Papa."

He smiled at her and left the room.

That evening, Allu pulled Mama's patchwork quilt snug around her, thinking about what Papa had said. Thinking about the newspapers she had read in her school library, in the shelter of the reference section. The house was still, and she could see the shadows of tree branches waving quietly across her walls, also refusing to succumb to the slumber of night.

Her thoughts awhirl, she remembered when she had first read the papers, the words had brought a slow kind of sting.

Japs Stealing American Jobs!

She felt a prickle that began in her fingers, before fighting its way into her arms and chest. It crept along, burning and radiating through layers of organs until it sank into her inner being. The tingle that had begun as a small prick suddenly overtook all her senses.

How to Tell Japs from Chinese!

Allu thought of the cartoon pictures in the papers from that day. Pictures of children with slanted eyes and teeth protruding from their mouths like tusks or fangs. The shame she had felt at smiling, wondering if her teachers saw her that way, hoping they hadn't read the comic section.

Slowly, ever so slowly, the feeling inside her turned over to numbness, leaving her void of any feeling.

Allu listened to the floorboards creak beneath the weight of her father's footsteps as he peeked in on her, and she quickly closed her eyes. She didn't want to talk to anyone. Not even Papa.

He stood for a moment, as if the decisions of the world rested on his shoulders. She wanted to call out to him. She wanted him to reassure her that everything would be alright. But she couldn't find her voice and not even Papa, the eternal optimist, could hide the worry in his face as he slowly pulled the door closed behind him.

She thought again about what he had said, and as he walked away, she tried to convince herself he was right.

Chapter Eight

Robbie held tight to the letter in his hands, reading the words as if his life hung on them. He must have read them a hundred times, but no matter how many times he did, they wouldn't answer all the questions he had.

"The timing's not right," he said to Jimmy outside the burger stand. Already, his car looked good as new and Robbie was somewhat relieved no one had mentioned the incident at the drive-in since it happened.

"But Robbie," Jimmy pleaded, "it's college ball. You know what guys like me would give to get a shot like that?"

"Jimmy…"

"No, listen," Jimmy said, cutting him off. "It's true and you know it. You're good, Robbie. *Real good.* And not just with baseball. You're smart. You'd be good at college." He leaned against the hood of the car. "You can't miss shots like this. I'd do anything to be able to go to college, but you know they're not fond of detention regulars."

Robbie chuckled. "True. And there's this thing about school that's important to colleges. Like *going.*"

"Well, at least I'm good where it counts," he smirked, taking a sip of his malt.

"Where's that?" Robbie asked. He scrunched his burger wrapper into a ball and tossed it into the garbage.

"With the ladies, *obviously.*" Jimmy took the lid off the cup and tipped it back, letting the chocolate ice cream slide into his mouth before tossing the empty container.

"I could never compete with you in that department," Robbie agreed, glad they'd changed the subject away from baseball and college.

"How are things with Daisy? Are you still sweet on her?"

Robbie shrugged. They hadn't hung out with Jimmy and Dee in a while. Things had been off since Pearl Harbor. A slight burning filled his chest.

"I don't know," Robbie said abruptly. It was true. He'd hardly saw her. He tried talking to her at school and she always had to get going somewhere else. He waited by her locker and she never showed to meet him in the mornings anymore. Heck, he didn't even know if they were still going together.

"I'm sorry," Jimmy said, a look of regret on his face. "This war has everything upside down and backwards. It's on everyone's minds. Hell, my old man even wants to help with the war effort."

"I suppose you're right," Robbie said, lost in thought, glancing toward the parking lot where a group of young boys were hitting rocks with sticks. "So, you thinking about it?"

"The war? Who isn't?"

"No," he interrupted. "*Joining?*"

Jimmy was quiet. "My cousin was drafted. He's twenty-one." He paused. "I'm going, Robbie. I already decided. I don't have the choices you have, the support. The old man doesn't even notice when I come home anymore."

Robbie didn't know what to say. It was probably true. He'd never met the man, but had seen him stumbling around town, mumbling to himself. He'd seen the bruises on Jimmy's arms, and on nights of defiance, his face. He thought of his own father who had never raised a hand to him in his life. A man of respect and honor, love and patience. He felt bad for Jimmy.

"Well, I'm joining with you," Robbie said, putting his hand up as Jimmy started to protest. "Baseball is great and all, but to serve your country, now *that* means something." Now more than ever, it was important to show loyalty and bring honor to his family.

Besides, plans change. He'd wait until after the war and re-evaluate. He knew what he needed to do, and sacrifice would become a part of everyone's life until the war was over. He had to fight for the country he loved. *His* country.

He wouldn't tell his father about the letter, who'd try to influence his decision, and Papa could be very persuasive. No, he'd tuck the letter into his pine box for safekeeping and show it to him when the timing was better. The last thing Robbie needed right now was one more person questioning his intentions.

Chapter Nine

January, 1942

Mama paced the floorboards, stopping long enough to pull back the curtains. She glanced from the front window to the clock which hung on the wall near the supper table, muttering in Japanese.

It was seven-fifty at night. Allu pressed her cheek against the rough wood of the table, struggling to keep her eyes open. She couldn't offer much support but stayed with Mama anyway. Robbie was Robbie after all.

She wondered if he was too old to get the wooden spoon and smirked, until she saw Mama's face, a twisted bundle of intersecting wrinkles and lines.

Mama reached her hand to her shoulder, squeezing the muscle in her neck as if to numb the pain that had settled into it. She scanned the driveway once again.

It wasn't unusual for Robbie to miss supper. Why was tonight any different? When he was late, Mama just teased him that he could eat with the chickens. And most times, Robbie had already filled up on popcorn and nuts from the ball game anyway. Except for the time he had snuck in around eleven after Allu had gone to bed. He wasn't allowed to attend any games for an entire week after that. But then, Mama had been more upset with him than worried. Tonight, she was downright anxious.

Headlights seeped in through the window, casting strange shadow shapes across the wall.

Mama had hardly reached the door before she began yelling in Japanese. There was only one boy in town who drove a car like that.

Jimmy Hanson.

Following Mama, Allu saw Jimmy throw his hand up in an effortless wave, wearing his deviance as a badge of honor. Allu strolled out to the porch casually, feeling her cheeks warm as he tipped his hat and winked. He was a gentleman like that—always escorted by a new sweetheart who was much more eager to gain his attention than Allu was. Regardless, she straightened up and gave her cheeks a quick pinch of color, then went back inside as Jimmy drove away.

"Robbie Noguchi!" Mama's voice was sharp and demanding as he strode through the kitchen door. "It's nearly eight o' clock. *Where* have you been?" She didn't give him time to answer. "You know the rules! What's so important to risk your life over?"

Robbie dropped his book bag onto the floor and pulled a glass out of the cupboard, pouring himself a cup of milk. "You worry too much, Ma. The game got over late, that's all."

Mama scanned him with narrowed eyes, her face torn.

"Besides," he went on, "I'm practically an adult."

Allu held her breath, knowing their mother all too well.

Robbie hesitated, leaning against the counter as if to ready himself.

"*No,* Robbie," she exploded. "You are *not* an adult! You are seventeen-years-old and *far* from being an adult." She shook a finger in his face, her cheeks a mess of red splotches. "Do you know where all the other adult Japanese American men were tonight?"

He opened his mouth to reply, but she cut him off. "At home with their families. Obeying legal curfew."

Robbie rested a hand on her shoulder. A good foot taller than her now, it was hard to believe he'd been born prematurely, once fitting easily within the crook of her arm. Or so Allu had been told about a million times.

"I'm fine, see?" he asked, his voice gentle and calm.

Mama studied him for a moment, her shoulders beginning to relax.

"They're getting so much stricter." Mama sighed. "I overheard Mrs. Yoshimo telling the grocery clerk that five more men have been taken. That's *fifteen* Japanese American business owners in two days."

Robbie set his glass by the sink and glanced at Allu, as if noticing her for the first time. "Just hens clucking in the henhouse." He winked. "The FBI was probably questioning them, that's all. Besides, we have nothing to hide. Let them question us."

"See?" Mama walked over to the windowpane, sneaking a quick glance outside before pulling the curtains shut. "That's exactly the thing I've been talking about, Robbie. Your opinions are going to get you in trouble."

He slung his bag over his shoulder. "Don't worry, Ma. Luck is on my side." He ruffled her hair on the way to his bedroom, and Allu noticed something slip up out of his back pocket. Without hesitation, he quickly tucked it back in, glancing at Mama, who had already moved into another room.

Allu sensed he hadn't been at the game. "So, what was the score?" she asked.

He pulled his eyebrows together in surprise, confirming her suspicions. Two could play this game.

"Close," he said, climbing the stairs to his room.

"How close?"

"Seven to six," he called over his shoulder.

I bet. Mama had gone back to doing the dishes, her mind a million miles away, but not Allu. It would take a lot more than dimples and smooth talk to work on her. Something was off. She couldn't say what exactly, but he was definitely hiding something. And even she knew that luck could only last so long.

Chapter Ten

"You know, my old man doesn't want me hanging around you," Jimmy confessed one day in January while Robbie was riding in his car. He was one of those guys who liked to state the obvious, but really, there was nothing to say. Robbie felt bad enough about the drive-in incident, and every time he saw the buffed-out door, he was reminded.

"But," Jimmy said, raising his eyebrows, "he's nothing but a drunk, and when have I ever listened to him?"

"Never," Robbie said with a smile, grateful for his own father.

"So, you think Dee will wait for me?"

Robbie was about to make a smart remark, but changed his mind when he noticed the gleam in Jimmy's eyes.

"Sure, Jimmy. Who could ever replace the great Jimmy Hanson? You're downright charming."

"And don't forget the good looks. Irreplaceable good looks."

"Yes. And the good looks."

Jimmy laughed, pulling a pack of smokes from his front pocket. "Anyway, they say the ladies like the uniforms." He lit a cigarette. "Don't worry if we're not in the same unit. We'll meet back up and take the girls dancing once this war's over."

"Sounds like a swell plan," Robbie said, cracking his window.

They drove in silence, not wanting to say what they were thinking. Which would be worse? Imperial Japan or Hitler's troops of Italians and Germans? Robbie had heard of the atrocious things those soldiers had done. Unspeakable things. They didn't just conquer, they hurt and devoured with sharp teeth and an insatiable appetite, taking over the world one slice of a country at a time.

Robbie's father hardly spoke of his war days. There were a few pictures of him in uniform, kept in a box along with old family slides.

Robbie had snuck the box into his room a time or two, careful to replace it before its absence was noticed. He didn't know what all the fuss was about, anyway. When he served, he would proudly frame and display his pictures.

Jimmy turned into a filling station.

"I'm grabbing a soda," Robbie said, climbing out of the car.

"Grab two," Jimmy called from the pump. "I'll meet you inside."

The gas attendant looked up briefly as he wiped down the countertop. Had Robbie missed any signs outside? He hadn't noticed any, and hoped he was allowed in. It was hard to tell these days—every innocent look felt like an interrogation.

Feeling a bit uneasy, he quickly grabbed two bottles of Coke and handed the clerk some change before walking out.

It was eerily quiet for a Friday evening, but not unusual since the bombing. Most people stayed inside. Even the ballgames had cleared half their spectators. Getting Daisy out of the house had taken a lot of convincing, along with a lot of slight lies to her parents on her end.

Seeing Jimmy wasn't by his car, Robbie set the bottles of cola on the roof and waited. A set of headlights pulled in, glaring him in the eyes as it parked on the other side of the pump.

Hurry up, Jimmy.

"Hey, what do you know, it's my favorite Jap!"

Robbie recognized the voice immediately. Knots formed in his stomach.

"What? You're not happy to see me?" Calvin got out of the driver's door, shutting it loudly behind him.

Robbie clenched his fist at his side. *Where the hell was Jimmy?*

Calvin sauntered over, his buddies now getting out of the car. Were there two or three more? He didn't want to look away from Calvin. At least two.

Calvin stood in front of him, his face twisted in a satisfactory smile, his dark hair slicked back.

"Look," Robbie said, "I don't want any trouble. We just stopped to fill up and get a soda." Robbie tried to sidestep him, but Calvin shifted with him, blocking him against the car.

"Oh, you asked for trouble when you started eyeing my girl," he sneered. He was close enough to see the gap between his front teeth. "Or when you ignored my little warning sign on your friend's pretty car. Huh, Jap?" He grabbed the front of Robbie's shirt, jerking him close enough that he could smell the liquor on Calvin's breath.

"So, you're after my girl," Calvin said, his dark eyes fixated on his.

Robbie smiled. "Technically, I've already got her."

Calvin's eyes narrowed as he looked at him for a moment, as if trying to decide something. A slow smile snuck across his mouth. "Wise ass, huh?"

"And what are you going to do about it?" Robbie asked. He clenched his hand into a tight fist, ready at his side. He was about three inches taller than Calvin and in a lot better condition. He knew he could take him down.

"Oh, it's not *me* who's going to do something about it," he snickered.

Robbie shifted his eyes above Calvin's shoulder. There were three guys approaching, baseball bats in hand.

His stomach dropped.

He tried to sidestep Calvin. His only shot was to run.

Before he could budge, Calvin shoved his hands into his chest, pushing him against the car. He held Robbie's arms behind his back.

Robbie kicked at his legs but was off-balance without his arms. A force to his nose knocked the wind out of him, turning the sky into a black sea of stars. And then came a blow to his mouth, filling it with the metallic taste of blood.

He tried to think against the endless blows to his face, but all that registered was pain. Something heavy struck his side.

"You think you're the only one with a good swing?" Calvin laughed. "Do you? Well, I'll make sure you never play again, pretty boy."

The blows hit Robbie in different parts of his body, like relentless factory machines. He couldn't feel past the pain. And then, he couldn't feel at all…

It must have all happened in a matter of minutes, but it felt like an eternity as his legs buckled out from under him. He felt the hard pavement rough against his cheek, kicks thudding against his ribs.

"Hey!" yelled a gruff voice from the storefront.

Robbie heard footsteps running nearby and tried to open his eye, but couldn't against the swelling.

The male voice grew louder. "Get outta here before I call the police!"

"C'mon, Calvin. Let's go," urged another voice.

Robbie pulled his right eye open and tried to focus on a blurry pair of brown boots, just inches from his face. Every movement radiated pain in his ribs.

Squatting down, Calvin locked his dark eyes on his. "You didn't think I'd lose my girl to a *Jap*, did you?"

Robbie shut his eyes, bracing for another blow.

He heard Calvin sneer as something wet hit his cheek, running down his neck. He smelled soda. Cold and sticky, it covered his hair in a drench of sweetness mixed with blood.

He thought he heard Jimmy's voice in a delirious echo.

"You're gonna pay, Calvin! You hear me? You're gonna pay!"

He heard more footsteps, probably Calvin and his gang going to their car, leaving Robbie in a pool of blood, unsure of which body parts hurt worst. Then, he heard Jimmy's voice as he ran past him and chased the car from the parking lot.

But none of that mattered.

Robbie peered as they drove past him, and the world slowed down from a spinning blur to a slow-motion of every movement. His senses heightened, his ears hummed. And as the car rolled slowly past, he got a good look at how many people were in it.

Five. There were five.

Four guys and one gal.

And in that moment, his good eye met Daisy's as she watched from Calvin's window—the final blow. He let his body slump to the ground. *Let me die,* he thought.

"We'll whip them all, Rob," Jimmy said, out of breath. But in that moment, Robbie didn't care. He didn't care about anything. He just wanted to disappear.

Jimmy slid his arms under his own and pulled him up, propping him against his side. Robbie winced, the pain in his ribs feeling as if they were broken. "We'll start on the home front, then make our way to the Germans," Jimmy went on. He looked over at Robbie. "What do you say?"

"Okay," Robbie said, knowing how persistent his friend could be. Jimmy helped him into the car. "Okay…"

Chapter Eleven

When Allu first saw him, it was like someone stabbed her in the gut. She wanted to go after them. Who would do that to her brother? Didn't they know who he was? He was their star ball player and more than that, he was good. He was truly good, inside and out. But Mama shushed her and went right to work, applying ice to the purple blotches that covered his face.

No one asked what had happened. Not even Papa. He spoke gently to Robbie, a sad look on his face.

Allu sat quietly, watching them. She couldn't shake the vacant look that had filled Robbie's eyes where sparkling mischief once lived. There had to be something they could do! But what? What could *they* do?

Robbie would heal physically, she knew that, but would he ever be the same again?

From that night, school was unbearable. Life was inescapable. The box they had been confined to was closing in tighter and tighter, leaving little room to breathe and even less room for hope.

Allu wanted to find an open field and scream. Spew out the anger and frustration that had built up and settled into the bottom of her stomach to fill every open space with it, make the trees wither in her sadness.

And then one day, she did.

It felt good, too—being able to yell at the world and everything in it, even if only the birds heard.

It was precisely five minutes until Papa found her. He regarded her with sympathetic eyes, and without a word, silently walked over and took her hand.

But instead of leading Allu home, he did a peculiar thing. He lifted his face to the sky and bellowed. A gut-wrenching, ugly yell that made the birds flee and the hair on her arms stand on end.

Then, he scooped her up as he had done when she was a child and carried her home through the field. Even the birds stopped singing.

***

Over the next several days, Allu watched Robbie spend much of his time holed up in his room, biding the time until he turned eighteen and could join Jimmy in the United States Army. She'd tried to talk to him a few times, but he was different now. Focused only on the war.

They were all there the day Jimmy left for training camp *without* Robbie. Allu imagined it was the first time the two of them had done anything without the other, and though Robbie didn't say much, she could sense his moodiness. It clung to him and pervaded everyone around him, keeping them at a distance.

Many locals had come by the bus station to send their boys off to war. Boys who had been playing high-school ball and attending formals just a few weeks prior had now become men who would fight for their country. But they looked so young. Too young to be men fighting. Tearfully, many spectators came to show their support, waving American flags in one hand and anti-Jap signs in the other.

Mama made Robbie and Allu stand so far back, it was hard to see around the people. They were first to leave as the bus pulled away.

***

One morning, Allu peeked out of her bedroom curtains to see what had woken her. It was early February and an unlikely time for any holiday visitors. A shiny black car was parked in the driveway, its silver rims reflected the willow branches that hung from the tree with the tire swing. There were unfamiliar voices in the kitchen. She couldn't hear Mama's or Papa's. Just men.

She straightened her covers before tucking the corners neatly under the mattress. Guests meant dressing neatly. She quickly changed into her best pin-striped dress and patent-leather shoes, tying her strands of long black hair into a ponytail. Then, she scrubbed her face.

It had been eons since they'd had visitors or anyone Allu would consider a friend, for that matter, and anticipation began to churn in her stomach. She would represent their family well.

Mama was in the kitchen kneading dough, her eyes swollen in her face. Was Mama crying? Mama didn't cry. Not ever.

"Outside, Allu," Mama said firmly.

Papa sat at the table with two men. Both wore navy-colored suits and had silver hair cut close to their head. One with a scruffy face looked over to where she was standing. He gave her a hard stare with piercing eyes; he looked like he hadn't seen sleep in quite some time. They were both much bigger than Papa but seemed to be the same age.

Allu glanced down at her shoes, unsure of whether to listen to Mama or wait for this man to give her an order.

The scruffy man shifted his eyes to some papers he was holding, then back at Papa. "It says here you were born in Hawaii." The man skimmed the page. "Your father came to Hawaii from Japan in 1880."

"Yes," Papa said, his hands crossed on the table in front of him.

"How many times have you been back to Japan since then?" the other man asked, giving a sideways glance to his partner. He had a narrow face and pointy nose.

"None."

"Do you have family there?"

"Yes," Papa said. "But they are old, and I haven't spoken with them in several years."

The man with the dark stubble jotted something down on the paper.

Why were they asking these questions?

Mama noticed Allu was still in the room and shot her a sharp look. "Outside!"

Allu did as she was told but didn't shut the door, so she could hear through the screen just the same.

"Do you have any property or money in Japan?"

"No," Papa said.

"How much do you think you are worth in this country?" There was a pause. "How much money?"

"Not much money. Maybe five thousand. I am a farmer." Papa's voice was insistent.

"Is your business a corporation?" the man interrupted.

"No."

"Who do you want to win this war?"

Dishes clanked gently. Mama always cleaned when she was nervous.

"I hope America wins."

The man scoffed. "You don't want to see Japan lose."

"I have no connection to Japan," Papa replied. "This is the country of my children."

The questions went on, and eventually Allu got up and went to the swing. She didn't see how any of this made sense to these men. *Why did they care if she could or couldn't speak Japanese, or what school they went to? Or how they felt about the Japanese-Chinese war?*

She bit the side of her cheek. Where was Robbie? He'd know what to do. He probably went to an early practice.

Just then, the screen door opened and the men stepped outside. The scruffy man pulled a handkerchief from his pocket and patted the drops of sweat from his forehead before loosening his tie.

Papa came out behind them and headed toward the shed. They must have been bankers, she decided. Only bankers wore suits.

She waved meekly to their guests, but neither of them acknowledged her. What was it with old men who wore suits? They never seemed happy.

With sadness on his face, Papa pulled the shed door open.

One of the men carried a cardboard box.

The chickens! They were taking the chickens!

Allu ran to meet them.

"The chickens?" she asked.

They couldn't take their chickens! They collected their eggs for the market. They needed them. Besides, they weren't used to being handled by men in suits.

"Allu-chan," Papa said, and rested his hand gently upon her shoulder as the men went into the chicken shed. His soft brown eyes searched her face. "I don't know how to tell you this."

"They can't, Papa! They can't take the chickens!"

His eyes dropped, and he pulled both her hands into his. "It's not the chickens, Allu-chan. It's me." He paused, his brown eyes looking into hers. "I must leave for a while."

"What do you mean?" Her heart dropped to the bottom of her gut with a thud. "Leave where? The farm?"

He nodded. "Yes. Those men, the FBI, they are questioning Japanese business owners and teachers in the community."

"But…" Her mind went blank. She could see Mama watching them vacantly from the window, her shoulders rising and falling as she pushed her strength into the dough.

"Does Mama know?"

Papa nodded sadly.

"But…you don't own a business, Papa," she said, trying to keep her voice level. "There must be some kind of misunderstanding." He didn't even own a suit. Why did they want *him*?

"Is it because you were in World War I? Do they need you?" It was all she could think of that made sense. He fought with Americans.

Papa smiled sympathetically.

"I'll tell them," she offered. "I'll tell them you fought in World War I. They'll understand. I'll tell them you're a farmer now. That you grow beans and peas and corn and sometimes even watermelon. I'll tell them right now!"

Papa pulled her to his chest and held her tight. His heartbeat thudded gently against her cheek, and she felt safe in his arms. She could smell the familiar smell of his aftershave, and she wondered how long it would be before she smelled it again.

"Shhh," he whispered. "It will be okay, baby girl. I'll come back." His flannel shirt was wet from her tears.

But Allu didn't care if the men saw her cry. This was their fault. The men who took fathers away without reason. What kind of job was that?

She wiped her face with the back of her hand.

"Take care of Mama," Papa said. "She puts on a good act, but she's not as strong as she looks. Not as strong as you are. Take care of Robbie, too," he said, giving her a wink, but his eyes glistened with unshed tears. "Promise me?"

This was all happening too fast. They hadn't even had a warning. She'd heard rumors of other men being taken away, but those were other men. Men without names or meaning to her. Not *her* father.

"No Papa," she sobbed, shaking her head. "No." She felt helpless. How would they get by without him? He was her favorite person in the world. He was her safe place. He made everything okay.

"Allu," he said gently, stroking her hair. "This will get worked out."

But she doubted him. For the first time in her life, her father who once held the moon, was just a man like anyone else. And there were so many things she needed to say, but the words became trapped in the cage of her chest.

***

The men gave Papa forty-five minutes to say good-bye. Forty-five minutes for Papa to pack a bag. Forty-five minutes later, they stood on the porch, a family of three.

Without Papa.

Mama stood motionless in her dress, her apron covered in bread flour as we watched Papa get into the back of a stranger's black Cadillac.

Allu wondered if they got paid based on the number of fathers they stole from their families, just as her family did for their produce. She was angry she had put on one of her best dresses for these monsters.

Before they pulled away, Papa's eyes locked with hers through the dusty back window and he gave her a faint smile in silent agreement.

Robbie, who had recently walked in, held her back in confusion as Allu tried to jump off the porch.

"No, let me go, Robbie!" Allu cried. Robbie looked to Mama, unsure of what was going on or what to do.

"Let her go," Mama said quietly.

She raced behind the car, following them down the driveway, past the little brown mailbox. The one she had made with Papa when she was nine. "Jap" had been written on it in sloppy red letters only a couple of nights before.

She stopped suddenly when the car paused at the end of their driveway, and knocked loudly on the side of the window, waving frantically to Papa.

Then, the scruffy man turned the car onto the old country road.

Her lungs burned as she sucked in gasps of chalky gravel kicked up by the black car. She saw the man in the passenger seat glance at his side mirror and say something to the other man, but they didn't slow down.

Papa placed his hand upon the glass of the back window, his face twisted with emotion. *Would she ever see him again?*

Allu ran a little further, but her legs struggled to keep up with the car as it picked up speed. The car got smaller and smaller, until it became a pinprick in the distance. And then, all she could hear were the birds.

Papa was gone.

Suddenly, she hated the birds. How dare they sing when everything had been ripped away from her. They knew nothing of men or war. Allu didn't want to feed them or care for them anymore. She wanted them to feel deprived and hurt. Angry—just like her.

She wanted to hate everything and everybody. She wanted someone to need her or ask her for help, and she wanted to be powerful and important enough to say no.

The men had not only taken Papa, but anything deemed "spy tools" by the government, including her binoculars, the kitchen radio they used for news updates, and the family camera they had bought after a full summer of saving money from the farmer's market.

Also gone were pictures of both sets of grandparents, whom Allu had never even met, letters they had written, and anything else proving them to be "un-American."

For being a Japanese American, they sure gave Allu's family a lot of credit—as if they could run a spy center capable of launching World War II with common household items. She laughed, but it was a cynical laugh, not the childish giggle she made when she was happy. According to the U.S. government, their life in this house was enough of a threat to have her father taken away. To call him a *high-risk Resident Enemy Alien*.

And to think, he was just a farmer.

She stared a long time at the empty road, a lone tear streaming down her cheek.

Chapter Twelve

Allu stood in the driveway, numb to the pelting rain attempting to erode whatever was left of her soul. Lucille hadn't spoken to her since the attack…even her teachers seemed afraid of her. Her hands trembled as the same bus that had picked her up for the past eight years approached. Everything was different, everything a threat.

"Looking for a bus buddy?"

She whipped around to face Robbie, surprised to find him out of his room. He'd been tardy almost every day for the past week since Papa left.

"Aren't you biking?" she asked. He could no longer rely on Jimmy's rides with Jimmy gone, and the car didn't have much gas since their family money had been frozen by the government.

"Nah." He slung his bag casually over his shoulder. "Thought I'd take a little break from physical exertion." He smiled weakly, his eyes wincing slightly against the yellowish-purple still lingering on his cheeks.

At least Allu still had him. She drew in a deep breath as she grabbed his hand and turned away from the bus of window-gawkers.

"I'm a much better driver than that old coot anyway." Robbie smirked, giving her hand a squeeze.

"Well, it doesn't take much, does it?" she teased. Allu rolled her shoulders back and held her head high as the bus approached. *Let them look. Let them look all they want.* They could ride that old bus. She got into the car with Santa Ana's star ball player, who just happened to be her brother.

***

Over the next several days, more Japanese men began to disappear around town, and by the middle of February, most Japanese businesses were boarded up. No one knew where the men were taken, or when they would return. *If* they would return.

Allu refused to believe Papa was dead.

Surely, he'd told the FBI men that he'd fought in World War I. That had to stand for something, didn't it? They still had the American flag hanging from their front porch. Had those men noticed when they had taken him away? It was right by the door to their house.

Of course, they had seen it. Papa had earned a Purple Heart and a permanent limp defending that flag. He was more American than most. Allu wouldn't have been surprised if they'd asked him for help.

Either way, she missed him terribly and regretted not having more to say to him the day he'd left. If she'd known he was leaving, she would have told him how much she enjoyed their walks. How she liked the way he'd walk slowly to keep pace with her, and how he made her feel like their conversations and her opinions were important—even if they weren't loud opinions. How he made her feel like *she* was important.

She wanted to tell him how safe he made her feel when he took her hand in his. How she had always waited up in bed, unable to fall asleep until *he'd* checked in on her. How she wanted to be an illustrator because he believed in her. Because she wanted to make him proud.

But these days, she hardly slept, and Mama was often too preoccupied to tuck her in. She was probably too old for it anyway, Allu reminded herself.

On many occasions, she snuck into Mama's room, listening as Mama stifled her cries with flannel shirts that still had Papa's scent embedded in them. If Allu closed her eyes, she could almost pretend he was there with her, embracing her in a hug. And for all she knew, maybe the ghost of him was.

But as the days turned into weeks, the smell on Papa's clothes began to fade and so did Allu's hope of him returning. Even so, she waited every day by the mailbox, squinting against the brightness of the sun to see the postman as he pulled up their road.

It became increasingly hard to separate reality from the rumors that had grown rampant. One day, their neighbor, Mrs. Yoshimo was over, talking with Mama after school. She told them she was thankful she had only herself and her cat to worry about. She never had any children, and all the better for her now. She'd heard at the salon they were rounding up all the Japanese men, keeping them as potential hostages if needed, against the Japanese forces.

Though much of the conversation was in Japanese, Mama's face was readable as she sipped her tea with a slight tremble. It was ridiculous Mama even drank tea when Papa was gone, but she said they had to try and act like a "normal family" with "normal routines."

But things *weren't* normal, and Allu didn't see the use in pretending. And she didn't like Mama much for trying.

Mrs. Yoshimo helped herself to a few more cookies and another cup of tea before finally getting up and passing on her knowledge elsewhere up the road.

Mama walked her out and momentarily disappeared into the shed. She didn't go there often, as the outdoor chores were usually left for Allu and Robbie, and Mama hated the chickens.

She came out with a pile of empty seedbags folded neatly over her arm. "Allu-chan, go fetch Robbie," she said, draping the bags over the porch railings. There was an urgency in her voice that didn't leave room for questions.

Allu wasn't surprised to find Robbie's door locked. What was so private that he needed to lock the door? If the FBI wanted to come in, the FBI was going to come in. Apparently, she was the bigger threat.

"Robbie!" She tapped her knuckles against the wood.

"Busy," he replied.

Allu rolled her eyes, wondering what could keep him so *busy* all the time. "Oh, Robbie-chan, Mama wants you to come down to the porch!"

There was a heavy sigh, followed by a bit of stirring.

Downstairs, Mama gave them each a seed bag.

Allu was confused. They had a full stock of seed supply in the shed. Papa had had the bags filled before he left. Had he known he would be pulled away?

Allu pushed the thought aside. There was no time for speculation now. Besides, it was no longer safe in town. Even Robbie had ditched his bike for the school bus. Coming home with black eyes seemed to be the norm for him these days.

"Fill these bags with as many necessities as possible," Mama said, her forehead gleaming with drops of sweat. She'd clearly lost her mind.

Allu looked to Robbie, but he looked just as puzzled.

"Are you seriously…?" Robbie started, but Mama's look cut him off mid-sentence.

"Mama, are we running away?" Allu asked.

It seemed logical. Maybe she knew where Papa was, and they were going to meet him.

"Mrs. Yoshimo said to be ready for anything," Mama said and

unfolded her bag, shaking it out over the front steps as they stared at her in disbelief.

"Running away would make more sense," Robbie interjected. "Why don't we just move beyond the boundary?" He looked at their mother with expectant eyes. "We could go to Seattle. Or hell, we could even go to Montana. I could find a farm to work on until things settle down with the war."

Allu watched him, noticing how pale he'd gotten since Papa had gone. There was a sort of puffiness in his eyes that hadn't been there before.

"Robbie-chan." Mama sighed, resting her hand briefly on his broad shoulder. "They've frozen our accounts. There's no money for that."

She brushed her hands on her apron, ridding them of the powdered residue from the seed that had once filled the bags. "Besides, we don't know anyone there. Where would we go? I don't want to be separated." Her face was set in determination. "We must stick together and be prepared for anything."

Allu looked to Robbie for explanation. They were hiding something from her. She wasn't a kid anymore and she hated it when they treated her like one. "Robbie?"

He glanced at Mama, who averted her eyes.

"There's talk we're going to be sent away," Robbie confirmed.

A surge of air caught in Allu's throat. *"Away? Away where?"*

He shrugged. "No one knows. They think it would be better to keep all of us *spies* in one place, where they can keep watch over us. The War Relocation Association is calling them *pioneer communities* with protective services, but I know better."

Mama shot him a look and his smile faded.

"How will Papa know where we are when he comes home?" Allu started to panic.

Robbie looked down at his feet, avoiding her gaze.

"We can't think of that now," Mama said.

Mama had *no idea*, Allu realized. She was just as much in the dark as the rest of them. How could they leave the farm? Allu had never lived anywhere other than the farm.

"Go to the hallway closet and pack a sheet and blanket," Mama instructed. "Roll them so they fit tightly in your bag."

Was she serious? Allu would never leave the farm—the men would have to drag her out! But then, she thought of Papa and knew they could do exactly that.

"Allu-chan," Mama said sharply. "Take your head out of the clouds, girl!" She shook her finger at her. "Sometimes, I think your mind has grown wings and flown away with the birds. This *is* important. You need to listen."

Allu tried to focus, wishing she could be a bird. She would fly away, and…find Papa.

"Grab the extra toothbrushes, combs, and whatever else you can think of for daily needs. When you're sure you've grabbed enough clothes and all the essentials, you can choose five small personal things to take with you," Mama instructed.

Enough clothes? How should she know what *enough clothes* would be when she didn't even know where they were going, or for how long? Allu wondered if anyone would notice her absence at school.

"And five chickens don't count as your five personal things." Robbie began to smirk, but stopped when he saw her face.

Allu hadn't even thought about the chickens. What would happen to them? What would happen to the farm, and everything they left here?

***

Allu sat on the bed and surveyed her room. Mama shuffled loudly around the kitchen downstairs, opening cupboards and closing them as if preparing for the end of the world. Allu's room seemed smaller than it had that morning, and all of a sudden, each of her belongings had acquired sentimental value.

She snatched the gum wrapper from her garbage can, remembering it was from the last piece of gum her father had given her before he'd left. Thank God she hadn't emptied the garbage. She smoothed out the creases and folded it neatly, placing it in her pocket. She'd treasure it always.

Her room was the only place in the house that was all hers. Mama even let her decorate it herself. Pale pink walls gave backdrop to the many pictures she had painted of birds and flowers on the farm. Mama had framed a few of them with old barn board picture frames Papa had made, a gift for her last birthday. They were painted a sunny yellow and made every painting look as if it was from summer.

She wondered if each picture counted as a separate item, or if Mama meant five *categories* of small things. Deciding to be safe, she pried open the frames and rolled the prints, securing them with a hair binder. She refused to look at the empty space on her wall where their family *kamon* had once hung before the men had taken it away. Their family *mon* had hung in different places around the house, and Mama had stitched them all herself.

In the design, intricate pieces of feathery wheat arched protectively over a budding flower. They were gone, but Allu could draw them from memory. She placed a few prints in her bag, along with her bird identification book, sketchpad, and water paints.

Next, she sifted through the things on her dresser. There was a pin she had earned for being one of the top readers at school. Mama and Papa had been so proud as they sat among the other parents and watched as school officials pinned it to Allu's shirt. Was it important enough to bring with? It was small. Did it even count as one of her five things? Maybe she could remind Mama how proud she had been of her that day, and she'd decide to take the pin as one of *her* five things.

Allu began picking up and setting down things at random, each trinket with its own memory she couldn't forget. But what if she did forget? Most of her memories were from these possessions. Where would she be without them? *Who* would she be without them?

She hastily placed the pin in her bag.

Sliding open the drawer of her dresser, she wondered if they would have dressers or closets in their new place. She noticed as if for the first time how much her clothes smelled like cedar and remembered Papa had made the dresser when she was a baby. If only she could take the furniture! But it would be there when she got back, she reminded herself. Surely, they would only be gone a couple of days. Weeks at most. *If* they went at all. After all, this was all just a possibility. Surely it wouldn't actually happen. *Would it?*

Allu gently ran her fingers along the lace trimming of her white dress. It was the one Mama made her wear for special occasions, like school performances or trips to town. Now stained, it fit tightly and the lace made her arms itchy. It really had been a beautiful dress when Mama had first made it. Was it hand-sewn or by machine? Allu had never asked. Despite blotches of yellow here and there, she folded it neatly before tucking it between the other items in her bag.

Then she noticed the wooden pocket mirror that had once belonged to Lucille, sitting in the bottom of the drawer. It was the first gift she had gotten from a friend. After a moment, Allu pulled the pin out of the bag, replacing it with the mirror instead.

But what about her books? There were so many to choose from! Would it be more important to take the first book she had ever read, or her favorite book? Or the ones she hadn't read yet? Examining each one, she flipped through the pages before tossing each on the bed, packing them and replacing them, her hands moving as frantically as her thoughts.

In the end, her bag turned out to be an over-stuffed, haphazard mess of things. Her life had been reduced to a seed bag full of whatever remnants she could fit inside. Why couldn't it be as easy as it was for Robbie? All he probably cared to take was his beloved ball glove. Though the more she thought about it, she couldn't remember seeing him with it since the war had started.

That night, Allu waited in bed for Papa to come in and tell her everything would be okay. To tell her the war was over, and he had come home. She watched the door with a heavy heart and wondered if she'd ever see him again.

Later, a whistling noise awakened her, sounding like wind forcing its way through the barn boards of the shed in a hollow cry.

Somewhat dazed, she realized it wasn't the wind at all, but Mama's cries seeping through the crack of her closed door.

Chapter Thirteen

Oahu, Hawaii

February, 1942

Yukio and his grandfather sat in silence, trying not to think of the thousands of men trapped inside the *Arizona*, the *Oklahoma*, and the *Utah*, among others as they sank. The *U.S.S. West Virginia* had sunk upright after torpedoes had torn open its hull. Salvage workers had set out to repair the ship, working with divers in the murky waters; toxic fumes and oil intermixed with the smell of decaying flesh. But a sense of comradery overpowered. The men all believed the water would return to normal again.

Even as they sat, recovery teams ordered remains to be quickly buried in temporary graves. Oahu would never be the same. *Yukio* would never be the same.

"I still don't understand," Grandfather said, shaking his head. "How could they do this?" It was especially hard for him, having been born in Japan. "We work so hard in sugar cane fields. We American in heart."

Yukio realized he was referring to the U.S. government. "They're scared. It's not right, we know. They're focusing on Kibei leaders on the island. They figure that even though they're born in the U.S., being educated in Japan makes them a threat. Martial Law."

"But they not threat." Grandfather rubbed his eyes. "They priests and school teachers on the island. This our home. We've worked their sugar cane plantations for hardly any money."

Yukio rested his hand upon his grandfather's, the outside wrinkled and softened by time, but still calloused by hard work underneath.

"You are a good grandson. You take care of us and help your father on the farm." He tapped Yukio's military patch with his finger. "You show good *sekinin*—responsibility contributing to all of us. The community, the country, fulfilling obligations and not thinking of self. I proud of you."

He kissed his grandfather on the cheek before grabbing a couple of boxes of vegetables from their garden.

Yukio didn't understand it, either. They were Americans. They taught American History in schools and ran grocery stores. Most of them had never been off the island. He held a college degree as a teacher. That had to count as something, didn't it?

The sugarcane recreation hall was about a five-minute drive and the young kids ran to his jeep when he arrived.

"Yukio! Yukio's here!"

He climbed out and grabbed the boxes of produce.

There was a shortage of food on the island and his family was one of the fortunate ones far enough from the harbor to not have to leave their home.

He handed a box to a boy about the age of twelve who eagerly peeked inside. "Is this from your Victory Garden?" he asked.

"Sure is," Yukio replied. "Are you helping with the war effort?"

"Yes, sir," he said. "Some of the other boys and I have walked around the neighborhood collecting tin cans and pots to turn in for scrap. We even found a few tires." He looked at Yukio eagerly.

Since Japan controlled the Pacific Ocean, the rubber trade had been cut off from Asia, leaving the U.S. without a supply.

"Good job, soldier," he said, patting the boy on the head. He reached into his pocket and pulled out a stick of gum for him.

The boy's eyes lit up. "Thank you, sir!" He unwrapped the stick of gum and split it with another boy, carefully smoothing the tin foil wrapper to be saved for the war effort.

"I've been collecting stamps," another said enthusiastically as they made their way to the door of the hall. "I almost have enough to buy a war bond."

"Is that so?" Yukio asked with a smile. "Well, we all have to pull together to win this war now, don't we?"

The Rec Hall was noisy with the clamor of several families who had been pushed out of their homes in the harbor. Yukio scanned the group until he found her, assisting an elderly woman. Leinani was still the most beautiful woman he'd ever seen, her sun-kissed skin and thick dark hair evidence of her Polynesian roots of the island. She caught a glance of him and smiled, waving him over.

"Hello, Private," Leinani said. "More produce?" She took the vegetables from his arms and set it by the other supplies.

"We have more than enough."

"Thank you, Yukio. I feel so bad for these families. They've lost everything and the rationing makes it twice as hard."

"Yes," he agreed. "It's a tough time, but the war can't last forever."

"No, it can't." Leinani turned away from him, toward the woman she was helping. "Are you okay for now?"

The woman nodded and smiled at the two of them. "Go talk to your sweetheart," the older woman said, and the two of them slipped out a side door and into the fresh air.

His heart hurt for these families. The many who lost their homes due to fire or simply by living too close to the harbor. The Rec Hall was crowded and noisy, but safe.

"Thanks for coming, Yukio. You know how these kids look up to you. Besides, I don't mind seeing you in uniform," Leinani said, winking.

"Well, that's motivation enough then," he said, wrapping his arm around her and drawing her in for a kiss.

"I was looking at some dresses in a magazine today."

"Oh?" he raised his eyebrows.

"Yes," she confirmed. "I think I found the one. I'm going to try to find some similar fabric. I know I can make one just like it."

He kissed her forehead, wondering how he'd gotten so lucky.

"You're the best thing that came from college," he said.

"Maybe. Your degree isn't half-bad, either." She gave him a coy look and smiled.

"Let's do it right away," he said eagerly. "Right the minute this war is over. We'll get married on the beach if we have to."

"Hopefully, the barbed wire will be down by then." She took his hand, squeezing it tightly.

Barbed wire now surrounded all of the Oahu beaches to protect against any other raids.

He held her left hand to his lips and kissed her ring gently. "I'm sorry this whole thing happened, but I promise we'll have a big luau just like you wanted, Leinani. It will be even better than before."

She looked into his eyes. "This war isn't your fault. You'd think pretty highly of yourself to believe otherwise. It will all be alright. Anyway, I better get back. See you tonight?"

Yukio pulled her to him and kissed her playfully on the cheek. "Of course," he said.

He watched her walk away until she passed through the door and into the building of people waiting for her. These were the ones who were allowed to stay, despite not having homes. Most of them were natives to the area. Several hundred, maybe even a thousand, people had been forced to the mainland to make room for the many servicemen who now occupied the area.

Seeing the kids playing in the dirt, he felt a familiar feeling of uneasiness creep in. It wasn't the island he'd grown up in. Things were changing. Suspicions were high. Goods were scarce and grocery stores were nearly empty. Yukio knew it was just a matter of time before he'd be sent overseas. The war had disrupted so many lives but was so critical to the safety of their nation. Everyone had to do their part, even if it meant putting their lives on hold.

But for how long?

Chapter Fourteen

February 20th—his first birthday without Papa. Robbie was finally an adult, yet he'd never felt more like a kid. Mama made a cake, but it didn't seem right celebrating anything.

He stuck to himself at school these days, trying to avoid Calvin and his crew. He'd bumped into Daisy in the hallway one day and for just a moment, there had been a flicker of something in her eyes. Sympathy? Regret? He'd never know. She hadn't given him time to find out.

But now that he was eighteen, he could get out and do something important. He'd join up with Jimmy overseas. He felt bad for not being upfront with Mama.

It took a little convincing for her to let him go out. Ever since he'd gotten pounded by Calvin, she wasn't as tolerant as she used to be.

He spent the drive to the recruiting office wondering where he'd be stationed. He'd heard Jimmy was somewhere over in Italy, but who knew? Jimmy's dad wouldn't know Italy from California when drinking—which was all the time.

Italy would be something. To see the colosseum and walk on stone roads and bridges older than this country… Robbie could hardly imagine it. Mama had never been much of anywhere. He'd have to send postcards. Postcards with pictures of all the places they'd read about in history books. Maybe someone could even take his picture there, and he could slip it into a letter to her.

Outside the office, Robbie saw a few older men in uniform talking. They looked like they'd seen a few deployments. He wondered where they'd been, and if they had joined at eighteen and made a career of it.

They glanced up briefly at him, and Robbie tipped his hat to them respectfully on his way in.

A woman sat at a booth inside, shuffling a stack of papers. Robbie waited patiently, holding his hat in his hands. She was oblivious to him, even as he stood in front of her.

"Excuse me," he said, after clearing his throat hadn't gotten her attention. "I'm here to enlist." He'd worn a simple white t-shirt and made sure to tuck it in. He'd seen enough to know they were sticklers when it came to appearance. Hell, he'd even used hairspray.

The woman set her papers aside and folded her hands on the desk in front of her, looking him up and down. "I'm sorry, I can't enlist you at this time."

He must have heard her wrong. "Pardon?"

She leveled her eyes to his. "You don't qualify."

Robbie dug in his pocket for his wallet, pulling out his license. "I'm eighteen." He pointed to his birthday. "Eighteen today." He smiled.

The woman hesitated, moving the stack of papers to the other side of the desk. "We are not allowed to enlist Japanese."

Robbie stared at her face, watching the way it turned different shades of pink as she looked uneasily from him to her hands. He couldn't believe it. He could not *believe* it. Surely this was a mistake. He was willing to risk his life for this country. *His life wasn't good enough?*

Robbie could think of a thousand things to say, but none of them would bend the military.

"I'm sorry," she said again. "They removed all Japanese Americans from active duty when Pearl Harbor was hit."

But he'd already stopped listening.

Chapter Fifteen

Robbie threw open the screen door to the kitchen, letting it slam behind him.

Allu jumped, knocking over the bowl of shelled peas. "Look what you made me do!" Peas rolled across the counter.

Without so much as giving her a glance, Robbie stomped off to his room, slamming the door shut. He usually got into moods like this every few days after checking the mail, and though none of them said anything, they were all waiting. It had become a sort of routine: Robbie got the mail and placed the pile on the table for Mama to sort through. Allu assumed he'd already shuffled through the letters, and knowing Papa hadn't written, left Mama alone to her own disappointment when she did the same.

Allu longed for the radio. For any sort of noise. The sky was an ominous gray, as if God Himself was crying upon their fields. The house was so quiet. *Too quiet.* Silence had settled into the floorboards and walls in a slow but deliberate overtaking, and she had realized that silence carried its own sort of noise. A deafening hum of numbness creeping and crippling in its own manner. There was a power in the silence that was enough to drive her mad. A weapon in itself.

***

Later that evening, Allu heard Robbie and Mama's voices rise and fall from the kitchen in a lulled rhythm of whispers, and she couldn't help but listen. Besides, if they had news about what had happened to Papa, she deserved to know.

She crept to the hallway and pressed her shoulders flatly against the wall, holding her body still and drawing in deep, quiet breaths.

Mama's voice was stern. "Are you enlisted?"

There was a pause.

Allu held her breath, imagining what kind of punishment Mama would give her if she found her listening to their conversation. The clock ticked, and she nearly jumped out of her skin.

"No," Robbie said flatly. "Turns out the U.S. Military doesn't need Japanese volunteers."

"I'm sorry, Robbie-chan. This war can't go on forever. Besides," Mama added gently, "your family needs you."

"I know, Ma. It's just—" Robbie paused. "Jimmy and I had this big plan, you know? We were going to join together. It's always been him and me taking on the world. How can they pretend *I'm* not a citizen?" his voice rose. "They're letting the German-Americans fight. Even the Italians, for that matter."

So that was it. Robbie wanted to leave them, too. Allu's heart burned in her chest like a woodstove of ashes. She wanted to punch her fist through the wall and barge in and…

"Robbie," Mama's voice called out after footsteps that grew louder as they neared where Allu stood.

Quickly, she padded her way to her room, closing the door behind her. *How could he even think about deserting them? At least Papa hadn't had a choice!*

She felt her jaw pulsate and her cheeks heat, and she wanted to explode. She wanted this all to end. To go back to the way things used to be. Pretend this was a nightmare in some other place of the world.

Throwing herself down on her bed, she sucked in a deep breath and stared at the ceiling. It was her own fault for eavesdropping. Besides, maybe the war would end first. Maybe they wouldn't need Robbie. Maybe this wouldn't last long, and they could all go back to the way things were.

But deep down inside, Allu knew that was an outlandish dream. Life would never be the same.

She heard Robbie's bedroom door slam close and lock behind him.

Chapter Sixteen

Late February, 1942

"Allu-chan!"

Cold fingers clutched her arm, followed by the thud of feet hitting the floorboards. As far as Allu Noguchi could tell, it was still dark outside. She rubbed her eyes wearily as her mother pulled her from the bed.

"Get up!" Mama cried. "It's time!"

Allu forced her eyes open as the words hit her full force and her fear lurched to her stomach. She'd known this day was coming, but now that it was here, a sheer panic settled in, squeezing her heart tight, threatening to choke out any air from her throat or hope that remained.

"Where's Robbie?" Allu asked.

"Downstairs," Mama said. "Hurry. Grab your bag!"

She dressed quickly, taking one last look around her room. Her beautiful bedroom with sunny walls that had been painted yellow the summer before and floral curtains she had begged Mama to make. Stripped down, it could have been any girl's room, and Allu imagined important men in suits walking through it, saying to themselves, "This was a mistake. This girl is just like mine. She can't be the enemy. Look, she likes to paint. She even made her bed."

And how silly it was, that she had made her bed as if she would return after some vacation. A beach vacation, perhaps—

"Allu!" Mama's voice cut through her thoughts.

Without another glance, she flicked off the lights and hurried to where her family waited.

In the kitchen, Mama held a seed bag as she threw open the cupboards, shoving random objects inside as she went.

"Allu! Robbie!" she called, without looking up. "Get your bags and put as many jars of produce as you can in them!"

Allu looked to Robbie in disbelief, but his blank face showed he was just as confused by their mother's frantic gestures as she was.

"What kind of produce?" Allu thought of the hundreds of jars in the cellar.

"No matter! Go!"

"Robbie?" Allu's voice was desperate as they descended the stairs in the dark. "Where are we going?"

He hesitated. *He knew. He knew!*

"Robbie!" Panic rose inside her. "Tell me!"

"A relocation center," he said, without looking up.

Her mind raced. "*What? Why?*"

"A relocation center—camps for Japanese Americans."

Her shoulders tightened. Going to camp meant leaving the farm. But how could they? The chickens needed them. Sure, they were ugly and loud and selfishly indifferent, but they still depended on her family to feed them. Apparently, no one had informed them they were Japanese— and the chickens were probably the only ones who would notice their absence.

"Where?" She grabbed a jar of peaches she had canned last spring with Papa.

"I don't know, Allu," Robbie said, agitated.

"What…about…Papa?" She could barely choke out the words.

Robbie cocked his head to the side, stretching his neck. "More than likely, Papa's already there."

Allu was old enough to know when she was being lied to. She was quite used to it, in fact. Lucille lied, Mama lied, Robbie lied. They all lied! They lied to her like the government had lied when they made her believe once she was a U.S. citizen.

She tossed one more jar in her bag, and without another word, left Robbie in the dark cellar.

***

They left, carrying the remnants of their life from the farm in nothing more than seed bags meant for chickens. Mrs. Yoshimo met them in the driveway. She would not stop crying at the idea of leaving her cat behind. One stinking cat! Allu had five chickens and a missing father.

How *dare* she cry?

Allu forced her face forward, refusing to look at the house. The farm. The gardens. The tire swing. Refusing to feed the hunger of regret with images of the life she was leaving behind, knowing she might not ever sit beneath the apple trees again. Never run through the woods again. Never sit on Papa's porch again.

Her world had been robbed, and the damn chickens wouldn't shut up as they called out stupidly behind them. Allu had emptied every last bit of seed for them and still they called out, oblivious to what was happening. What would become of them? If no one cared about Allu's family as people, why would they care about some dumb ol' chickens?

She caught Robbie glancing back at them a couple of times before she took his hand in hers. She didn't say a word or look at him, but noticed he didn't look back once they began to drive away.

***

Towering piles of bags and blankets and luggage were scattered throughout the train station as people herded into the building. Sobs from adults mixed in with oblivious children's laughter in a confused state of chaos. And all around, there was a feeling of heaviness, pushing Allu down into the cement as her family pressed through the sea of people.

"Robbie," Mama said, and stopped by a large pile of suitcases, looking up at her son, who stood a near foot taller than her. "Do you have the tags?"

Robbie nodded, pulling out three vanilla cardboard pieces from his side satchel, each displaying their last name.

"Kind of an early driver license, hey?" He smiled meekly, pulling the necklace over Allu's head.

She looked at the card in disgust. It distinguished them just above that of rounded-up chickens. She should've felt ridiculous, but glancing around, Allu realized it was a situation that called for no such feelings. Still, she hoped no one from school was watching.

A few hours in, Robbie joined a couple of fellows for a game of cards amid a pile of blankets.

Allu leaned against a luggage bag and pulled her knees to her chin, squirming until her back rested somewhat comfortably against its bulk. All around her, people ran around in an effort of forming some kind of organization in the unknown.

A woman to her left cried profusely. Some girls to her right stared at Robbie. Allu wasn't sure where she fit in, so she decided to sketch instead.

She was drawn to one of the guys who took up cards with Robbie. He had a hard face with eyes lacking in both color and emotion, making for a dangerous card player. Unlike the other faces she tried to sketch, his was steady and unchanging, making it easier to draw than those with constant fleeting emotions.

When he laughed, there was a sharpness to it that sent shivers through her spine. She was quick to look away, and had to erase his eyes several times before getting them right. Something about him made her uneasy, and she hoped Robbie wouldn't let on that she was his sister.

Chapter Seventeen

The steam engine was slow to arrive, as if to deliberately taunt them. It lurched forward, heavy and strong, throwing a shrill cry into the air as it skidded against metal railways.

This was it.

The turn of Allu's life. On a big, black train which led to God knew where.

"Round up!" a man called out loudly. Patches of whiskers covered his face. Was he a policeman? FBI? Soldier? He scanned the crowd with beady eyes.

Suddenly, it was all too much. Her stomach turned and sweat slicked her face. She pulled her shirt up over her nose to repel the stench, wishing there was a way to block the cries, realizing they were her own.

She looked to Mama, who struggled to load her bag, pulling and twisting the heavy mass awkwardly onto the train. They were surrounded and packed in, shoulder to shoulder, like cattle, but alone.

It was noisy. Loud shouts and applauding, coupled with crying babies and scared children. People cheered from outside the windows, and she wondered how many of them had once been their friends. A few she recognized from school, though she didn't know their names. For some reason, Mr. Benson from the hardware store came to mind, and she wondered if he had brought his kids to watch.

All the faces of those deemed *American enough* to stay. How many were of German ancestry, she wondered, and were relieved it wasn't them? No matter now. It was too late to stay.

Allu slumped down beneath the window, relieved to be away from their stares. Softly, she hummed her father's bird song to the sounds of metal gliding along the tracks as her mother slept next to her.

"It will be okay," Robbie reassured her.

The train jerked a few times before settling into a steady glide along the tracks. *How did he know? How did he know it would be okay?* Tears formed in her eyes.

"I don't know," she said. "I don't know."

She turned her head to look out the window at the countryside and the many small towns they passed through, some with steady onlookers, and others, quiet and without concern. The train had fallen into a hum of hushed voices and quiet sniffles.

Soon, her eyes grew tired and the towns grew blurred until they fell into a facet of her mind where time stood still and scary things weren't real.

When Allu opened her eyes, the sun shone through her window. Was the train slowing? Both Mama and Robbie were asleep. A suffocating feeling climbed up into her stomach, clutching at her throat. Outside the window was an expanse of pale sand with an occasional clump of colored cacti pushing through the dry terrain. Set against the mountains, it might have been beautiful, maybe even inviting, given other circumstances. Dust whirled in the wind, giving the sky the appearance of an ominous yellow. A wooden sign read *Camp Manzanar.*

To her relief, rumor was they were still in California, though it was hard to believe when looking at the desert that lay stretched out in front of her.

She began to see shapes moving through the sand.

Soldiers. The place was guarded by soldiers.

"Robbie," she nudged his ribs gently with her elbow. "Robbie, wake up."

Robbie rubbed his eyes and peered out the window, his face dropping.

They had arrived at their new home.

Chapter Eighteen

As a kid, Robbie was a climber. And though the memory of pulling himself up the length of the trunk of a tree often eluded him, the sense of freedom when reaching the top didn't. It was his favorite childhood memory and came to the forefront of his mind as he looked out the window of the train.

He remembered one time when he was about six or seven, he had built a tree fort in the thicket of pines behind the shed. Choosing the ideal destination wasn't much unlike choosing a real home. Examining each dwelling, he searched for a solid foundation, an adequate covering in the event of rain, and a bed of carpet soft enough to lay on as he looked at his books.

Carefully, Robbie smoothed the fallen needles, spreading them evenly across the dirt floor of his new home. His hands were sticky with sap, but he didn't mind. As a boy, his mother would have been more concerned if he'd made it to supper clean.

A certain pride came with creating something as a boy. Just like the first time he'd held a pocketknife in his hand and used it to change the shape of a shard of wood. He hadn't been able to wait to come home from school to work on it.

Over several days, Robbie snapped dry branches from the lower portion of the tree, leaving just enough to obstruct the view from outside. And when the place was finished, he pulled one of his father's produce crates from the shed to the fort, transforming the structure into a realized sleeping quarter.

On bright days, the sun would softly spill through the openings of the evergreen boughs and fall upon his face, the scent of fresh pine filling his senses.

But one day, as he lay on the crate, his arms bent above his head, instead of looking *out*, he looked *up* as a thought occurred to him. What if he could create an upstairs that was even better than this old dirt floor?

Looking at the many limbs that stood between himself and the view from the roof, it was almost a daunting thought. *But what if he could? What if he could make it?* Even if it took days of clearing and careful climbing, he knew in his heart it would be worth it.

As luck would have it, it poured rain the next few days as he watched from the window, his dream's ambition being challenged through forced patience.

The first day of sunshine, Robbie set out again, determination in his heart. He saw the old pine in an entirely new way.

The first few limbs were easily maneuvered as he steadied himself one foot at a time so that he was stretched out like a rock climber, pulling with one hand as he lifted the opposite leg to gain footing. Slowly, he moved each of his own limbs in deliberate fashion, always moving upward.

As he repeated this process upward, Robbie was often tempted to look down at the familiar comfort of his old pallet, but found it slowed him down.

Look up, he reminded himself with each step.

When he made it as high as the limbs could bear his weight, he forgot about the cuts that burned through his tender skin or the sap that clung to his hair. The view from the roof overtook the pain of getting there. And though apple trees were more easily conquered, they lacked the views of that rugged, old pine.

But once at the top, there was nowhere to go. Though the beauty of endless views gave a sense of peace to him, there was still something unsettling about the restriction of being contained to the tree. And eventually, Robbie found his way down again.

Scoping out his new home, Robbie thought of that old pine tree now. He looked at the towering wall before him, trimmed in barbed wire, guarded by men who carried guns meant to stop anyone who dared look up.

And for the first time, he realized it wasn't the constriction of the tree which had made him feel uneasy as a kid, but his reliance upon it for the view.

Chapter Nineteen

The first thing Allu noticed were the mountains. They were so large, she could see their white peaks above the endless line of people who stood in front of her.

Powerfully large, their presence cut into the sky, white and magnificent. The mountains dwarfed everything around them, taunting Allu with a freedom she could see, but not touch. Papa often referenced the Sierra-Nevada Mountain Range…how sad he would be to know this was her first encounter with them. The mountains made the neat rows of shack-like buildings look as if they were an ugly afterthought to a masterful painting, a competition of natural beauty and horrid human taste.

Allu tugged on Mama's sleeve, but her eyes were elsewhere. Not on the mountains at all, but on *something* else.

Barbed wire fence.

It was all around them. She wondered what kind of animals they were trying to keep in. Barbed wire was only used when keeping in animals—animals who attempted to escape and had to be stopped with painful consequences.

Mama's hands were cold as she clutched her bag with white knuckles. The noises around them made it real, the cries and murmurs becoming the buzz of bees as Allu's insides began to boil like one of Mama's hot stews.

"What the hell," Robbie said, looking out toward the building in front of them.

Allu stretched on her tiptoes to see where the line was going. There must've been a couple hundred people in front of them, all shuffling in unison as the line moved forward.

"What's going on?" she asked. "Robbie, what are they doing?" She felt a surge of panic.

"I don't know," he said, shaking his head.

The line moved, causing everyone to move forward. Distant cries of children from the other end of the line filled the silence. Up ahead, there was a worn building that seemed to be sucking the line into it.

"Robbie?" Allu asked, her voice rising. "Tell me."

Everyone shuffled forward.

"Allu," Mama said, "be quiet." Her eyes were hollow and unrecognizable as she followed the line closer to the building.

What was happening? Where were they going? She struggled to see around the people in front of her, but the line seemed endless.

Someone from behind nudged Allu forward.

She loosened her grip on Mama's hand, realizing her fingernails had left marks in her skin. Mama stood stiffly, and Allu doubted she even noticed.

The line moved again.

"Typhoid vaccinations," an older woman in front of them whispered.

What was typhoid? Allu imagined a long sharp needle stabbing into her arm and she began to shake. She looked to Robbie for help, but even he stared blankly ahead, creases between his eyes. She had to do something.

The line moved.

With her mind, she urged him. *Robbie, do something! Papa! Where was Papa? He would stop this!*

The line moved again.

She wanted to protest but couldn't find her voice. She glanced around frantically, looking for someone, anyone who would stop these men from hurting her.

Didn't anyone care? There were other fathers around—not many, but enough to help her.

The line moved and then they were in front of the building.

She watched Robbie stare squarely at the nurse. The pretty one who offered a sympathetic smile.

He extended his arm out, expressionless.

How big was the needle? Allu wondered. She looked away.

And just like that, Robbie was moving ahead, pulling the line with him.

Everyone shuffled forward until Allu was right in front of the nurse, sandwiched between a rigid line of people and nowhere to escape.

Fighting back tears, she squeezed her eyes shut and stuck out her arm. She thought of the farm and the chickens. Just earlier today, she had fed them. It seemed so long ago.

The needle pierced through the skin of her arm in a sharp poke, followed by a slow burn that slid through her veins like a trail of fire.

"Next." The nurse's voice was indifferent. Not the pretty nurse with the nice smile, but the one standing beside her, the one who kept the line moving.

Allu's teeth ached and she relaxed her jaw. And then, it was over.

The line moved her a step away from the needles and the nurses. Another minute later, she was back outside. Her head pounded and her arm throbbed.

"Nice hospitality around here," Robbie said, giving her a pat on the back.

She smiled weakly, feeling a bit better. He seemed to be back to his old self.

For the first time, she noticed how cold it was. Despite the long sleeves, her shirt was much too thin for the emptiness of the place. Rubbing her arms, she looked around. Rows of wood shacks with tarpaper walls stood abandoned and unwelcoming. Bits of tattered tarpaper blew in the wind, tapping against the sides of the ugly buildings. Along the edge of camp was a long trench coupled with barbed wire. All around them, families sat with heaps of bags from the life they were leaving behind, a look of both confusion and bewilderment across their faces.

Allu held her bag tightly as two guards approached.

They began to inspect the card necklaces, dividing them into smaller groups, forcing them into different single file lines. *Were they separating them?*

She grabbed Mama's hand. *Did they know she was only twelve?* Japanese, but only twelve.

She forced out a breath.

A guard with tan skin and wrinkled eyes checked the cards to her right. A dark gray gun hung from his shoulder by a strap, pointing to the sky. How many times had he shot it? How fast could he pull it to his eye and jerk the trigger?

He muttered something to the guard next to him, who sneered.

Allu drew in a quiet breath, slow and steady as she looked to the ground. Wretched sand was everywhere. Colorless and lacking.

Taffy, Red Beard... To calm herself, she began to recite the names of her chickens in her mind.

Boots stepped heavy in front of her, and someone grabbed the card around her neck. *Attila.*

Time seemed to slow. She could feel his eyes glance from the card to her face, as if trying to decide whether her name matched her appearance. *Taffy, Red Beard, Attila...*

The guard turned the card over again before he moved to Mama. Allu bit her cheek until she tasted blood.

The man said something to Mama, who remained still with questioning eyes.

"Move!" he barked.

This time, she did as she was told.

***

Their assigned guard was young, made older by his uniform. He had bright eyes that contrasted dramatically with the sandy color of the place. As they walked through the buildings, he pointed out the mess hall, where meals were served three times a day, an hour at each designated time. Latrines and other various buildings were located just beyond. He used the word "barracks" to describe the building they'd live in.

They listened quietly, those in the back straining to hear, reliant upon those patient enough to pass along the information.

Dust hung in the desert sky, encompassing the camp like a haze of smoke, brought to life by movement. The seldom breeze carried bits of it that clung to the inside of Allu's throat, nostrils, and eyes before settling upon her skin like a veil of scratchy lace. Her throat burned as she coughed. Dirt, belonging on the bottom of shoes, became a constant reminder of her place in the world.

Their guard hesitated, looking from his map to the barracks.

She'd counted. They had passed eight rows of barracks. Without street names to mark each strip of dirt, she worried about getting lost. She'd have to find their apartment based on counting.

"I wonder if he could find his way out of a paper bag," Robbie smirked.

Another soldier passed by and chuckled at his mishap.

The guard's face reddened, and Allu realized he must have been about Robbie's age. She wondered if Jimmy had been recruited to herd up and watch over others like them. She hoped the war wouldn't change him or make him feel any differently about them. These days, anything was possible. Even the unthinkable.

They were the last in their group to be dropped off. This couldn't be it, could it? The building they arrived at looked like it was about to fall apart. Even from where they stood, Allu could hear the wind whistle as it blew through the cracks between the boards. A few steps led up to a rickety door, and dusty windows hid whatever was inside. Their chicken coop back home was better built.

Mama grabbed her hand, warm and strong, and looked at her with fear in her eyes.

Allu tried to smile. She must be strong for Mama. She had promised Papa. But did he know this would be their new home? How could it be?

Chapter Twenty

Ordinarily, Richmond Miller wouldn't have been smoking a cigarette. He'd be lying if he said he wasn't in possession of a pinup magazine, but he certainly wouldn't subject his lungs to the mercy of a large corporation's profit stick. Although, he had to admit, it did make him feel more like a man to say he smoked. Or maybe it was the gun.

How ironic life was. Take for instance the fact that just six months prior, he had been on a football field with countless homecoming hopeful cheerleaders lined up at his disposal. And now, here he stood in the Manzanar watchtower, with a pinup girl staring back at him on the glossy pages of a magazine—the only girl among the soldiers he toured with. Stuck in a California hellhole, guarding a wall when the real war was being fought overseas.

He took a drag of his cigarette and adjusted his rifle as he looked out across the endless desert. For miles, there was nothing. Absolutely nothing, save for a few scraggly trees and the occasional rattlesnake. Richmond often wondered on which side of the barbed wire fence he would rather be—open freedom with the threat of dangerous predators or in captivity with food provisions. Surely, one would die in the desert. If not by predators, then by the relentless heat of the sun or the freezing temperatures at night. Yes, life was a regular prankster, setting people up for one punchline or another.

From where Richmond stood, he had a bird's-eye view of the detainment center. Camp itself consisted of several hundred buildings, which had been constructed and aligned in such a way as to promote extreme organization. From the sky, it was reduced to a series of black rectangular patterns separated by strips of colorless dirt.

He'd been inside the renovated horse stalls. His first assignment had been to compartmentalize the stalls into smaller living quarters, accomplished by hanging sheets of tarp paper. As those were extremely flammable, he was careful to take his smoke breaks outside the buildings. But nothing could rid the smell of a stall once it had been occupied by animals who shit wherever they wanted. Hang up a few tarps, throw in a few metal coil beds, and it might resemble a human camp, but in the end, it still smelled like shit.

A few days prior, the place had had an eerie quiet to it, not much unlike the abandoned gold rush towns of the west Richmond had read about. Ghost towns. To have ghosts, first a town required lost lives. And right now, this one crawled with Japs.

He had enlisted in the army because his father expected it. And here he was, a glorified Jap-sitter.

"Richmond," his father would say in a stern voice, "if you don't have honor of duty and doing what's right, then you don't have anything."

Richmond had learned his father's sense of meticulous habit the hard way at ten years old, starting with the consequences of not having polished shoes for church. The five scars on his hand served as a reminder of the importance of representing your family well.

Leaning back in his chair, he kicked his boots up and wiped away remnants of the desert that had formed a cake of orange dust around the soles. The dust that staked its claim on everything within a wind's breath away. Surely, he now understood his father's mad perfectionism of clean boots, even if he didn't understand his means of enforcing the idea.

He checked his watch, gave one last glance around the premises before calling it a day, and headed to supper. There was sure to be another train arriving tomorrow, and another after that. Hopefully, the trains would bring a little more excitement than seeing what kind of canned vegetable was for dinner. Again.

And with that, Richmond pinched the stub of his cigarette between his fingers and flicked it into the hungry sands of the desert.

Chapter Twenty-one

"Nice place," Robbie said, dropping his bag to the floor. The smell of musty fur was thick and overwhelming in the empty box they were to call home. No bigger than Allu's old bedroom and bathroom combined.

Allu walked to the bed and sat. It was the first time she'd been able to sit down since the train ride. Coils pressed round and springy against her bottom as the weight of her body sunk into the worn, thin mattress.

For a moment, no one said anything as Robbie inspected the place, tapping his toe against the wall or on a rotten board, examining the extent of repair needed. Nothing could make this shack feel like a home.

Just yesterday, she had been in class. Sixty days ago, she had been with Papa in fields of corn, and all had been perfect in the world. *How had this happened?*

"Robbie," Mama said, breaking the silence. "You take that corner. Allu and I will sleep over here."

"How long are we staying?" Allu asked. If her mother even knew.

Robbie laughed, cold and sharp. "As long as this damn war lasts, I imagine."

Mama tapped him across the back of the head with her hand. "Watch your language, young man."

A wounded look flashed momentarily across his face. "My language is the *damn* least of concerns in this situation." He threw his bag across the room to the other bed. "I'm going out to have a look around."

"Robbie" Mama grabbed his arm and looked at him with pleading eyes.

He hesitated before pulling his arm away and headed for the door.

***

Allu and Mama organized the place as best as they could. More than one bag a person never would have fit. Not for the first time, Allu wondered what would happen to the rest of their belongings back home. Back at their *real home*.

She pushed the thought from her mind and busied herself with dusting the dirt from the windowsill as Mama pulled sheets from their bags, fitting them around the limp mattresses. Each bed had been pushed to opposite ends of the room to provide as much space and privacy as possible. Once the place was cleaned, they would hang a rope across the walls, dividing the room with an extra sheet.

Allu carefully unrolled the jars of produce, lining them up neatly along the shelves surrounding the room. They were so beautiful...the only color in the room, really, and she wondered if they even had to eat them. Just looking at them made her think of Papa, and a sadness filled her heart.

Despite the emptiness, it was a loud place. The paper walls whistled with the floorboards as cold air pushed both wind and sand through its cracks, which scattered across the room in a thin sheet. Mama frantically swept, but not as quickly as the dust came in.

Robbie reported back sometime later with a layout of the camp. There were about five hundred barracks spread across thirty-six blocks. The mess hall, laundry building, and latrines were located a few blocks from their barrack.

They sat and listened, wrapped in army blankets. There was one per bed. Allu's skin itched against the abrasiveness of the wool, and she regretted packing her books and not more blankets.

Mama began to moan, clutching her stomach.

"Mama, are you okay?" Allu asked. She looked ill.

"Typhoid shot," Robbie said.

He walked over and placed his hand on Mama's back. "I overheard people talking about it all over camp."

Allu grabbed her hand with a sudden urgency to locate the latrines. Night had fallen, pouring a sheet of stars among the heavens, leaving the mountain air bitterly cold and the wind an insult to their lack of warm clothing.

"Hurry," Mama whispered.

Robbie insisted on escorting them, although Allu knew it had less to do with his sense of direction and more to do with his sense of responsibility as the head of the household.

"Just a bit further," he confirmed over his shoulder.

They struggled to keep up as Mama clutched her stomach and had to stop every few steps. Sweat beaded across her forehead.

"Almost there," Allu said gently, trying to stay strong for her mother. "Just a few more steps."

Mama's shoulders dropped as they reached the latrines and saw a long line waiting. Either the typhoid vaccination had affected many residents about the same time, or they were hoping for the privacy a night visit would offer. Mama looked as hopeless as most of the women in line.

"I don't think I can wait," she whispered to Robbie, her eyes scrunched together. She had begun rocking back and forth.

"Allu-chan, stay with Ma." Robbie made his way to the front of the line, where a couple of older women stood. For a moment, they spoke amongst themselves.

She wished they'd hurry up. Even from where they were standing, the stench was undeniable. Mama was strong and prideful, but Allu didn't know how long she would make it.

Finally, the women ahead shook their heads in agreement.

"They're waving us over!" Allu cried, but her mother didn't answer.

"Ma?" She turned to find Mama silently wiping tears from her cheeks, her head hung low. She tried to remember the last time she'd actually seen her mother cry, which made the situation that much more unbearable.

"What is it?" Allu asked softly.

Mama's sniffles grew louder, and a few women looked over.

Robbie seemed to notice as well, a look of concern on his face as he left the women at the front of the line.

"Too late," Mama said sheepishly.

It took a moment for Allu to realize what Mama was saying until she saw the wet sand beneath her, the dignity leaving her body in a muddled mess in the dirt, surrounded by strangers.

"It's okay, Mama," she said, wrapping her arm around her thick waist. "No one even notices. It's okay."

But it wasn't okay. None of this was okay. And it hurt. It hurt her heart, her pride, her dignity. It hurt more than losing her friends. More than the shots. More than being fenced in. Mama's spirit, always strong and prideful, was slowly dying, and there was nothing Allu could do but watch.

Chapter Twenty-two

Order and efficiency soon regimented their lives. Standing in line had become a significant necessity required for basic needs Allu had always taken for granted. Going to the restroom had to be planned and neatly tucked into the schedule between a maximum of two-hour chunks of time.

Mama was adamant they eat as a family. Whether it was knowing it helped her maintain a level of normalcy, or the fact that neither Allu nor Robbie had anyone else to eat with, they agreed. And so that morning, like most, they walked as a family to an unknown breakfast.

The mess hall was about a fifteen-minute walk away. The line met them only ten minutes into that walk as Mama cursed under her breath, claiming a spot behind an elderly man who barely acknowledged their presence.

"Allu," she said, peering around the people in front of them, "see that man wearing the black hat?" She pointed to a man who stood only five people from the counter. "Go ask him how long he's been waiting."

She opened her mouth to protest, but quickly closed it again. Mama looked as if she had aged years within the days they had been here, and looking at her now, her eyes were red and apologetic. Her ability to protect her babies had been taken away. Her role to cook for and nurture her family had been reduced to a dependence on strangers to serve them whatever foods could be produced and prepared for large quantities of people. Usually, that meant canned goods. Or hot dogs. And Allu had never even liked hot dogs.

Nodding, Allu squeezed her way into the building, past the long line of people who seemed just as tired as Mama. They watched her with narrowed eyes but said nothing.

"Thirty minutes," she reported back a few minutes later.

Mama's eyes scrunched slightly.

Allu couldn't remember the last time she had seen her smile.

"I'm not that hungry anyway," Robbie said, placing a hand on their mother's shoulder. "Do you want to stay or go back?"

Allu knew he was lying. He'd never pass up a meal of any kind. Even hot dogs. She guessed Mama knew, too, as she tilted her head to one side and raised her eyebrows.

Robbie glanced at Allu expectantly.

"Me, neither," she said, a little less convincing.

They had missed supper the evening before, and her stomach now rumbled in protest. She wondered how many days a person could go without eating before withering away into the dirt.

Mama held her hand to her cheek, rocking back and forth. "It will be at least another forty minutes," she said. "I suppose we could go back and eat some of the jarred fruit."

Allu glanced to Robbie, who nodded in agreement, as she reluctantly gave up her place in line to a girl just a few years older than herself.

Not long after, they sat inside their apartment and shared a jar of sweet cherries for breakfast. Neither of them mentioned Papa's name as they plucked the sweet red fruit from the jar, but despite how small the room was, an emptiness filled its corners. Allu knew life would never be the same or that cherries would never taste as sweet.

Chapter Twenty-three

It didn't take long for camp to break apart families, and by late March, the binds of tradition began to fray one strand at a time. It started in the mess halls, where children ran wild and mothers ate solemnly, their roles as caregivers ripped away, replaced by soldier's commands.

They ate on pie tins, trying to forget the lives they left behind. Lives promised by the American dream.

Some mess halls were lucky enough to permit detainees who had been chefs and restaurant owners to cook. They created soup bases with ketchup and water. Fried bologna was sugared for dessert, and hot dogs were sautéed with rice or added to eggs in breakfast bakes.

But, Allu hadn't been fortunate enough to be assigned to one of those halls, so she waited in line, hoping for some kind of variation.

A guard dug his metal ladle deep into a steamy pan and pulled out a pile of mixed vegetables without looking up. A hot dog dropped on her plate, slick with sweat from sitting in a pan of water. Hopefully, she'd gotten in line early enough to get her hands on some ketchup or soy sauce to make the food edible.

"I think you're a little too old for milk," a scratchy voice said from behind the counter when she reached out for a cup of milk.

She grabbed water instead, thinking he was much too old to be serving it.

Mama and Robbie were consumed with plans of building some furniture for their barrack when Allu plopped down next to them. If they noticed her disappointment, they said nothing. There was extra scrap lumber near the slaughterhouse, she heard Robbie say, and he could grab a few pieces a little at a time to make a table. What was the use of a table without any food to eat on it? But the glimmer in his eyes made her keep the thought to herself.

Someone tapped her on the shoulder. "May I sit here?"

The girl looked about Allu's age. She balanced her pie tin in one hand and a glass in the other.

Allu noticed her cup was filled with milk and felt her cheeks burn. She didn't need any friends. She didn't want any friends. It wouldn't be much longer and they'd be back home, and she could tell Lucille about this dreadful place and Lucille would feel bad and—

"Free country." Allu smirked, sliding closer to Robbie.

For just an instant, she felt a bit ashamed of herself, and looked to Mama, thankful she hadn't heard.

Instead of moving on to another table, the girl giggled and squeezed in beside her. It was going to be one of *those* days.

"I'm Kiko," she said, extending her hand. "Block nine, barrack two with my mother, father, and…"

"Your father's here?" Allu interrupted the girl, who already seemed to have everything she didn't. She shoved a forkful of rice in her mouth, trying not to despise her.

"Yes," Kiko said slowly, "but he hasn't been much like himself since becoming sick."

Ungrateful girl. At least she *had* a father.

"Aren't they eating?" Allu looked around the mess hall, wondering if she would take a hint.

Kiko shrugged. "My brother's napping, and Mama didn't want to leave him." She neatly picked at her hot dog bun. "I'd give anything for salted butter." She sighed.

"I'd give anything for fresh vegetables," Allu mumbled, looking to her mother, who was too busy talking with Robbie to notice.

The girl was quiet, watching her with patient eyes.

Allu shifted uncomfortably. "My father was a farmer."

"Really?" Kiko asked. "What did he plant?"

It was the first time anyone had asked about her family. About their real life. The life they'd had *before*. Thoughts and conversations at the camp had slid away from such topics and more toward a constant worry of whether there would be enough food to eat or whether the latrines had installed curtains yet. Or had even been pumped that day.

Allu's heart clenched inside her chest, and she was about to change the subject when Mama looked over and smiled at them. She dropped her shoulders. "Whatever was in season, I guess. Butter lettuce, green beans, sugar-snap peas sweet enough to eat plain. Mama would scold us for eating all the veggies before she could steam them."

"You're lucky," Kiko said, taking a bite of the colorful pile of mush.

"We had to buy our vegetables from the market on special occasions. Most the time, we stocked up on canned vegetables."

If the girl wanted her to feel sorry for her because of that, she was mistaken, and should go find someone else to dump her sob story on.

"Or maybe you're the lucky one, because it makes eating *this* so much easier," Allu said.

Kiko turned out to be relentless for a skinny scrapper, making room for herself next to Allu again the following day. Either that, or she was completely dumb to the fact that Allu didn't care about her or her family.

She didn't need any friends. She didn't want *any* friends. She only wanted to get back to the farm. Back to where everything would be the same as it had been. Where she and Lucille would go to the junior high fling together and all would be as it always had been. Lucille would curl Allu's hair with her rollers as she had promised. People would realize Japanese American citizens weren't the enemy, and they'd win this war together.

Designing a flower out of peas, Allu half-listened to Kiko rattle on about her old life back in San Francisco.

Despite her best efforts, Allu would have to be blind not to notice the girl had a pretty face. A face that looked young enough to still get milk at camp, but old enough to get boys' attention. She gestured dramatically when she spoke, her two glossy black braids swaying, long parted with great precision down the center. Obviously, her mother had done it.

Allu tried to remember the last time Mama had braided her hair. Was she too pre-occupied to offer, or was she waiting to be asked?

Kiko glanced over to make sure Allu was listening.

Allu broke apart the flower before mashing the peas with her fork.

The next afternoon, she wedged herself between Robbie and Mama at lunch.

"Allu, what on earth are you doing?" Mama asked.

Robbie's back was to them so he could face some girls who had sat next to him. It was cramped. Mama looked at her with raised eyebrows but moved over as much as she could. Every time she reached her fork to her mouth, she knocked into Robbie's back.

"Do you mind?" he finally asked.

What a grouch.

Allu glanced around the hall, but Kiko wasn't at any of the tables or even in line. Probably found someone else to interrogate, or maybe she was with her perfect family.

It was a quiet lunch as Mama spoke with the other women at the table

95

and Robbie flirted with his new admirers. No one seemed to care enough to talk to her.

Good, it's better this way.

Chapter Twenty-four

The only consistency in camp was the dust. Dust that swallowed Allu and her family whole like a swarm of bees.

They swept every couple of hours: a constant assault against the orange dry sand. Allu thought Mama might go crazy trying to keep their barrack clean as she ordered them to wipe the windows with damp clothes. Though it was a worthless effort, they complied for the sake of Mama's sanity.

And just when things had slowed into the familiarity of routine, things began to change too quickly to keep up.

Another train of families was dropped off at camp. Allu knew there'd be more, but she was still surprised when she heard the train. Maybe because deep in her heart, she was hoping it was coming to bring them back home to the farm.

Robbie was quick to see *what was going on*, which of course meant he was going to check out the population of new girls.

There was a low murmur of commotion as confused groups were led throughout the camp. Allu looked out the window and watched a guard make his way to their row.

"Huh," Mama said, throwing a hand on her hip. "These barracks are full. They must've moved some people out up the row."

Allu heard a light tap, and she and Mama both looked at the door. The soft tap began again. Deciding to check it out, Allu set her broom to the side and made her way over.

An older man with worried eyes and a slow smile stood in the doorway, a bag in his hand. Behind him stood a woman with peppered hair cropped just below her ears, holding the hand of a man who seemed much too old to be holding hands with his mother. He mumbled noisily to himself as he rocked back and forth.

Allu was relieved when Mama came up from behind her and greeted them warmly.

"You must be mistaken," she said, crease lines forming on her forehead. "This apartment is occupied. My daughter and son and I are staying here. See?" She pointed to the decorated interior of the place.

The old man shrugged apologetically. "That guard walked us over here himself."

Mama stepped outside and looked down the dirt strip between barracks. The quiet of the place had been replaced by chaotic cries and murmured voices as people filled the empty spaces of the area.

For a moment, they just stood there. The man looked to the wife who was too busy soothing, who Allu thought to be their son, to notice.

It was no use. There were families standing at the door of almost every barrack on the block.

"I could move our beds over to one side of the room," Allu offered.

Mama shot her a look of disappointment but gave her a nod.

Allu quickly pushed the metal bedframes to one side of the room before sitting territorially on her bed, in case anyone thought that was up for sharing as well.

The three newcomers quietly pulled their belongings out of their bags, tossing glances her way every so often. The boy must have been about eighteen or nineteen and seemed content when humming to himself as he sat on his bed and watched his parents unpack. She wondered if she'd be able to sleep with the noise.

How would they share this space? It was an animal stall, after all, not meant to be occupied by humans, let alone shared with strangers.

Chapter Twenty-five

From what Robbie could tell, there must've been about nine hundred people dropped off, excluding children who ran around too quickly to count. There were rumors of other camps located around the West Coast, and he wondered if they were as shitty as this one.

Tar paper walls with dirt or plank floors could not justify a home in the United States, could it? Robbie couldn't help but think of his old baseball team and wondered how many of the boys were left besides him and Jimmy.

Jimmy. What the hell happened to Jimmy? A void opened up in his chest, the kind he imagined he'd get when someone died.

They'd been through everything together. Everything but this damn war. What the hell would Jimmy say about a place like this, if he could see him now? What a waste Robbie had become.

He circled the area, searching the faces, trying to shake off the thought of his best friend and focusing on the task at hand.

"Excuse me, sir?" Robbie tapped an older man on the shoulder, then pulled out a worn picture from his back pocket. "Have you seen this man?"

Gently pulling the photo from his hands, the man looked at the picture as he shook his head just like all the others had done. "No," he said sadly before handing the picture back. He rested his hand on Robbie's shoulder. "Good luck finding your father."

Robbie believed he sincerely meant it.

***

By the time Robbie made it back, Mama had fixed some sweet tea and was talking politely with the guests, who she quickly introduced to

Robbie. Johnny, the man sitting upon the extra bed, said nothing. He stared at his hands, clasping and unclasping them. He glanced up at Robbie, making eye contact with him briefly before fixing his eyes back on his hands.

"Robbie," Mama said, "Mr. and Mrs. Kato tell me they were instructed to unpack here."

It was more of a question than a statement. Based on the number of new arrivals and the number of vacant barracks, Robbie figured it was true. He extended his hand out.

"But there's no room," Allu protested, fixing her eyes on Mama.

Mrs. Kato adjusted her teacup nervously, while Mr. Kato went and sat beside their son and wrapped his arm reassuringly around his shoulder.

"Allu—" Mama began.

"Don't even *try* to fix this. You can't fix this. You can't fix any of this," she yelled, storming out of the room, slamming the door behind her.

"Allu!"

"Ma," Robbie said, grabbing her arm gently. "Let her go."

He found Allu sitting on the steps outside, her face resting in her hands. She gave him a sideways glance.

"This is unconstitutional," she muttered without looking up.

When had his little sister grown up?

"That may be so," Robbie said gently, "but it's happening." He paused. "You know, I remember the first time I ever beat Papa playing chess." He smiled, remembering how proud he had been. "Ma was always the one to boost my confidence by letting me win. Gave me enough self-confidence to keep coming back to play Papa. But it was him who taught me the determination to persevere…to keep trying."

Allu dropped her arms and rested them across her knees.

"Every Sunday," Robbie went on, "we would return to our table on the porch to pick up where we left off from the week before. We'd been doing that since they gave me the set for my tenth birthday."

"I remember you yelling at me if I went anywhere near it," Allu said, still not looking up at him.

"So, over the years, I must've played him at least two hundred times. I began to think he was unbeatable."

"What did you do when you finally beat him?" she asked, finally meeting his eyes.

"I was fourteen. At first, I did what any fourteen-year-old would do." He shrugged. "I gloated. I jumped up and down and made my own winner's dance."

Allu's mouth turned slightly upward.

"But then, he told me something I'll never forget," Robbie said.

"How bad you are at dancing?"

"Not quite," he chuckled. "He said, *'Robbie-chan,'* in his calm voice, of course."

"Of course," she agreed.

"'Respect is not something given to you but is something earned.' I've replayed that over and over in my head in many different situations, and it seems to apply to everything."

Allu looked down at her feet.

"And so…" Robbie reached his arm behind his back and grabbed his seed bag, digging deep within it. Past his ball glove. Past his pictures. Past a yearbook of faces he may never see again. He pulled out the last personal item he'd chosen to pack. "I thought we could carry on his tradition."

"Papa's chess set!"

"Well, technically it's mine. But yes, Papa's chess set."

Allu wrapped her arms around his waist, taking him aback. Things would be okay. Soon, this war would be over and Allu could go home and beat Papa at checkers. The thought warmed his heart and nestled into his mind.

"You know…" She grinned, tracing the king's engravings. "Papa might say those things about respect, but he still hated to lose."

Robbie smiled, knowing it was true. "And I'm more like Papa than anyone else in this world."

Chapter Twenty-six

As Richmond lay in bed, he couldn't stop thinking about his mother. Not the looks of her, but glimpses of memories from everyday moments that had become the sum of her in his mind.

She had an elusive lust for life, and he wondered if it was attainable—something he could acquire, or something only a lucky few were born with.

Richmond was like his mother in all other ways, and no one could deny he was her child when looking at him. It wasn't a bad thing, as his mother had features typical of Scandinavian descent—features anyone would envy. She had grayish-blue eyes that sparkled when she laughed, inviting people to read her thoughts. Eyes that entranced and captured the attention of many. Eyes Richmond now found to be to his benefit when courting the ladies. And though his hair matched the pale yellow of his mother's, he had never been allowed to grow it beyond an army cut and couldn't say whether it held her natural curls.

His thoughts of his mother slid into thoughts of Emma Thompson, a girl from his hometown, and a smile crept up the side of his cheeks. He'd marry her, if she was available after the war. And the best part about it was that his mother liked her, even if his father didn't approve of her family.

All was still on his side of camp, as most of the military police were either asleep or on watch. He appreciated the quiet of the night, and could almost believe he was back in his North Carolina hometown when he closed his eyes. It was a rare occasion for him to wake up back home without the smell of flapjacks and sausage wafting down the hallway, the smell of syrup so thick, it seemed to make the air taste sweet. A smile would spread across his mother's lips as Richmond entered the kitchen, as if he was her single motivation for life itself.

"That boy needs to start getting up earlier and taking a little responsibility around here," his father would comment without looking up, forking a piece of a pancake. "We're not raising some kind of flower child. Not in my house. If you're going to be somebody someday, then you need to sit up straight and look like somebody."

Ignoring his father, his mother would slide her hand across the table, resting her neatly-polished nails on top of Richmond's, giving him a wink. Her nail color was the only thing inconsistent with the memory, changing from bubble-gum pink to cherry red. Her smile always remained the same.

Richmond did his best to cut the flapjacks, always cognizant of his father's judgmental watch. He held his fork upright with a shaky fist, effectively pinning the pancake to the plate as he had seen his father do, severing it into neatly sliced strips with each slide of his knife. But his hands struggled, leaving awkward, jagged pieces as it scraped clumsily against the plate.

In his memory, his mother took a sip of coffee, giving him a quick glance before clearing her throat. "There's a town social set for two Fridays out," she said, dabbing her lips with her napkin.

The attention was off Richmond as he watched cautiously from beneath dark lashes. His father chewed slowly, deliberately, before taking a sip of orange juice, his eyes set indifferently. A side-effect of the war, he now had the ability to mask his facial expressions. Only whiskey could break through.

"I thought it might be fun to go as a family," his mother offered, blowing gently on her coffee as she studied Richmond's expression.

The boy allowed a quick glance toward his father, admiring his mother's tenacity. John Linden was going to the dance with his family, and if he was lucky enough, Martha Landry would be there, too, wearing that red polka-dot dress that accentuated her waist and...

"Damn it, Eloise," his father snapped. "Life's not a country club." He put down his fork, wiping his hands neatly on his napkin as Richmond's mother's mouth wavered with her eyes. "Besides, I'm not in town that weekend."

At the age of fourteen, Richmond wasn't too young to know his father was having an affair and wondered if his mother knew.

"Very well then," his mother replied with forced cheerfulness. "Would you like another pancake, dear?" She pulled one the size of a silver dollar from the pile and placed it on his plate.

His father had already left the room when she gave the boy a wink.

That next day, so long ago, would always remain in his mind. It was the day of the dance.

"Rich," his mother called out the back door as he ran through the grass, a football tucked under the safety of his right arm. It was a hot day, and the perspiration only added to the authenticity of his imagined football persona.

He eyed his mother from across the yard. Dressed in a cobalt-colored dress made of silk, he wondered what his mother had up her sleeve.

"Yes, Mother?" he asked, wiping trickles of sweat from his forehead.

"Wash up." She placed her hands on each side of his face, kissing him on the forehead with pink lips he was sure he'd have to scrub to get off. "And put on your best clothes."

Even then, it didn't take a scientist to know his mother was pretty. Even without the makeup, she had a natural beauty that, when accentuated with the effort of cosmetics, provoked sideways glances from women and caused men to rush to relieve her from small tasks, such as opening the door or helping her take off her coat.

That night was no exception as she and Richmond walked through the crowd of the Recreation Hall to the dance floor, the jazz band encouraging everyone on the floor to break out the jitterbug.

Mother laughed as she danced, her blond waves meticulously pinned to her head, flashing dimples Richmond had never seen before.

He made his way outside, past a group of men who puffed on cigars, thankful for an escape from the noise and pressure of dancing. The music resonated in his ears, giving the night a soft hum, replaced by a voice he recognized as John Linden's, a fellow from his class.

"Truth or dare," John taunted.

Mark Hamilton, Henry Johnson, and a few boys Richmond didn't recognize from school sat across from him under a tall oak as they shared drags of a cigarette.

John nodded at Rich as he sat down beside him. His usual baseball cap and white tee-shirt replaced by a yellow and blue striped tie and navy blue suit, making him barely recognizable and almost laughable out of the context of his everyday clothes.

"Dare," Mark declared weakly as a smile snuck up on John's face.

"Go sneak under the bleachers and look up Miss Gable's dress," John said in a low voice.

Mark's eyes widened. "But, what if I get caught?"

"Look." John stared intently in Mark's eyes. "Would you rather go play with the girls?" He nodded to the group of girls up the trench, who were bouncing between the rhythms of laughter and whispers.

"Oh, alright." Mark sighed, then made his way up the hill in slow steps.

"And tell us the color and pattern to be sure you're not lying!" John yelled after him before turning to Henry.

"Truth or dare?"

"Truth," Henry said quickly.

"Hmm." John rubbed his chin in mock contemplation. "What bra size does your sister wear?"

They all laughed, except Henry, who was the only one of them with an older sister who was cute enough to notice.

Henry's cheeks reddened. "How the hell am I supposed to know that?"

"Oh, come on Henry." John stifled a laugh, keeping a straight face. "You've never noticed any of her laundry laying around?"

Richmond could feel his ribs about to burst.

"She's my sister, for Pete's sake."

Unable to hold back, Richmond and John broke out in laughter, barely able to choke out words.

"Fine," John managed eventually. "Dare, then."

Looking at the group of girls, Henry took a deep breath. "Okay, okay. I don't know my sister's, but I have seen Susie Anderson's."

The boys leaned in closer.

"She was staying over one night, and when they were downstairs listening to the radio show, I went to my sister's room looking for something."

"And?" John encouraged him.

"And, well, I couldn't help it. It was right there in front of me, laying on her overnight bag—as if she wanted me to see it."

John laughed. "Sounds like Susie, alright."

"B cup."

John nodded his head in approval while the other boys joined in, having no idea what that meant, but not wanting to be the ones to ask.

Next it was Richmond's turn. He pulled himself up to his feet. "Dare," he declared loudly, scared of being asked any questions regarding his mother's undergarments.

"Ooh, I've got one!" said one of the boys he didn't recognize. He thought maybe it was Mark's younger brother—he had the same big ears. "Go kiss Jean Linehan."

The boys turned their heads in unison to look at the group of girls, which included Jean. They waited in silence for Richmond's answer, hanging on his every word.

"Easy as pie." He heard the words escape from his mouth. His mind raced quicker than his heart as he made his way over to the group of girls, who had noticed him approach.

He looked back at the pre-adolescent blank faces of four boys, who were staring. It was now or never. He grabbed Jean's hand and pulled her up to her feet before leading her behind a tree.

"Look, Jean," he said, praying she wouldn't notice the scarlet shade that had crept into his cheeks. She was two years older than him, and at sixteen, knew a lot more about this than he did. "I was dared to kiss you." He dropped his eyes, wanting to be struck by lightning at that very moment. "But we don't have to. I could just maybe tell them we did."

For a moment, she looked at him, as if debating what to do. Her dress was tight-fitting, accentuating her waist, even as it covered her knees. Her usual straight hair had been replaced by curls pinned along the sides of her face.

He picked at a piece of bark. And then, without warning, her lips turned up into a slow smile and before he could think, she leaned into him so closely, he could smell the minty flavor of her gum. Rich felt her lips push up against his. His eyes closed briefly, and he thought his heart might leap out of his chest. He placed his hand on her hip as he had seen other men do on the movies, and to his surprise, it fit perfectly in the swell of her side.

When he opened his eyes, she gave him a quick peck on the cheek.

"For good measure," she teased.

He rummaged his brain for words more appropriate than *holy hell*.

"Oh," she added, grabbing his arm casually. "Here's a piece of gum. Put it in your mouth and tell them it came from me." She unwrapped the piece of gum, placing it in his hand with a smirk. "They'll like that."

She slipped back to her group of friends and gave him a wink as he walked away, a bit taller, to the awed silence of admiration from his group of friends, chewing mint gum with her lipstick smeared across his lips. Now *that* was a memory not to be forgotten.

The dance that night seemed to have the same effect on Mother as it did on Richmond, as she twirled around the kitchen after they'd returned home. She grabbed his hand at random as a means for spinning or dipping.

Richmond allowed himself to laugh a little, playing into his mother's joy as he abided. What they hadn't noticed, however, was his father sitting in the chair next to the bay window in the sitting room, regarding them with a tense jaw.

When Richmond's father switched the lamp on, his mother froze momentarily before dropping his hand, a blank expression sweeping over her face.

He'd never forget the glimpse of fear in his mother's eyes, nor the forced smile which quickly preceded it. A pleading, polite smile he recognized from every interaction he'd ever seen between his mother and father, and one that lacked in every way her dancing smile hadn't.

That night, he obeyed his mother and locked himself in his room after his father was too dizzy to hit straight. He had pulled his pillow over his ears, muffling the sounds coming from the room next to his, feeling like a cowardly kid, but vowing to wake up a man.

Chapter Twenty-seven

After dodging Kiko for several days, Allu had gotten comfortable eating alone. Well, basically alone, as the Katos sat by Mama, and Robbie sat with whichever girls favored his attention. But this morning was different. This morning, Kiko was back.

Allu hardly recognized her as the same girl who had insisted on pestering her daily. This girl sat alone, her head slumped over her tin. If it weren't for the double-plaited braids, Allu probably wouldn't have even noticed her.

Hesitating, Allu shifted her feet uncomfortably as she gathered her food and sat beside Mama and Robbie. Not that they noticed her, really. Her eyes were drawn to the sadness in Kiko's demeanor. *What was wrong with her?* She couldn't help but feel a little guilty at the way she had treated her.

"Ma?"

Mama went on talking about the possibility of a seamstress shop opening in camp.

Allu cleared her throat. "Mama?"

"What is it, Allu?" Mama asked, clearly irritated.

"Do you mind if I sit with someone?"

Mama looked around. "Who?"

"A friend."

"Oh!" Even Mama was surprised. "Of course."

Allu made her way over to Kiko, gently setting her tin down on the table.

"You don't have to pretend to like me," Kiko said, shifting her eyes from her plate to Allu's face and back to the plate again.

Allu felt a sharp pang in her chest. So, she had noticed her attempts of steering her away. "I know," she said hesitantly, sitting beside her.

She waited for Kiko to say something, but the girl focused her attention on the table instead.

"I haven't seen you around." Allu now wanted to be her friend more than anything in the world. Well, almost anything.

Kiko shrugged, without looking up. "Father's been ill."

Allu shifted uncomfortably. "I'm sorry. Is he…"

"Dead? No, but just the same."

Allu told Kiko about her father, speaking of him for the first time in weeks. How they both shared a love of birds and singing. How they took long walks, and worked the market together, and how he would always reward her work with a bit of the profit for a sweet.

Kiko listened quietly as Allu explained how FBI men took her father away in a big black car.

There was a long silence before Kiko spoke. "My father was a laborer in a sawmill. Best carpenter around. When he wasn't building things for other people, he'd build things in our garage for our family. The dollhouse was my favorite." Kiko looked whimsically at her fork. "It reminded me of a gingerbread house, with its shutters and shingles neatly trimmed and painted my favorite color of blue."

Allu listened, and Kiko went on. "He even made these itty-bitty beds and chairs and any other furniture you can imagine. Mother sewed all the blankets and people." Kiko held her smile for just a moment before her lips turned down.

"That sounds beautiful."

Allu had never had a dollhouse, though sometimes she had snuck off to Robbie's fort with her best doll and drink tea as high-society people did.

An idea popped in her head. "Hey," she said, excited over the idea, "maybe we can build a dollhouse together."

Kiko sat up, looked into Allu's eyes. "Really?"

"Why not? We've got nothing else here worth doing."

***

Falling asleep to unfamiliar rhythms of strangers' sleeping habits was a skill Allu hadn't mastered and wasn't sure it was one she ever could. Mama was already asleep, her body at the mercy of the air she sucked in and out as her chest rose and fell indifferently. With Mrs. Kato's blessing, she had draped a linen sheet across the room, splitting the apartment in half and offering what little privacy it could.

Allu stared at the sheet, which had once been the sail of a ship on many star-filled nights back on their porch long ago. As much as she tried, she couldn't imagine the sheet being anything more than what it was—a sheet on a rope.

And no matter how many sheets of tar paper had been put up, an animal stall was still an animal stall. But maybe she and Kiko could design something beautiful within it. The type of house they wished they could live in. Maybe it would even be realistic enough to pretend it *was* their house.

She wondered if Robbie could help them find paint. Yellow. She hadn't seen the color in months. She would paint the front door yellow. And they would love the new house and take pride in it.

Even if they were too old for dolls.

Chapter Twenty-eight

Generally, the Katos kept to themselves, which was nice, because on most days, Allu didn't feel like talking much. Mr. Kato was a retired fisherman who'd worked in the canneries on Terminal Island for a solid thirty years before retirement. Like Papa, he had come to the U.S. by ship, along with two older sisters and his mother and father, in hopes of a more prosperous life. Allu liked to secretly pretend the Katos were her grandparents. It made the situation a little more normal, and she'd never met her own, so it was kind of a win-win.

Mrs. Kato explained one day over tea, how she had been a teacher for a couple of years when she had met her future husband at a dance with her friends. Not long after, they had married and learned she was expecting.

Naturally, they had imagined raising a son who would be like his father. They joked over whether he'd like baseball as his father did or art and literature like his mother. Pregnancy had been a joyous period of preparation and reflection as she had come to love the little kicker within her tummy.

It was a cold, rainy day the afternoon Mr. Kato had been called from his boat to meet his wife at the hospital. He had raced there, hardly noticing the stop signs he passed or the fact he still wore his mucky waders. His wife had already been lying in bed, her hair damp and matted against her forehead as she pushed air forcefully from her mouth in dragon-like puffs. Without any comparison, the labor seemed to go smoothly, and an hour later, baby John arrived.

In fact, Mrs. Kato explained, Mr. Kato hadn't realized anything had gone wrong until the doctor had frantically began pulling at the umbilical cord, shouting commands to the nurses who hustled in and out, passing medical instruments to the doctor who hardly acknowledged their presence.

The baby's face had taken on a purple hue as the doctor's expert hands fumbled with the cord, which had wound its way around the baby's neck. Once yanked free, the baby was quickly handed off to a nurse's arms and rushed out of the room. And just like that, the air had gone still and quiet.

Mrs. Kato's eyes glistened, and Allu could tell she was about to cry.

Mama handed her a handkerchief and placed her hand on Mrs. Kato's arm, waiting patiently for her to compose herself before going on.

She told them how she had begun to sob, demanding to see her baby.

Mr. Kato had helplessly stroked his wife's arm, reassuring her it would be okay, though the look on his face reflected her own.

It had been easy for Mr. Kato to believe his baby was not unlike any of the others. Through the glass window of the nursery, baby John slept, neatly tucked within the security of a cotton blanket. His face had been the most beautiful face Mr. Kato had ever seen—round and perfect with little ears no bigger than the size of his thumbnails.

He opened his eyes for the first time as Mr. Kato held him, and the man was positively smitten.

"We soon began to see the difference between Johnny and the other boys," Mrs. Kato said. "While other mothers were chasing their active toddlers around the room, looking worn-out, I was desperately encouraging mine to walk. Or explore. Or do *anything* other than cry."

Truth was, Mrs. Kato told Allu and her mother, John didn't do much. He slept a lot and sat a lot. She had faithfully brought him to his checkups, as any diligent mother would have and asked many questions. The doctor had reassured her that he was on pace with his growth projection and on track to be big for a Nisei boy. Still, her maternal instinct told her something was off.

"As John grew, it became more and more obvious that something wasn't right. He was easily frustrated and often cried, only subsiding long enough to revert to yelling. We tried everything to correct his behavior: positive incentives with treats, negative incentives with isolating him in his room, and everything in-between. By age ten, we had accepted the idea that John was different. Neither better nor less." She shrugged. "Just *different*."

Their hopes of cheering for him during baseball games or watching him chase kids on the playground had finally died. And no matter how much Mrs. Kato tried, she struggled to fit in with all the *mom* conversations. She had so desperately wanted to find companionship and bonding with them, desperate for someone to say the things on her mind. *My son often needs help brushing his teeth. He hates loud noises to the point of locking himself in his room and hums as he rocks. Yours doesn't take showers, either?*

Mrs. Kato would have laughed in understanding, as mothers do when confiding in the shared joy of parenting challenges. *They are boys!*

But those conversations existed only in her mind, while the other mothers arranged carpools for birthday parties Johnny wasn't invited to, or discussed sports politics on why so and so hadn't been playing such and such position on the little league team.

Mrs. Kato had smiled politely and told herself that she was in fact a mother as well. Maybe even a better one for the patience her child demanded—and who needed friends outside of their little family, anyway?

But she couldn't shake the feelings of guilt when acknowledging her grief over the boy that would never be.

"Now that he's an adult, he's learned to control his emotions, and mostly keeps to himself," Mrs. Kato said.

She took a sip of tea to compose herself. "But sometimes, I feel so alone. I wish he would give me a hug or do anything to reciprocate affection. Johnny doesn't show a preference of being with others or being left to himself."

Allu listened carefully. Already she'd heard Mrs. Kato cry herself to sleep on several occasions, but assumed it was more to do with their internment than with their son. Now, she realized, perhaps it was both.

But still, she loved him with her entire being. God had trusted her to care for him. And he was incredible, she told them. He could recite many species of fish—something Mrs. Kato wished she could take credit for, but that was her husband—and had more humility than most adults she knew. He said hi to every person they passed on the street, and if they didn't say hi back, he'd assume they didn't hear him and said it louder. He had told her he loved her exactly three times, but it had been in the right context, and the best words she'd ever heard.

Mr. Kato often walked with their son. It was hard for Allu to imagine him as an unruly child. She'd heard nothing more than humming come from him, and only when he played his music. She figured it helped to calm him down. Ella Fitzgerald was his favorite, and Allu thought he might even be sweet on her. They often listened to Mr. Kato's record player, which brought life to their little apartment.

***

A few days later, Allu came home from lunch with Kiko to find Johnny on the front porch, jumping up and down and clapping his hands. It was so unlike him; she felt her heart speed up with anticipation.

"Come see, come see," he said. He grabbed her hand, his own much bigger than hers, but very gentle. He pulled her to the corner of the barrack.

What on earth was he so excited about?

He reached underneath the wooden planks, pulling out a cardboard box. "Look," Johnny said, lifting the lid.

Two balls of leftover yarn were wrapped haphazardly in the box. Not quite as exciting as Allu had hoped, but she tried to show enthusiasm. "Are green and blue your favorite colors?"

"No. Look!" He gently pushed the yarn to the side of the box with his finger, exposing something gray and very much living!

"What is it?" Allu resisted the urge to reach down and pick it up.

"Mouse." He clapped again. "Yeah, yeah. Mouse. John Mouse."

Allu felt a twinge of pleasure and wanted to clap herself. "Where did you find it?"

He pointed.

"The rafters?" she asked.

He nodded.

"He's so tiny. John Mouse?"

"John. John Mouse," he confirmed, his mouth twisted in a lopsided grin. "You. Hold him."

"Really?" A spark of warmth ignited inside her chest.

John clapped, unable to keep from bouncing on his feet.

Allu scooped up the creature and stroked his fur as he quivered at the mercy of her careful hands. Suddenly, all the world seemed a better place, and all that mattered was keeping this tiny thing safe. How did it ever stand a chance, she wondered, if it felt the pull of the largeness of the world while trapped within four walls.

They stood there for a while. Just the three of them. John had been saving bits of crusted bread in the pocket of his sweater, and pulled out a pinch, placing it in the box.

When the dinner bell rang, it signified a renewed sense of purpose.

Johnny, of all people, had given her something the government couldn't: something to care about. And John Mouse made a lot less noise than the chickens.

Chapter Twenty-nine

"I miss the farm," Allu said one day to Robbie.

It had been almost three months since leaving. Allu was scared to say what she really thought. *I miss Papa, but he's most likely dead. What did we do to deserve this? How could grown-ups treat families this way? Didn't people become nicer when they turned into parents?* But all the words got jumbled and came out as "I miss the farm."

"You know, Allu-chan," Robbie said, following a stint of silence, "the farm was never really ours."

"What?" She snapped up in bed. What was he saying? Of course it was theirs. Or Papa's, at least.

Robbie sighed, his silhouette rolling over to face her. "Allu, we rented the farm."

She struggled to understand, feeling the blood pump into her temples and all the places it shouldn't be.

"Papa's Nisei," he went on. "He's technically not even an American citizen, which means he could never own a house or buy land."

Allu felt her breath hitch in her throat, giving rise to an anger that bubbled in the pit of her stomach. "Then what happened to it?" She didn't care about waking Mama. Was she in on this, too? "Robbie!"

"I don't know," he snapped. "It's probably been rented out again."

"What? They can't do that!"

"Would you quiet down? Of course they can. If they can load us up like a bunch of cattle and fence us into a camp, they can take our farm. Look, I'm only telling you this because I think you're old enough to know."

"What about our belongings? What about Papa's stuff? What about the chickens?"

Robbie sighed. "Ma and I sold most of the valuables before we left."

How dare they? Her cheeks burned as a pulsating pain beat in her temples. That was unforgivable.

"We had no choice, Allu," Robbie said sullenly. "Even with as little as they paid out, if it wasn't sold, it would've been stolen."

His harsh words hurt her heart and stung her eyes with tears she thought she'd run out of crying. She would *never* forgive them. *They were liars. They were all liars!* Papa would have told her. He would've sat them down at the kitchen table and talked it over as a family.

But Papa was gone.

Ignoring her brother, Allu rolled over to face the wall, tucking her legs into her chest. Her heart physically hurt.

She remembered hearing once that feelings didn't actually come from your heart, but from chemicals made by your brain. But her heart ached anyway, and her entire soul felt as if it had been ripped out of her body and exposed. A wide-open hole gaped where her heart once had been, leaving nothing but a hollow cavity for the harsh truth to settle into.

How many believed that had ever had their dad and their home stripped away from them? How many had ever had their identity and past nearly erased? Allu missed her old self, the one that roamed freely on the farm, blissfully unaware of the truth that lurked in its shadows.

She missed the sounds of nature. The way the wind blew through the openings of pine trees older than she was, whistling. The sound of orioles singing as they perched beside her bedroom window.

Her bedroom window. She'd once had her own room. The memory almost seemed surreal. Her own space—a place where she could read with the windows open, inviting the sounds of Earth's creations to fill the room.

But at camp, there were too many sounds and not enough space. Sounds of hammering, and bells signaling what to do next. A constant clamor of people talking and yelling, of neighbor's whispers heard through thin walls and babies crying. And there was nowhere to go to get away and think, and nothing but sand to draw.

That's what camp was. A whole lot of nothing. No birds—Allu couldn't remember the last time she'd seen a bird. No books, other than those that passed military inspection, and no identity without any family photos or heirlooms.

Her past depended on her memory of it, but the more she tried to remember Papa's face, the less she could. She began to forget the details in his laugh lines and the way his face changed when he frowned. The exact shade of his hair. She felt less and less connected with her past. Where did she even belong?

She couldn't find much in common with anyone. The government assumed because Japanese people looked alike, they were alike. The government liked sameness, neatly categorizing people and things—which they deemed interchangeable—into groups of the same. Even daily schedules in camp looked the same.

Yet at the same time, the future was unnervingly unpredictable, and there was too much danger in dreaming when too much had been taken away.

Chapter Thirty

Oahu, Hawaii

June, 1942

"I don't know where we're going," Yukio said. "I'm afraid they'll send us to Japan." The words were blurted out before he could think about how his grandfather must be feeling. He didn't want to worry him.

Earlier that day, all second-born Japanese Americans serving in the guard had been recalled to Schofield Barracks, their weapons taken away. They'd been told under strict orders of confidentiality that they'd be heading overseas.

His grandfather frowned at him. "General DeWitt, he not like us. Who knows what he has in mind. You remember to make your family proud and not bring shame."

Yukio gave him a nod. This was a man who had left everything to come to the United States when his family had been starving on their farm under the modernization of Japan and its massive taxes and debts on to farmers.

"It won't be for long, I hope," he told Leinani, holding her hand tight. He could tell she was trying not to cry for the sake of his grandfather, but her lip quivered. Her eyes welled with unshed tears as she squeezed his hand.

"We'll win this war," he said, shifting his eyes to his grandfather. "We have to."

He tried not to worry even as his insides twisted. Serving in the Hawaiian National Guard, Yukio was sworn to protect the islands and guard its barbed-wire beaches from another attack. He had been in the thick of the attack and did his best to defend what was left of the Pacific Fleet and Hawaiian citizens.

That had to count for something, didn't it?

Chapter Thirty-one

In June of 1942, parents got together and decided it was important to create as much normalcy as possible for the kids. Several teachers were hired, along with any internees who had teaching experience, and they had themselves a school. Without books, it didn't seem much like a school to Allu, but it made the parents feel better and gave the kids something to do.

Allu's teacher was a lovely young internee who had gotten her teaching degree before the war. She played learning games and quizzed on history facts, arithmetic, and anything else deemed important.

Allu and her classmates sat in the dust against the tar paper walls or on boards they found. There must have been about forty kids in the class, and fortunately for Allu, Kiko was one of them. They sat together, partnering up to practice lessons and learn more about each other. It was a slow and comfortable sort of friendship.

"Ready to go?" Kiko asked as they stood outside the building on the first day after school had been dismissed.

Mama had strict instructions. "Well, I'm supposed to wait for Robbie—"

"We can wait," Kiko interrupted.

Allu sighed. She'd seen that look before. What was it that girls found so irresistible in her brother? It was annoying. Still, she couldn't help but feel sorry for Kiko.

"Okay." She shrugged.

"How was school, Allu-chan?" Robbie asked as he arrived, messing up her hair.

She quickly glanced around to make sure there weren't any boys her age watching. She hated being treated like a kid. Kiko giggled, and already Allu regretted waiting for him.

"Okay, considering we didn't have any books or chalkboards," she replied.

"Isn't it swell?" He grinned, which sent Kiko into a fit of girlish giggles.

Allu shot her a look of warning. "Yes, if you don't like to learn, I guess it would be."

"The boys were talking in class. I guess there's a baseball team building." Kiko's cheeks blushed slightly.

"Robbie plays ball," Allu said. "He was one of the best in town."

"*Was*," Robbie emphasized. "There are more important things than baseball. Besides." He shot them a sideways glance and raised his eyebrows. "I don't know if they could handle me."

Kiko stifled another giggle, and Allu rolled her eyes in disgust. It would be a long walk home. She made a mental note to talk to Mama about walking alone the next day.

"When are try-outs?" she asked.

"Hell, if I know," Robbie said.

Allu glanced at Kiko, who didn't seem bothered by his language.

"I'm not trying out."

She stared at her brother. "What? What do you mean?"

Just then, footsteps thudded behind them. The boy with dark eyes from the train station came running past with an evil smirk on his face as he knocked Robbie's hat off.

That guy.

There was something about him Allu didn't like. Instinctively, she grabbed Robbie's arm as the boy ran off. Robbie's jaw clenched, his cheek muscle bulging out.

"Now *that* is the opposite of a gentlemen," Kiko said, grabbing Robbie's hat from the ground and slapping the dust from it before handing it back to him. "His name's Haruto. He's in our block. Rumor has it, he makes his own *saki* with rice leftover from the kitchen."

"Really?" Allu let go of her grasp on Robbie's shirt.

"He keeps it buried in the dirt. Under the barrack." Kiko looked satisfied at having their attention.

"And I hear he's bad company," Robbie added seriously. "Stay away from him." His voice hinted at knowing something Allu and Kiko didn't.

She began to open her mouth to ask.

"Allu. I mean it."

"Okay. Fine, whatever."

His gaze shifted to a group of senior high girls.

Allu sighed. "Go ahead."

"Really?" he asked.

"Go ahead."

"Ma said—"

"Never mind what Mama said. I'm not a baby anymore."

"If you're sure," Robbie said, positioning his hat, his attention on the girls across the dirt road.

She guessed he hadn't really been listening. "Go," she ordered him.

Not long after, it was just her and Kiko again. "Boys," she sighed, shaking her head.

"Boys," Kiko agreed quietly, her gaze still following him at a distance.

Chapter Thirty-two

Over the summer, things fell into a different pattern, and with each passing day, Allu's life on the farm became a distant and foreign memory.

She had an understanding with Kiko that if she were to get to the mess hall first, she would save her a seat, and vice-versa. The food had gotten better as they allowed each block to choose a cook, and though there were still far too many meals consisting of hot dogs, the rice and ketchup sauces made it more bearable. Soy sauce became an elusive best friend.

Kiko was a good friend, but Allu couldn't help but compare her to Lucille. Lucille was everything Allu wanted to be, but couldn't. Kiko was everything she was, but didn't want to be. But unlike Allu, Kiko seemed content with who she was. Sometimes even proud. Anyway, her friendship with Allu gave her a much-needed separation from Mama and Robbie and the Katos.

They spent most of their free time sitting in the limbs of pear and apple trees in the abandoned orchard Camp Manzanar was named after, talking about boys. They had learned about Manzanar's history in class. It was hard to believe that dry, dusty patch of nothingness had once been a beautiful garden ten thousand years ago when Native American Paiutes had taken care of the land with respect, building unique irrigations systems using water from snow-fed Sierra streams. Under their care and mutual respect for nature, they had nurtured the land, and it had produced pine nuts, fruit, and other indigenous foods, in addition to their hunting and fishing efforts.

They'd been taught greed, the monster of men, had destroyed everything beautiful about that place. Gold and silver were discovered in the 1860s in the Sierra-Nevada, attracting ranchers and farmers. Conflict had broken out, and eventually the military had intervened and forced the Paiutes into relocation at Fort Tejon in 1863. Most of the Native Americans who had cared for the land, and made it their home for thousands of years, were forced to be hired back as workers to the farmers. Allu thought she knew how they must have felt.

Farmers had continued to grow apples, pears, potatoes, and even alfalfa until 1910. But land rights and water rights had been bought out, and Manzanar was completely abandoned in the 1930s.

Allu's teacher suspected there was some kind of sweet deal between the military and Los Angeles, who held the water rights to Manzanar. All of this was, of course, spoken of quietly, but Allu thought her teacher was smart. Plus, Robbie filled in the details.

Whenever they talked about boys, sitting among the few resilient trees that had survived decades of neglect, Allu tried to be patient when Kiko slipped in casual questions about Robbie. She doubted her brother even remembered Kiko's name, but she answered her questions all the same, trying to recall his favorite kind of music before the war, along with other trivial information like what he had eaten for breakfast.

Kiko's reaction was always the same: a slow smile, as if she'd been invited into a deep secret that exposed the essence of life itself. Allu wouldn't have been surprised to learn she kept a journal of notes.

***

"Father has stopped talking," Kiko said softly one day. The October air had grown colder, and they could almost see their breath against the mountains.

"What do you mean?"

She shrugged. "Just stopped."

People didn't decide to just *stop talking*.

"Did something happen?" Allu asked.

Kiko looked at the ground. "Can't say. Mama doesn't talk about it when I'm around, but sometimes, I hear her whispers through the wall when she goes outside and talks to her friend." She lowered her voice. "She mentioned him having a cold of the soul."

"A cold?" Allu had had colds several times, and none of them had prevented her from talking.

"Of the soul," Kiko confirmed. "You know, *extreme sadness*. Since his stroke at the mill, he hasn't been able to work."

Allu didn't know what to say, so she just nodded.

"And that was his passion in life. Woodworking. Mama says if you take away a man's passion, you take the soul right out of the man, and he's no longer the person you know."

Allu thought of her father, and how much he had loved to farm. "Is there anything we can do?"

"Don't know."

Kiko's voice sent a pang to her heart. That settled it. She couldn't bring Papa here, but she could help Kiko save her own father.

She grabbed her friend's hand and gave it a reassuring squeeze as a plan began to formulate in her mind.

***

Robbie wasn't as enthusiastic about Allu's plan as she'd hoped, but a few days later, he came back with a box of small pieces of lumber he'd grabbed from block ten, along with a sheet of plywood. Earlier that fall, he'd built Mama a couple of chairs and side tables from scrap wood he'd found by chance on the way to their mess hall for a second lunch. Allu hoped it would be enough to inspire Kiko's father.

There was just one more favor to ask, and much to her surprise, Robbie agreed, though he seemed distracted at the time.

Allu presented Kiko with the box full of wood that following Wednesday, and was excited to go to school Thursday, expecting a full report of her father's miraculous recovery. But Kiko shook her head quietly, as she did on Friday and the following Monday.

Allu was grateful Robbie never asked if it had helped.

***

Robbie watched a boy a few years younger than him swing at the ball and miss.

"Open your stance," he called out to the boy.

The boy widened his legs and took another swing, cracking the ball into the air.

A baseball team had formed, and it seemed every boy old enough to play had tried out. Part of him wanted to. Robbie loved baseball the way he loved summertime, but he wasn't a kid anymore, and some things weren't as important as they used to be.

Baseball was one of them.

It was like Allu said one night, when he had asked why she didn't draw anymore. What was the purpose in it? It wouldn't end the war, and it wouldn't get them out of this place. Hobbies were for kids.

Besides, he'd proven himself. He had the college recruitment letter. He didn't know why he'd kept it, even. He used to carry it with him, as if it defined him worthy somehow. Now, it sat with his other collectibles he'd managed to save from the farm, in a little wooden box under his feedbag beneath the bed. He regretted Papa would never see it. It would have made him so proud.

Papa had been a humble man who had done whatever he could for the family. Still, they could never afford much. Watching Robbie play ball had brought so much joy to Papa, and that had been the best gift, to see him sitting among all the "professionals" in town. Robbie owed it to him to play his best—to gift him with as much pride as he could.

Still, his father had never gotten to see the letter and it meant so much more to him than it did to Robbie. He'd never gotten to share that feeling or see the look on his father's face seeing that they had won.

He tried to feel useful where he could, but it didn't fulfill him. He couldn't shake the undeniable feeling that he should be doing something, anything, to help with the war effort.

Robbie watched another kid hit the ball before strolling through the camp. Mama was back at the barrack taking care of Mr. and Mrs. Kato, who'd fallen ill, a commonality among residents eating in crowded conditions. She'd fixed them a soup with Papa's vegetables and a bowl of hot water she'd managed to bring back from the mess hall.

There were stories of other internees who could often be heard yelling at each other in Japanese, their spirits wild with the confinement of the tight space. Their privacy had been stolen, and they took out their anger on each other. It was even sadder when those wild spirits transformed into silent helplessness.

Robbie passed a couple of guards, about his age, who were talking amongst themselves and hardly glanced his way as he passed. He thought of Jimmy. It should be him and Jimmy fighting together overseas. Where was he now? He hadn't heard anything about him since they'd been sent to camp. All he knew was that he was with the army, along with a few other guys from their old ball team. He managed to track down a few extra wool army blankets for the Katos and headed back to their barrack.

"Do you need sweeping done, Ma?" he asked.

His mother gave him a shrug, her eyes etched in concern.

A nagging feeling of emptiness filled every crevice of his soul. The barbed wire fencing was nothing in comparison to the invisible boundaries that separated him from the other boys his age who were deemed worthy to serve their country. But he was not.

He couldn't keep sitting around, playing house anymore. It'd drive him crazy. He'd wait it out, see what happened. There had to be a way for him to help, to do more.

Chapter Thirty-three

Mama was apprehensive about Allu's latest plan, but then again, she usually was.

"He's very gentle, and has better manners than anyone at camp," Allu said.

Mama gave a look of consideration before nodding her head. "*Only* the perimeter of the block. And be back before dark."

Johnny, it turned out, was fun to be around. Even if he wouldn't have had a pet mouse, Allu still would have thought so. He tucked the mouse neatly in his shirt pocket when they went outside, and she gave him a quick wink. No one else knew about John Mouse, and it was nice to have something of their own in a place where everything had to be shared.

"He's getting big." Allu watched him squirm around in Johnny's pocket.

"Yeah, yeah. He big boy like me," Johnny said, pointing to his chest with a grin.

It wasn't a half bad day out. She watched the sun cast shadows on the mountains, wondering what kinds of animals surrounded them in the desert. They walked in silence until they reached the second set of latrines, which had new privacy walls built between the toilets. It would be worth the extra walk to use them. That was where they decided the halfway point was for their walk, and a good place to turn back to avoid getting to their barrack by dark.

So, their daily walks began. Most days they walked in silence, trapped by their own thoughts, grateful to be released from the confines of small living and lack of privacy.

Johnny almost always brought John Mouse, tucking him in his pinned shirt pocket.

"Manzanar means 'orchard,'" Johnny said one day.

It was a hot day, but without the threat of the dust storms the mountain winds often brought, they decided to walk a little farther than usual.

"I heard something about that," Allu agreed. "It's amazing how pear trees can still grow in this desert after being abandoned all these years."

He looked over at her quizzically. "Pear trees?"

"Haven't you seen them? There's a few at the far corner of camp. The water table is high enough to keep them alive."

Johnny's face lit up and he quickened his pace.

"I can show you if you want to walk farther." Allu couldn't see any harm in it; she'd walked there several times after school with Kiko.

"Yeah, yeah!" he said, clapping his hands together. "Let's go."

Johnny squealed with delight when they reached the pear trees, plucking a juicy fruit off and taking a bite.

"Mauder. Yeah, yeah. And fauder, too," he said, picking two more.

Allu smiled. "They'll like that."

They were almost to the mess hall on the way back when she couldn't shake the feeling they were being watched. Allu didn't want to scare Johnny, but quickened their pace, leading him by the hand and throwing an occasional glance behind them.

Every time she did, the footsteps stopped. Something wasn't right.

She glanced at Johnny, who was fixated on the mountains and seemed not to notice. Gently placing her hand on the back of his arm, she led him by the elbow. They were halfway home, and she cursed the trip to the pear trees.

All of a sudden, a sharp voice piped up from behind them, causing Allu's heart to race and her mouth to go dry.

"Hey!" a voice sneered from behind them. "You're Robbie's kid sister, aren't you?"

Haruto. Johnny and Allu kept walking, as panic surged through her.

"Is this your *boyfriend*?" He cut them off. Then he faced them and began to walk backwards. "I hope I'm not slowing you down, but then again…" He sneered, glancing at Johnny. "He doesn't need any help with that."

Johnny began to hum, but kept walking, squeezing her hand tightly.

Allu seethed. "Leave us alone, or—"

"*Or what?* You'll tell your big, bad brother?"

Three more blocks to go. Johnny hummed louder.

"Shhh. Shshshsh. It's okay," Allu said gently. She couldn't tell if he was angry or scared. She wondered if Johnny knew what was happening.

Haruto snickered. "Sorry to interrupt your *intimate* conversation.

Tell your brother I paid you a visit, and that he might want to keep his mouth shut." He began to veer off toward the laundry building. "He'll know what you mean."

Allu's heart raced with newfound fear as they made their way to their barrack.

Chapter Thirty-four

Allu couldn't get Haruto's face out of her head, especially his cold, dark eyes—and was on guard the rest of the night.

A tap at the door the next morning was a good distraction when she saw Kiko standing in the entrance, a smile plastered across her face.

"What's the good news?" Allu stepped outside, pulling the door closed behind her.

Kiko took a wooden box from her pocket. "Father made it from the scrap wood!"

"That's great!" The box fit perfectly in the palm of Allu's hand.

"Look inside."

She lifted the lid and found three miniature dolls. The largest one was the length of her smallest finger and looked like something straight out of the window of a toy store. The doll was an old woman touting gray bits of yarn for hair and a long white gown. Beside her was a girl with long black braids and a bright pink dress. Where they had found the material in a dreary place like this, Allu didn't know. She picked up the second doll, admiring the detail.

"This one must be you," she said, turning it over in her hand.

Kiko smiled and closed her fingers around the doll. "No, Allu. She is *you*. I want you to keep her. You know, for good luck."

Allu couldn't remember the last time anyone had given her anything. "I can keep it?"

Kiko nodded and smiled the biggest smile Allu had seen on her friend's face in weeks. Her father was well again.

She should refuse something so beautiful, something which belonged inside a real bedroom or dollhouse, but Allu treasured the doll too much to reject it.

"Stay put one minute, okay?" Allu ran inside the barrack and returned a few minutes later with a jar of Papa's cherries. "Give these to your family."

"Oh, I couldn't," Kiko said. "Are those your father's?"

"Yes. And he'd want you to have them." She thought of Papa and knew he would've probably given out most of their jarred fruit by then, if he were here.

"Tell your father that Papa's passion was to farm." She handed Kiko the jar. It was the first produce of last season. A season that had begun with Papa and ended without him.

Kiko's eyes gleamed.

Allu knew she had made the right decision. Papa would have been proud.

In that moment, she found inspiration and her heart was full. "Stay here one more minute," she said to Kiko, who was still admiring the cherries. "I'm going to get my pencils and sketchpad."

***

"Walk?" Johnny asked her as they passed him outside. She had forgotten all about it.

"Not today," she said, feeling a little guilty. "Maybe tomorrow though, okay?"

"Okay," he said, nodding enthusiastically with a smile. "Okay."

On days he couldn't sneak Mr. Mouse inside, he checked on him at least three times a day. Part of her felt guilty for skipping their walk today, but he probably wouldn't mind.

That afternoon, she and Kiko drew several pictures of the mountains, but the pages kept blowing closed. She was having a hard time holding them down with one hand while trying to draw with the other.

Sandstorms came fierce and suddenly in the desert, and it was gearing up to be one of those days. Particles of dust began to fill the sky, blackening out the sun in a thick haze.

"I ought to be going," Kiko said, looking up at the sky after trading paintings.

"Okay. Wait here while I put everything inside, and I'll walk you back to your barrack."

Mama made Robbie come with, and Allu had to admit, she felt comforted by his presence. His broad frame and sense of humor had a way of making people feel safe. Already, the temperature had dropped quite a bit, and if she looked closely, she could see bits of sand being picked up by the wind and thrown into spinning circles in the sky.

There was power in circles. Allu had learned that when reading her Native American books. The seasons, the sun, the moon, and the stars were circular, as were her favorite rocks. They had been shaped by a river, or maybe the wind itself over time.

But today, the circles were not in Allu's favor. They grew stronger and louder, and they blocked out the sun. They took away her ability to see anything beyond her outstretched arm, which held tightly to Kiko, her face covered by a sea of black hair whipping wildly about her.

Particles of sand hit Allu's face. She narrowed her eyes and bent her head as she leaned into the wind and forged her way behind Robbie, grateful for his large mass. This storm was getting bad fast, worse than she'd ever seen before.

Chapter Thirty-five

Another God-forsaken dust storm.

As luck would have it, Richmond still had a couple hours until the end of his watch, going on hardly any sleep. He couldn't wait to give the boys a hard time after this one. He should've gotten some sleep the night before, but they'd rope-tied him into playing a few rounds of blackjack, which had turned into a few too many. But it was better than lying in bed, trying to sleep, listening to them playing the rounds without him. The war had sucked the fun out of most everything, but it couldn't take away a man's right to throw some money down once in a while.

Turns out, Richmond was damn good at it, too, and he ended up with most of their money by morning.

He smiled, thinking of those long bus rides to football games his senior year. That was when he'd *really* learned to play. He had a knack for it, though he doubted he'd ever be good enough to put any big money in. It was amazing to him what years of bus rides as a three-sport athlete could do for a competitive gambling advantage.

When he'd found out he'd been drafted, he had actually been relieved. He hadn't given much thought to college and hadn't known if he even had the smarts for it. Of course, the old man had said college was for pretty boys, and would probably have kicked his ass if he'd enrolled. Well, *tried* to enroll, anyway.

Richmond smirked at the thought. He wasn't a little boy that his father could slap around anymore. And if he ever laid a hand on his mother again… He clenched his fist at the thought of it.

Gusts of cold wind slapped his face, spraying sand into his eyes as he lowered his helmet. He could barely make out faces of people as their silhouettes hustled to buildings for shelter. More than likely, supper would be canceled, and he'd have to scrounge his barrack for leftovers.

What a hellhole of a place to be stationed.

His number one duty when standing guard was to ensure no one tried escaping. Not that anyone with half a mind would. Threats beyond the barbed wire came in the form of rattlesnakes and sub-zero temperatures during the dark desert nights.

And everyone knew not to screw with Mother Nature.

But every once in a while, a dimwit would come close. Whether out of curiosity or rebellion, they'd slowly approach the fence and get just close enough to feel the weight of their conscience telling them to turn around. Either that, or the surge of electricity waiting to zap the hair off their ass. They were teenage boys most of the time, doing the same thing Richmond would've done at that age, trying to impress a girl or show off their defiance of death on a dare or something stupid like that.

Usually, he'd yell down to them to get the hell away from the fence, and that would send them running. They were lucky it was him on duty and not Howard, who had much less tolerance for Japs and always thought it was fun to shoot a few rounds at their feet.

This damn sand.

Setting his gun down, Richmond shook the sand from his uniform. His eyes burned, and when he rubbed at them, fine particles scratched like bits of glass. He opened his eyes wide and squinted them shut several times. It was going to be a long shift.

He grabbed his gun from the floor and propped it against the rail.

A dark shadow stretched across the ground, out in the dirt patch just beyond the barbed wire fence. Was that dark shadow there a minute ago?

Shit. He strained his eyes and leaned forward. It was hard to tell what it even was. A wooden box of some sort, or some kind of structure he'd missed earlier in the daylight. Strange how things got obscured by the darkness and messed with people's minds.

Nonetheless, Richmond found himself staring at the shape, straining his eyes. The shape twisted from a sloppy square to more of a taller rectangle.

Or had it?

The wind roared in his ears, throwing gusts of sand at his face as it laughed.

He stepped closer to the rail. The shape definitely grew in size, as if approaching. It was about fifteen feet from the fence, and shapeless in the thick fog.

He grabbed his gun and waited.

Chapter Thirty-six

Robbie listened as Mr. and Mrs. Kato called out Johnny's name against the howl of the wind.

"He's not back," Mrs. Kato told Mama. "He should be back." A worried look crossed her face.

"It took us longer than usual to return," Allu offered, feeling guilty. She debated whether to tell them he asked her to walk with him. "It's difficult to see anything with all the dust. It's even difficult to breathe. Maybe he's running late."

Mrs. Kato didn't seem convinced. She called Johnny's name again while Robbie grabbed some cardboard from the barrack and carried it against the wind.

"Allu!" Robbie called as he pushed the cardboard against the window with his shoulder, half of it flapping with the wind. Sand had seeped through the cracks already, forming a layer of dust resembling carpet inside.

"Hold this," he said, frantically pounding a nail in each corner as she leaned her hands against the cardboard. "Is there anywhere he'd go?"

Allu paused. "Maybe to check on Mr. Mouse."

Robbie gave the nail one last hit and slumped his shoulders before turning to look at her. "I told you. Mr. Kato already checked. The box is gone."

A worried look crossed her face, and Robbie felt pulled in different directions. Should he stay and protect Allu and Mama, or help find Johnny? Mr. and Mrs. Kato didn't get around that easily. He couldn't just sit here and wait.

"Stay here with Mama," he decided. "I'll look around camp."

***

Richmond pushed the stock of the gun firmly against his shoulder, just as he had so many times while hunting. "Turn around," he urged under his breath. "Turn *around*."

His hands were shaking, his non-shooting eye closed.

Whatever the shadow was, it wasn't a deer. The thought made him sick to his stomach. He clenched his hand tighter around the foreign feel of a barrel he had held several hundred times.

Richmond watched and waited, focusing his eye as if it could burn through the layer of dust.

He cleared his mind, breathing slowly to a steady calm beneath the noise surrounding him. In a few short hours, he'd be back at camp, laughing about his paranoia with the guys.

Surely the thing had left. Most likely, it had been one of the camp animals the government had brought in for the makeshift farm they were starting. A pig, maybe. It was probably a damn ol' pig.

He slumped his shoulders as he set the weight of the gun on his lap and felt the muscles in his back loosen. What he needed was a nice hot shower to get rid of all this dust.

And a beer. He'd give anything for a beer.

If the guys back at base could see him, he'd never hear the end of it. Especially, if they knew it was just a pig or goat on the loose!

He pushed the safety button in, feeling it pop with the push of his thumb as he listened to the wind.

***

Robbie called out Johnny's name. He'd checked the latrines. Both of them. He had run all the way to the orchard and back. Hardly anyone was out of their barrack, and those who were, were too frantic to stop.

Where could he be?

Pieces of tar paper blew in front of him. He'd be lucky if he didn't get knocked out by all the scrap blowing around. He couldn't see two feet in front of him or make out where he was. Curse this damn place.

Bang!

The sound of the shot stopped him cold. It was the first gunshot he had actually heard since the war had started. It was hard to tell with the wind which direction it had come from, and a chill ran down his spine.

Dear God, no. No! No!

He pushed his legs forward, running through a storm of sand, praying his family was safe.

Chapter Thirty-seven

Mrs. Kato ran toward the sound of the gun and found herself several blocks from her own barrack. Breathing hard, she stood in the firebreak between barracks and screamed. Her words were mangled between Japanese and English, but her wailing was universal.

Curled up in a limp ball, the body lay motionless, barely visible through the sandstorm.

She stood away, fearful to look. It couldn't be him. She refused to believe it was Johnny. Not her baby. Of all people, not her baby.

Just this morning, he had eaten bread for breakfast, and she had wiped the crumbs away like she had a hundred times and would a hundred days more.

She pressed her hand against her mouth. *No, it couldn't be him.* She couldn't be the poor mother whose kid this was.

But even through the storm, Mrs. Kato couldn't mistake her son's hands. Though they were large, even for an adult, they still resembled those of a child's—chubby with dimples, just as she remembered them. Hands she would hold when he was too tired to protest. Hands she would cover in soft kisses as she rocked him to sleep. Hands that had once fit neatly into the palm of her own. Hands that even as an adult, he would use ever so gently to carry around the thing he may have loved most in the world, Mr. Mouse.

Get up! Damn you, Johnny-chan, get up!

Mrs. Kato waited for him to pull his oversized body up with that goofy smile of his. To laugh and ask her what was wrong, and why she was standing in the bitter cold without a coat, her face wet with tears and dirty with sand as it filled the creases of her face.

She went to him, his body motionless in the dirt. Then she noticed a dark, wet spot in the center of his chest.

They'd shot him, her baby. The realization hit her like a brick to the head. Dust was piling on top of him, his dark hair now a dirty orange, as if the desert was trying to devour him, despite her frantic sweeps across his face with her shirtsleeve.

"*My baby*," she cried, rocking him in her arms. He was big and clumsy, but still her son.

And suddenly, everything was different. Everything was wrong. This wasn't her life. Not the one she had five minutes ago.

How could he have died alone? Like a wild animal.

Johnny had always been the least threatening creature gifted to this world. Hadn't he already been dealt a hand of tough cards? Wasn't it enough to sit alone in the corner of the playground day after day as a kid? To be laughed at and called names and not understood as he laughed with them—a look of joy on his face? Didn't wanting to fit in make him like any other boy?

Her body shook with dark emotions her soul had kept hidden. In the end, she had failed as a mother to protect him. *Did this mean she was no longer a mother?*

Heavy as he was, she sat beside him in the dirt and wrapped her arms around his lifeless body, placing kisses on his dusty forehead, something she could only do when he had slept as a child. How many nights had it been since she'd last held him? How many nights had she gazed at him, wondering if others saw him sleep, if they could tell he was different from other boys?

Mrs. Kato thought these things as she gently rocked Johnny back and forth, even as tears streamed down her face and she hummed her baby boy a lullaby, setting his spirit free.

Chapter Thirty-eight

Rolling on his side, Richmond leaned over the edge of the cot, thinking he might get sick. Bile had caught in his throat and stayed there, leaving a sickening feeling lurking in the pit of his stomach. He heaved once. Nothing. He might as well drag his ass out of bed for a cigarette.

A cold moon clung to the darkness of the night as he exhaled clouds of smoke into a clear sky. There was a stillness to the air after the storm. He ignored the sliding movements of his thoughts and the rings of smoke he carefully wrapped around the distant moon. What a day.

How the hell was he to know the kid was different? Would other kids wander around in a sandstorm? Desert sandstorms could be ruthless. Everyone knew that.

And why the hell were there women and children and elderly people here, anyway, when the real enemy was overseas? Real wars were fought between men. Shit, Richmond didn't even know that type of people were here. He had never seen any. At least not from the tower.

He had known he had killed *it*, whatever *it* was, even before the bullet had left the chamber and before he watched the shadow fall. It had surprised him just how quickly he reacted when the shadow lunged toward the barbed wire fence.

Instinctively.

Another split moment had been all it took to click the safety off and pull the trigger. *And then. And then,* he froze up.

Richmond had met other veterans who had killed before, defending their country, but he now wondered when the glory came in. They would walk in parades with heads held high, though they were reluctant to tell specific stories in even the most intimate settings. For his father, glory had been trapped in a glass bottle of booze, unattainable and elusive despite the number of bottles he finished in effort of finding it.

Still, if he'd known the kid was slow, would he have shot him? The question dragged repeatedly through his mind. He kept coming to the same conclusion: *he'd had to*. Those were his orders. It wasn't his job to ask questions. It was his job to do his job.

To obey. To honor his country. Honor his position, not question it. It was his duty to shoot anyone who attempted to escape or threatened the safety of others. Safety and order were based on rules.

If the kid had obeyed the rules and stayed a safe distance away, not gone running around the fence looking dangerous, he would be in bed right now. Had Richmond not shot him, it was his ass on the line, not to mention the disciplinary action that would follow. Which would mean dealing with the old man. Surely, he'd find out.

Still, those things hadn't even crossed his mind when he'd taken the shot. He had thought he was shooting a damn animal. And animals didn't have feelings. Or mothers.

He lit another cigarette and felt a pat on his back. "Congratulations!"

Great. Howard. He was the last person Richmond wanted to see about now. Or ever really.

"Thanks for protecting us all. *That* was definitely a spy for the Japs." Howard laughed.

Before another word could come out of his mouth, Richmond snapped.

A surprised look crossed the fellow soldier's face as Richmond grabbed his collar, his cigarette within a few hairs of burning the guy's face.

"Easy, easy," Howard said. "I'm just having a little fun. It's just Jap blood."

"Don't ever talk to me about this again," Richmond threatened. "*You hear me?* I did my job."

A terrified look momentarily crossed Howard's face before he retreated inside.

Richmond pushed the rest of his cigarette into the dirt. Yes, he could live with a little bit of blood on his hands. *Jap blood. That's right.*

He tried to convince himself it was part of his job, but he felt unsettled just the same.

What would his father have done? He would've shot, that's what he would have done. But would his father live with regret?

He doubted it. He wouldn't even be thinking about it anymore.

But Richmond wasn't his father. Thank the mighty God for that. His father was one of the worst men he'd ever known.

Chapter Thirty-nine

Camp McCoy, Wisconsin

Winter, 1942

Yukio had never known this kind of cold in his life, but he welcomed the beauty of the snow.

Snow.

The first time it had snowed, how crazy they must've looked out there in camp, throwing armfuls of the cold glittery stuff into the air. There had been even a few snowmen made in camp. It was another thrill of surprise after witnessing the extravagance of autumn leaves' transitioning colors. He made sure to write Leinani about it and vowed to take her to see it someday.

He'd been here for weeks, and now thought back to Oahu with its expansive beaches. Thought back to passing underneath the Golden Gate Bridge on the *S.S. Maui* to dock in Oakland, California. It was a magnificent structure, a brilliant red connection between San Francisco and Sausalito. He would always remember that image, and the feeling of relief that they were in the United States and not unloading in Japan.

They had left secretly during the night on trains heading to Wisconsin, with the orders to *keep the window shutters down* to avoid potential confusion from civilians who might have become distressed at seeing Asian soldiers. It would've looked really bad after all, for them to be seen passing through areas where anyone who looked Japanese was interned in camps.

Training was difficult with long days and longer nights, but Yukio thought of Leinani and carried on.

Many of the men were in their late twenties to early thirties. Several were college graduates, and a few had been excited when they passed San Francisco, traveling near colleges they had attended. They knew the mainland. But now, they were far from the sun and the beaches.

From Sparta to Tomah and then La Crosse, Wisconsin had welcomed them with open arms. Hell, many of the guys even played ball in intermixed teams and found rural sweethearts.

But one night, word came of a few men gone missing from camp. Rumors had floated they'd been shipped down on a secret training mission to Cat Island in California. One officer had said they were training attack dogs, training them to attack anyone with an Asian scent, hoping it would be a strategy against the Japanese Army.

Yukio thought about how this whole war brought out the best, worst, and most ludicrous ideas in men.

When he finally had time, he wrote to his family.

> *They've asked me to be a part of a new battalion, and we're going to make things right again. Prove our loyalty. The 100th Battalion. One puka-puka. Because I was Hawaiian National Guard before the attack, I'm allowed to fight.*
>
> *We're building a solid reputation as a cohesive unit. We're quick and strong and have exceptional training records. Heck, I think we even surprised the Texan Division here. They might be bigger than us, but they don't have the martial arts training we do. Competition is fierce, and fights break out over who got the best test scores or who is the best boxer.*
>
> *Overall, we have gained everyone's respect, and we are being prepared for battle. We will prove our loyalty.*

Yukio traced the patch with the elephant leaf, symbolizing protection from ancient times, along with the chief's helmet.

> *I will write again soon.*
> *Your loving son,*
> *Yukio*
>
> *Remember Pearl Harbor.*

He'd signed off with his battalions' motto, rereading the last three words. How could they forget?

Chapter Forty

Johnny was dead.

And it was all her fault. Allu should've been with him on the walk. *Had he been smiling when she'd last seen him? Had he seemed disappointed she had chosen to be with Kiko instead? Had he known the difference?* Allu couldn't shake the thoughts from her head.

It had been that damn mouse. He was probably chasing that stupid mouse around and didn't realize how far away he'd run. And for what? It was just a little, unimportant thing. Not important enough to go and get yourself killed over. And that mouse had probably lived.

Well, Allu hoped he had died somewhere in the desert.

Johnny should've known better to be more responsible. He'd been at least twenty-some years old. And he had probably been smiling when he'd died. Why had he been so damn reckless?

The joy he'd brought with him had made Allu's life more bearable, almost happier. *But Johnny was dead.*

Holidays became almost non-existent, marked by nothing more than the date. Robbie insisted on having supper in the barrack as a family. Since Johnny had died, he'd made every attempt to pull them together.

Most days, Allu avoided the place. It had become too quiet, and it physically hurt her insides to look over at the empty space that had once been occupied by Johnny.

Mr. and Mrs. Kato had asked for a transfer, and just like that, they were gone. Then, it was just the three of them again, and the Katos were nothing more than a memory.

Mama spent most of her time working at the camp hospital, which allowed them a little money to buy things like fabric for floral curtains.

On Thanksgiving, Robbie held a bag in front of them, wrapped in a ribbon.

"What's this?" Mama asked, wiping her hands with a towel.

Allu could tell the bag was heavy, the way Robbie had it slung over his shoulder. She felt a flush of anticipation.

Robbie shrugged. He'd always been one for building up surprises.

"Come on, Robbie! Tell us!" Allu couldn't help herself. They never received anything special in camp and it had been ages since she'd unwrapped anything.

"I figured since it is Thanksgiving and all," he began, "I'd contribute a little something to the meal."

Mama raised her eyebrows as Allu crossed the room to where Robbie was standing. How beautifully absurd he looked holding that bag with an old faded blue ribbon, but she was excited nonetheless.

He began to hand the heavy bag to Allu and then stopped, setting it on the floor between them. "But first, little sister, you must promise to save me the first bite."

"Robbie!" She slapped his arm before pulling the ribbon loose. Peering into the bag, she could see it was some sort of frozen bird.

"Duck," he answered, with a half-cocked smile. "We butchered a few from one of the camp farms a few days back."

"Duck! Robbie, you're the greatest!" Allu wrapped her arms around him. He'd been working here and there on the farm but had never brought anything home.

Mama came over and joined them.

Mama hadn't sung in ages, but softly hummed that afternoon as she dressed the bird with leftover bits of bread, soy, and butter packets she saved for special occasions. Fortunately, she knew of a family who had been assigned to a barrack with a small stove. To imagine that!

They ate in silence, other than the occasional mention of things that didn't really matter much, pretending not to notice the three empty chairs that had been pulled away from the table and sat in the corner of the room.

The meat of the duck was juicy and tender, and Allu thought she might never stop eating. Mama had saved Papa's last jar of cherries and put a spoonful on each of their plates before dishing up plates for the friends who had been so gracious as to let her use their stove.

Things were getting better, it seemed. But she'd learned not to place too much hope in times like this.

Chapter Forty-one

December, 1942

Richmond had become a joke. Excluded from card games and conversations.

He'd had to smack a few of the guys around, and it was enough for them to keep their mouths shut. He still saw the smirk on their faces, heard the whispers when they thought he was asleep.

Just like his father did. He always said Richmond would amount to nothing. That he couldn't handle a soldier's life like a real man could. But this wasn't a soldier's life, was it? No, Richmond had signed up to fight the enemy and put his own life in danger. Not watch a camp full of kids and families who didn't know much about the war on the outside of the fence.

Could the old man have handled this? Probably not, because he wasn't much good at handling anything without a gun or his fist or a bottle of booze.

Still, Richmond could imagine the humiliation of going home and having to face him, and face what he'd done.

And he couldn't get that idea out of his head.

First, he wrote a letter to his mother. Apologizing for not standing up to his father—for not being able to protect her against the man she believed she loved. He hoped she could forgive him.

Next, he polished his boots, scrubbing them until his elbows ached and his fingers stung with freshly-formed blisters.

He passed a few fellow guards who acknowledged him, but not without hesitation and downward glances.

"Another one down," one said.

He recognized him as the cook from barrack twelve. A real asshole. Richmond tipped his hat and walked past them without a word.

***

The orchard was empty.

Richmond sucked in a deep breath of dry air before exhaling loudly. The air was sweet in a way that almost made him forget where he was. The mountains were notably more beautiful than before, their silhouette softened by the smearing of white snow. Pictures in magazines definitely didn't do them justice.

There was a perfect spot in the sun, against the outer edge of the orchard, and he imagined what the place must have looked like before L.A. Water and Power Department had bought up most of the water rights.

Despite the high water tables, it was impressive that the trees continued to grow, as if part of a bigger plan that not even humans could screw up.

His mother would've liked the orchard. A small piece of beauty amidst the desert. A place to forget about the war. Forget about his father.

He imagined his father's face when he read his note and realized what Richmond had done. *Was about to do.* He wondered if his father knew how he felt about him. If he saw it in his eyes or felt it when they occupied the same room—the thickness suffocating any neutrality between them.

Richmond tried to avoid him for the sake of his mother. He knew it pained her to watch other fathers playing catch with their sons or coaching their baseball games that she attended alone, taking on the roles of both parents.

"He'd love to play if you have room," she'd casually say to the neighbor dads, trying to get Richmond involved.

He'd heard her crying so many nights. Yes, his father would know what he'd done, and would pay for it. That was how justice worked.

Richmond took one last look at the sky and lifted the barrel of the gun to his head.

Chapter Forty-two

She'd thought the orchard was empty.

Allu plucked a pear and turned the fruit over, inspecting it for wormholes before carefully placing it in the burlap purse Mama had made her. It could fit approximately four pears—just enough for her, Mama, Robbie, and Kiko. She stood on the tips of her toes and reached her arm high up into the branches, but then something caused her to pull back. An overwhelming sensation filled her body, covering her arms in goosebumps.

She wasn't alone.

She released a slow breath, letting the pear slip from her hand and hit the dirt with a quiet thump. Should she run to the entrance or creep slowly?

Panic filled her body. *Run.* But how could she run when she couldn't get her legs to move?

That was when she noticed him.

The soldier's silhouette was still against the mountains, the gun jutting out from his side. *Ready. Deadly.*

And then, he turned his head in her direction, noticing her for the first time. A shot rang out, causing her heart to nearly jump into her chest.

Her body let loose and she bolted into a dead run as she searched the sky for planes. Had the Japanese overtaken the West Coast? More shots fired.

Men of all ages crowded the firebreaks, shouting in Japanese over the sound of bells. Allu's stomach twisted as she desperately looked for a familiar face. But she wasn't anywhere near her block.

"Robbie," she yelled, her voice useless against the louder shouting that came from the dirt streets. "Robbie!"

Her breath was short. She could make it to the latrines and hide out.

Why was everyone running? What were they running from? Where had the shot come from?

Nazis? Japanese?

It became difficult to breath. She bolted between people, feeling others hit her shoulders and shove her about in the crowd. The mob was growing.

"Get back to your barrack," a man yelled as he passed her.

She was almost to the latrines. She should have told Robbie she was going to the orchard. Would Kiko remember?

People were running and bells were ringing. They were all going in the direction of the hospital. She turned around and broke out into a run.

***

"Allu!" Robbie yelled. Johnny's face flashed in Robbie's mind as he ran through the bustling streets to find his sister. He couldn't live with himself if anything happened to her. *Where was she?*

All around him, men were shouting and yelling.

Haruto had finally done it. There had been talks of riot, and though Robbie hadn't been included in any of the conversations, everyone could feel their unavoidable approach. A sharp line drawn between those who were bitter for being imprisoned and those who were part of the Japanese American Citizens league, known as "friends" to the War Administration.

Haruto, along with many others, suspected the Caucasian cooks of stealing sugar and meat from the warehouses and then turning around and selling it on the black market. When a few infants in camp had suddenly died, many had speculated it was due to the use of saccharin substitutes, and the heat of Hell began to build. The War Relocation's response?

Jail anyone who had the tenacity to accuse any of the Caucasian cooks. And this had only fueled Haruto's fire.

Allu had told him he'd threatened her and Johnny one day while walking. Robbie had overheard the rioters were going after one of the internees thought to be aiding the Administration, rumored to be hiding in the hospital.

A new panic flooded his body. Was Ma working? No, it was Monday. Mama was not working.

"Allu!" he yelled again.

He followed the firebreak in the direction opposite of the commotion, hoping Allu was smart enough to seek safety inside a barrack.

A man shoved into him as he ran past without looking back. Already, several military guards were shouting commands, but no one paid attention.

Where could she be?

Images flashed in his mind and his stomach twisted. Allu was young, and though she put up a good front, not very strong. Or at least not strong enough to protect herself against a rioting group of people.

"Allu!" His only hope was for her to hear him.

***

Allu panted, but there was no time to stop. If she kept up her pace, she could make it to the school in maybe ten minutes. She'd never been a fast runner, though.

All around her, people yelled and shoved their way through the crowd. Mostly men, they were charging toward the hospital.

She glanced over to see a couple of guards running toward a group of men who were throwing rocks. The sounds of shooting stopping them.

There was no time to look. No time to slow down.

Two more blocks to the school. And then one. She stopped to catch her breath, feeling light-headed.

What should she do? She should have stayed inside. She should have learned her lesson from Johnny. Now, she was going to die right here in the sand.

All alone. Without Robbie or Mama.

She began to breathe quickly and noticed how hot she felt. Unbearably hot. Dizziness began to take over. She needed water. *Desperately*.

She saw a soldier with a gun running toward her, his form beginning to swirl and contort into a sea of blackness as she felt herself hitting the ground.

Chapter Forty-three

Chaos filled the streets as Richmond made his way toward the hospital from the station. They had known this day was coming, but it was great shitty luck that it had happened to be at that very moment in the orchard, right when he was about to end it all. As he'd thought before, God sure had a sense of humor.

Riot bells rang out and it was the guards against two-thousand protestors. He was filled with some sort of sense of purpose. At least for the time-being. He quickly reported to his station and was handed tear-gas bombs and grabbed his rifle.

He had to hold the sling of his rifle to keep it from sliding off his back as he jogged. That was all he needed—an internee to find his weapon and kill him with it. The idea made him laugh. He couldn't do the job himself, but just his luck he'd be killed by an internee.

He rounded the barrack. If he cut through the latrines, maybe he could cut off the mob.

He was running faster than he'd ever run. Even in football.

When he got to the latrines, he realized it was full of people. Many faces of women and children who were seeking shelter from the riot. He'd have to go around the building, going through would only slow him down.

Kicked-up dust was everywhere, filling his lungs as he sucked in, making it difficult to see where the shouting was coming from and just how close he was.

His foot caught on something, hurling him into the air. He hit the ground, knuckles first. What the hell had happened?

He looked back to see what had stopped him.

A body was slumped over, laying in the sand. A memory of the boy he'd shot surfaced and he thought he might be sick.

It's not him. He stumbled closer to where the body lay.

A girl? A teenage girl.

Go figure, he was in the only action he'd seen during this war, and he had tripped over a girl!

He looked toward the direction of the riot and then back at the girl.

Shit. Today was *not* his day.

Reluctantly, he crawled back to her and checked her pulse. He'd never been so close to any of the internees before. The girl had glossy hair and was quite beautiful.

He glanced up the road before scooping her up in his arms, turning away from the hospital and toward the school.

Chapter Forty-four

Allu recognized the poster-plastered walls and desks, a few books stacked neatly on the front table. She was in her classroom in the school, but how? When? How had she gotten here? The last thing she remembered…

The soldier in the orchard.

Her side was tender to touch, a bruise growing, though she wasn't sure why. Bells outside reminded her that any attempt of escape would be unwise.

"Allu?"

Robbie! What a relief. Her brother gently scooped her up into his arms.

"How did I get here? What's going on?" she asked, looking around.

Through the window, she could see men running around outside, their voices yelling angrily.

"There's a riot going on," Robbie whispered. "It's not safe out there. At least not yet."

It didn't matter. Her brother was here. He was warm and comforting and she didn't want to let him go.

"Mama?" she asked.

"She's safe," he reassured her.

Then, she buried her head into his chest and began to cry.

"It's okay, Allu. I've got you. I'll protect you."

Chapter Forty-five

January, 1943

Johnny's death had made the guns real and the men in uniforms a threat. Ten men had been wounded, and two had died in the riots. It could've been him. It could've been Allu, or any of them. A feeling of uneasiness clutched Robbie's stomach thinking about it. It'd be a lie for him to say he wasn't relieved to have Haruto gone. It turned out, he was among the lead rioters and had been deemed disloyal to the U.S. Rumor was, he had been sent to Tule Lake before being permanently removed from the country, along with several other protestors—sadly, many who Robbie knew were World War I veterans.

Tensions were high, and getting worse. He felt helpless, as if the life were being sucked out of him by the minute, but what could he do? How could he help? Why wouldn't they let him serve and prove his worth?

And then, his chance came in the form of a loyalty questionnaire.

Rumor around camp was that the military were pulling together some internees to form a battalion. Robbie could hardly believe it. It seemed so long ago that he and Jimmy had sat at the recruitment office and he'd been rejected by the U.S. Army. Now, they were going to take on the world together, and whip the Nazis.

He smiled. Whenever he imagined Jimmy, he was always the way he was, sweet-talking some dame in a foreign country, but using his uniform to get the ladies.

He hated to admit it, but damn it, he missed him. None of the guys at camp were quite like Jimmy. He wasn't naïve enough to think the war hadn't changed him, but he wondered how.

This new regiment, the 442nd, would join the 100th Infantry Battalion. He'd read as much about the 100th as he could from what little information circulated camp. He knew they were extremely successful in training and were made up of all Japanese American volunteers from Hawaii, mostly National Guard servicemen.

Six months after Pearl Harbor had been attacked, the army had requested fifteen-hundred Nisei volunteers from Hawaii. More than ten thousand had responded, and the 100th Infantry Battalion was formed. They were a passionate bunch, who had seen first-hand their homes destroyed by Japanese Imperial forces.

The government now wanted to test the loyalty of *non-Hawaiian* Japanese Americans as well. Already, this new regiment was building quickly, and many of the young guys were volunteering to leave camp— which, Robbie suspected, was exactly what the War Relocation Group wanted. To lessen the numbers and prevent more riots.

But it was so much more than that to Robbie. For him, this was his chance to prove how much he loved this country.

Not everyone felt the same as him. Men all over camp were talking about it, many of them enraged. The questionnaire fueled both fear and anger. If you were unwilling to fight in the war, there was a chance of being shipped to Japan, a country many of them had never even seen. And if you pledged loyalty to the U.S., then you would also be revoked by the Emperor, which if the U.S. sent you to Japan anyway, then you were facing the consequences of a harsh Emperor who led the Imperial Army.

Robbie read the questionnaire carefully, his heart pounding. How he answered the questions would determine the course of his life from this day forward.

He thought of Allu and Mama. Who would take care of them if he left? Would they be okay? Would he see them again? And if so, where? How would he find them if the camp broke up?

Hell, Allu was practically more responsible than he was. It saddened him to think of how unfair it was that she'd had to grow up so fast and was losing her teenage years to this place. Joining the battalion would be a better way to take care of not only Allu and Ma, but their entire country, wouldn't it?

It was his right, after all, to serve and prove his loyalty just like anyone else. And that was more than he could ever give his family back here, but could they ever forgive him?

***

Robbie waited for a good time to break the news, gnawing at his cheek at supper.

"Why the special occasion?" Mama asked, dumping the rolls in a bread basket for the table. It wasn't often they ate at the barrack, but he'd insisted.

"Well," he started, clearing his throat. "I've enlisted."

Mama froze, her face going blank.

"*What*?" Allu snapped.

Robbie had known she wouldn't take it well, and had expected this. He walked toward her, but she threw her hand up to stop him.

"Allu, I've—"

"No! Robbie, no!" she cried.

He could see her hands clenched in fists at her sides. He plopped down on the chair, guilt weighing down on his chest.

"Robbie," Mama said, "are you *sure* you need to do this? Why don't you think it over?"

He sighed. "I've been thinking this over since the war began. I need to get out of here and feel useful again." He searched her face, hoping his words hadn't offended her.

"Robbie-chan, you *are* useful. Useful to your family." She looked around, lowering her voice. "Why defend a country who won't acknowledge you, other than as a tool for fighting?"

"Yes!" Allu interrupted. "Papa fought for this country. Look what happened to him." She shoved her chair into the table before stomping out of the room.

Robbie stood up to go after her, but Mama motioned for him to stop. "Let her go."

He rested his hand on top of hers. The weight of the world hung beneath her eyes, and for a moment, he questioned whether he was doing the right thing. "Ma, I need to do this."

Mama sighed, but then nodded. "Okay. Then I will try to understand."

Allu wouldn't be so forgiving. He knew how much she counted on him, though she'd never admit it. She was stubborn like her mother and wise beyond her years.

"Look, Allu-chan," Robbie said as he sat beside her on the porch. "I'm sorry."

She had those red blotchy spots on her skin that she only got when she'd been crying. This was even harder than he'd thought it'd be.

"Look. I know you're angry, but I'm doing this for our family. For *all* Japanese American families. For the first time, I feel important. *Empowered*. I need to do this, Allu."

She seemed to consider his words, turning her head away as she wiped her face with her sleeve.

There were so many things he wanted to say to her.

I know this hurts. I know this isn't fair. None of this is fair.

But instead, he wrapped his arm around her shoulder as they sat together for what could be the last time.

Chapter Forty-six

Robbie was deserting them, that's what he was doing. Deserting them to get out of this place.

Kiko listened quietly to Allu's rant, her eyes downcast as she clutched her hands.

"It's irresponsible," Allu said. "To volunteer for a war where you're not needed or valued. Hell, there's plenty of other Nisei men who could be soldiers. Old men who don't have siblings to look after. Or mothers."

It sounded a bit ridiculous, even to her as she said it out loud, but that wasn't the point. *It didn't* have *to be Robbie.* He had responsibilities here. She looked over at Kiko, who was messing around with her laces. Was she even listening?

"Who knows when he'll be back?" Allu said, disregarding her. "What if he can't even find us? What if camp closes or he runs off with someone after the war?"

Kiko sniffled.

Good grief. She needed to get over her crush! She was years younger than him.

"Look, I'm sorry. I didn't mean to say that. He's not going to *run off* with someone." Although, Allu wouldn't doubt it, given how reckless Robbie was acting.

Kiko dabbed at her nose with a handkerchief. "That's not it," she said, turning her face away.

Was her father sick again? Shit. How selfish she was to go on about Robbie.

"Is it your father?" Allu asked, resting her hand on her friend's back. She could feel Kiko's body rise and fall with quiet sobs. Allu's cheeks got hot. What a horrible friend she'd be to go on and on and find out later her father had died.

"He's fine." Kiko sniffed.

"So, what is it?"

Kiko hesitated.

Allu really wished she'd tie her shoelaces and leave them alone already.

"What if...what if he doesn't come back?"

She looked at her for a minute. "Who?" Allu asked.

"Robbie. I mean, what if?"

That's what she was worried about? She laughed in disbelief at her friend. "It's *Robbie*. Of course he'll come back. We're the only family he's got." It wasn't like Robbie would just fight the war and then forget about them.

Kiko shrugged, seemingly unconvinced.

A thick stillness filled the space between them, and Allu's irritation with her began to grow again.

"I mean, what if something happens to him?" Kiko asked, her voice cracking.

Allu laughed in relief. "That's what you're worried about? It's Robbie! One time, he fell out of a tree and didn't cry or anything. He even did chores that night, and no one knew his arm was broken. Another time, he got hit smack in the middle of his face with a ball and finished the game with a bloody nose." Robbie didn't get hurt, and when he did, he didn't stay hurt. If anyone would be a tough soldier, it would be him.

Kiko gave her a confused look.

"If you'd seen Robbie play ball, you'd know how strong and fast he is," she said. Kiko hadn't known him long enough to know what kind of person he was. Apparently, Allu hardly knew him at all. She'd been shocked by his decision to enlist.

Allu's temples began to pulsate. How did Kiko have the nerve to think something could happen to Robbie?

She stood up. It was time for her to go. Allu didn't want to talk anymore. "Maybe I'll see you tomorrow," she said, trying to keep her voice level.

Kiko said nothing but looked up at her with puffy eyes.

She almost felt sorry for her. She was just a naïve, emotional girl who liked Robbie but knew nothing about him. But she was her friend.

Things happened to *old* soldiers. Fathers. People Allu didn't know. Ones whose names weren't listed in the paper. Ones who were part of a number. Like the number of soldiers who were missing. Or the number of soldiers who were hospitalized. Or discharged. Or dead.

Not Robbie. He was much too young and strong to become one of *those* numbers.

Chapter Forty-seven

It was her. Richmond was sure of it.

The girl had dark hair that reflected the glare off the sun, tied up into some sort of twist or something. Had to be about fourteen or fifteen, he guessed.

He tried to imagine her in a different setting. Probably fifteen.

He wanted to make sure she had made it out alright from the riots. He hadn't heard of any girls in the death toll, but then again, who knew? There were a lot of people at camp and that whole day had been a mess. If not for her…

He shuddered at the thought of that day in the orchard. The day he was ready to end it all until he saw her watching him. Sure, he believed in afterlife of some sorts, but what? His parents weren't exactly the Holy Roller type, and with the things he'd done, who knew where he would have ended up.

Had she screamed before or after the riot shots rang out? He replayed the day in his mind like he had a hundred times since, but couldn't remember. Just her scream. The scream that had caused him to take the aim of his gun off from himself. She had saved him.

And there she was. At the orchard again. It had to be her. She carried the same bag.

But now that he'd found her, what should he say?

Richmond straightened his gun and casually walked to where the girl was sitting. She looked up at him, fear in her eyes.

Did she recognize him? He thought maybe he should've left the gun by the tree so as not to scare her.

"Great place, isn't it?" he said, picking an apple.

She looked at him quizzically and he quickly realized how ridiculous it sounded, even to him. "I mean, the orchard."

"Yes," she agreed, shutting her book.

It looked like a sketchpad of sorts. "Do you draw?" he asked.

Immediately, it felt like an intrusive question and he regretted it altogether. This was *not* going the way he'd imagined. Why didn't he just thank the girl and walk away before anyone saw him talking to her?

"Some," she said, her face softening. "It's okay to be here, isn't it? In the orchard, I mean."

Why was she asking him? That's right. The uniform.

His stomach twisted as he realized it was because of that damn uniform. "Yesss," he stammered. He glanced around to see if any of the guys were around, not surprised when he didn't see anyone. They would never be caught on this side of camp off-duty.

"So, what do you draw?"

She shrugged. "Not much to draw around the barracks, so I come here to draw the mountains. Or trees."

"Can I see?"

She glanced at him suspiciously, but then lifted the book cover so he could take a better look.

The drawing was good. Real good. It looked just like a pear tree, but without the color.

"Wow. That's impressive."

She quickly closed her book and tucked it into her bag, getting ready to go before he asked any more questions.

"I'm Richmond." He offered his hand, and the girl flinched. Shit, why did she think he was going to hurt her every time he moved?

Her cheeks reddened as she slowly extended her hand. "Alluriana."

"Alluriana. That's a new one."

"It's Japanese," she replied.

He felt his cheeks redden. *Obviously,* it was a traditional name. Pretty enough, though.

"I'd better be going," she said, pulling her bag across her shoulder as she stood. "I'm glad you're okay."

And the girl with the beautiful name and shiny hair left him standing amongst the pear trees.

Chapter Forty-eight

Strange, Allu thought as she walked home. It was almost as if that soldier had known her. Sure, he may have seen her that day in the orchard, but she'd ran away as soon as she'd heard the shots. Today was the first time a guard had talked to her, besides giving her orders.

Still, guards could never be trusted. No one in camp could, really.

She thought about the conversation all day, and again that evening, in bed.

"Allu-chan," Robbie whispered. "I know you're awake."

She inhaled deeply, waiting for him to leave.

"Look," he said, sitting on her bed. "I can't go away knowing you're upset with me." He sighed, probably rubbing his temples the way he always did when he was stressed.

"Anyway," he went on. "I've got something I'd like you to have. You can give it back when I come home." He set something on the bed and walked away.

Allu didn't give him the benefit of her curiosity, so she waited until she heard snoring to check it out, straining her eyes in the darkness as she felt around. Mama stirred in her sleep, mumbling something in Japanese before falling back into a peaceful rhythm of breathing.

The envelope was thick, and part of her was afraid to open it. She slid her finger under the crease of the paper until the adhesive let loose. She glanced at Mama and Robbie, making sure they were still asleep.

She gently shook the contents upon the bed. Several small negatives of film slid out. Her heart pounded as she picked one up, careful to touch only the edges for fear the faces might disappear under the heat of her fingertips. Holding it up next to the window, Papa's face smiled at her through the light of the moon. It was the first time she'd seen his face for some time.

There were several prints. Allu must have lost half the night examining each one. Her heart was a convoluted mixture between pain and loss, fullness and joy. There were pictures of the farm, the chickens. Everything.

There were even negatives she'd never seen before, of family she'd never known. A heritage she'd tried so hard to forget. To dismiss.

And Robbie had snuck these images, deciding it was a heritage worth risking his life for. Unbidden tears welled in her eyes. What would she do without her brother not around?

Chapter Forty-nine

April, 1943

The day had come for Robbie to leave. How could Allu forgive him? She tried to shake the anxiety that filled every part of her body, but it wouldn't loosen its grip. The buses were set to leave that afternoon, and he'd be gone. It would be the first time he'd ever been separated from them.

Part of her was angry he was leaving this place, and the other part of her selfishly wanted to hold onto him, even if it jeopardized his worth.

She needed to think. To get away from everybody and deal with this alone. But the orchard turned out to be as crowded as her thoughts, filled with laughter and talking and kids who ran around the trees while adults gossiped. She felt sorry for those kids who had grown up here. They had hardly any idea of what the world was like outside of this place.

At least she had that. But maybe that's what made everything worse.

She tried to recall every precious memory she had with Robbie but could only retrieve a few. Most of them were from outside of camp and had him holding a baseball bat. How foolish these kids were to be running and laughing when people were dying.

Robbie could've been anything. He was different from everyone else. Why be a soldier? What did he have to prove? There was no one left to prove anything to other than Mama and her, and they how valued Robbie was.

"You're not going to see the 4-4-2 off?"

The voice made her jump.

It was the guard. The one who had talked to her in the orchard. Richmond—that was his name. What did he want anyway? He stepped closer.

Allu froze and a troubled look briefly passed over his face.

"You know," the guard said, taking a seat beside her, "the day of the revolt was one of the toughest days I've had in this place. This war."

He glanced at her and she felt uncomfortable. What did this have to do with her? Why was he telling her these things?

"I was trying to do what I could, lost in the confusion. Trying to break the crowd, move the crowd, whatever I could." He shook his head. "I remember coming across one man in particular who wasn't following the crowd but going against it."

Avoid eye contact, Allu told herself. She wasn't in the mood for conversation, especially not with him. A few internees looked over, but she didn't care. They left the orchard.

"He was so persistent. Kept calling the same name over and over. In fact, I've crossed him a few times during duty. I asked who he was calling for, and it turns out, it was his sister's name. She went missing."

Allu tried to fight back tears, rubbing her cheeks with her hand. For a moment, all was still and the world was quiet.

"That's one of the only things I remember from that God-awful day— the look of fear in his eyes. The desperation."

She looked up at him and was surprised to see his eyes were kind.

"What did you do?" she asked. She didn't mean for it to come out sarcastically, but there it was anyway.

He shrugged with a smile, not too different from Papa's. "I told him I'd brought her to the school and assured him that she was safe."

Allu studied his eyes. Eyes didn't lie. They deceived, but didn't outright lie. Yet Allu couldn't remember anyone else being with her when she had been lost. Why would *he* have saved her? She had too much pride to ask.

"I was only eighteen when I enlisted," Richmond said, his voice distant. "Seems ages ago now. I remember feeling something pulling at my heart, knowing I was doing my part, doing what was expected for my country, and yet, I felt so alone." He paused. "My mother saw me off, and it's her face that carries me through when things seem too unbearable to go through alone."

Allu gave him a look. "Why are you telling me all this?" But a nagging feeling climbed its way up into her heart.

Richmond looked at her thoughtfully. "Because I think there's somewhere you need to be."

***

Allu's legs burned, revolting against the speed of her body.

She passed the school, then the mess hall, and didn't stop until she reached their barrack.

Empty.

Slamming the door, she struck the chess board with her hand, casting pieces all over the steps. Frantically, she snatched the king piece from the floor, leaving the rest of the pieces scattered, praying her legs would get her to the bus on time.

"Robbie!" Allu cried. She shoved through the crowd as many people embraced, saying their good-byes.

She scanned the crowd. Several men were boarding the bus.

"Robbie!" She panicked. *Was this the only bus, or had she missed him?* Oh, please say she hadn't missed him. She could never forgive herself. "Robbie!"

"Allu!" Kiko's voice called out from somewhere to her right. "Allu, over here!"

"Is Robbie there?" Allu yelled back, ignoring the sharp glares she got as she barged her way through to where her friend was standing.

"Yes! Hurry!"

Mama stood next to Kiko. A few girls who seemed to be Robbie's age were crying nearby. Robbie stuck his head out of the bus window and his lips turned up into a smile when he saw Allu.

"Quite a party, huh?" He smirked.

"He waited as long as he could," Mama said, prodding Allu forward.

She was still upset, but right then it didn't matter. "Robbie, I'm sorry." Tears burned her eyes and she didn't try to hide them. She handed the chess piece up to him. "For luck."

He chuckled, his eyes tearing up. "How will you play without a king?"

"I'm not playing until you're back," Allu said matter-of-factly.

Robbie smiled. "Then, I guess I'm undefeated until I return."

"I'll be waiting," she said. "And Robbie?"

"Yeah?"

"Thanks," she said, "for the negatives."

He winked at her.

As the bus pulled away, she shoved through the crowd to follow his wave, his smile blocking out everyone else as she watched it drive away. Despite all the people, she felt so alone. Empty and hollow and alone, with nothing but memories of the people she loved most but couldn't hold onto.

Robbie was gone.

When would she see him again? Allu closed her eyes briefly and ingrained the memory of him waving from the bus into her mind, hoping it wouldn't be her last.

Chapter Fifty

The mess hall was quiet that night for dinner. It seemed no one had an appetite. The clanking and scraping of silverware against pie tins was the only sound.

Papa was gone and now Robbie was gone, too. It felt as if the life inside Allu's body was slowly withering away and dying in darkness, rotting and leaving a hollow cavity within her ribcage.

"Rice today," Kiko mentioned casually, but her face looked concerned.

Allu sniffled, pushing the food around on her tin. She didn't feel much like talking and regretted even being there.

"He's going to be okay," Kiko said, placing her hand over Allu's. "It will be okay."

"Yes," she said quietly. But how could it? Everything was going to be different and she didn't like different. Different almost always meant bad things for their family.

"There's a lot of volunteers, Allu. They'll protect each other. They'll win this war for our country. They'll save thousands of people."

"Have you heard about the 100th, Kiko?" Allu asked. She wanted to believe her friend, but she'd come to grips with the possibilities. "Robbie told me about them. They are one of the most trained battalions of all time. You know why they are asking for volunteers now?"

Kiko shook her head.

"Because they know so many of them will probably die over there." She set her fork down. She wasn't hungry.

For a few moments, the background noise of the mess hall filled the silence. And then, Kiko squeezed Allu's hand again. "I'm sorry, Allu," she said. "Life isn't fair."

Allu sniffled, nodding her head. She felt miserable. No, life was not fair.

Kiko said, "Maybe we can do something tomorrow to distract you."

Allu gave her a weak smile. "Maybe."

Chapter Fifty-one

Camp Shelby, Mississippi

Summer, 1943

After a year of field exercises, physical training, and marksmanship lessons, Yukio was ready to fight the Nazis. His battalion had been drilled longer than any other battalion. Just as the old Asian proverb went, "With crisis, also comes opportunity." In this case, opportunity meant *training*. And more training. Heck, as long as they were off the West Coast and busy, the government was happy to look the other way at Japanese Americans serving—even though they were all born in the United States, like other second-generation Americans, such as the enlisted Norwegians and Germans.

They were pushing out now, and boy, was he glad. Camp Shelby was nothing like what Camp McCoy had been. Yukio almost missed the cold weather and snow. Segregation and turmoil was everywhere. People of color were forced to sit in the back of the buses, and when the enlisted men stepped on the bus, he and the other men were urged up front by the drivers because of their military status. It tore at his soul to see discrimination happen so openly.

And the place was full of *chiggers*. His arms burned from scratching, and many of the guys had gotten infections. Besides that, there were ticks and snakes. Nothing like the poisonous frogs he was used to in Hawaii. Although, he had to admit, he kind of liked the armadillo steaks that were common to the area.

The terrain was a challenge for his company, but it'd help prepare them for the tough maneuvers during the war games they'd participate in when they moved to Louisiana for the next stage of training exercises. It was critical they did well there. If the 100th battalion performed, he and his company would take to combat in Italy with the 34th Red Bull

Infantry to face the Nazi Regime.

Yukio prayed he was ready. Prayed the battalion was ready. When he'd joined the United States National Guard, he'd never thought he'd have to fight in a war, but now that the time was near, he had to be confident in his skills and those of his comrades if he ever wanted to see Leinani again.

Chapter Fifty-two

A llu's first letter came in mid-summer, 1943.
Camp had begun to transform. Since the riot, internees had come together in a sort of unspoken oath to create their own community. Heck, there was even a beauty parlor and sewing facility now. Gardens began to pop up around camp, displaying bridges and intricately-placed pebble. Outside of their barracks, Allu and Kiko had designed their own landscaped patterns—mostly on weekends when they weren't in class.

Allu thought it was funny how her first notion was to run and tell Robbie himself: *Look, we've received a letter!*

In a way, some days it felt like he was still there at camp, that if she looked hard enough, she'd find him with that smirk on his face. She laughed to herself, imagining him hiding out in the laundry area with some pretty girls his age.

She wanted to be alone when she opened the letter. Maybe, because, it was the first she'd ever gotten with her name written on the envelope. Mama, though hesitant, gave Allu permission to read it in one of the gardens so long as it didn't get lost or ruined.

The envelope was delicate. Girly. A fine tear in its seam indicated where camp officials had opened it for screening. But still, it felt sacred. Personal.

Holding her breath, Allu slid the letter from the envelope. But there wasn't any writing on the sheet of paper itself. Rather, there was a picture of the most beautiful bird she'd ever seen painted. The initials *"LP"* were in the corner.

Lucille Peterson.

Allu turned the envelope over to make sure it was addressed correctly. It appeared so.

Oh, how she had missed Lucille those first isolated months after the bombing. She hadn't understood what she'd done so wrong to turn her friend against her. It had only taken a few years for her to realize it was their differences that had scared Lucille. Differences that weren't even evident to them until society made it evident. And now, she suddenly felt sorry for Lucille. Sorry she had been raised by parents who didn't encourage individuality, or free thought, for that matter.

But there was hope. Hope in the form of a bright yellow bird painted across a cloudless sky, addressed to her.

***

"I've got some exciting news." Richmond looked around, as if it was private information that could be stolen at any time.

The orchard smelled of apple blossoms and a pink canopy of flowers almost made her forget they were encamped.

"War's over?" Allu suppressed a smirk. It was easier to be friends than to pretend not to know each other every time they ran into each other—which turned out to be often.

"Just as good," he said. "Meet me after supper. East-end garden."

She gave him a confused look but agreed to see him later.

***

The east-end garden had become less busy than the orchard, so Allu didn't mind going there to talk. Still, she was hesitant to meet up purposefully. Sure, things had gotten more lax at camp, but there was always the chance of Mama finding out she was with one of the guards. Or worse, officials punishing Richmond. Although, she knew he feared himself more than anyone. He was so hard on himself. He didn't say so in direct terms, but she noticed the sleepless nights that marked under his eyes and sensed the anger that sometimes laced his words. The war was hard on everyone, and he was no worse than any of the other guards.

Richmond walked toward her in the garden, soldier-like, but she noticed how his eyes twinkled under the bill of his hat, even if he didn't smile much. She imagined him wearing regular clothes and tried to picture what he would look like. Maybe he'd smile without the uniform.

"So, what is it?" Allu asked, sitting down on the ground.

He sat down next to her, leaving the slightest distance between them.

"I've found your father." He blurted out the words, leaving them to hang in the silence between them.

She must have heard him wrong. "*What?*"

"*Your father.* I found him."

Allu swallowed hard. It wasn't like Richmond to kid around with her, but she was incredulous with this news. He was going too far. Maybe this whole time he was befriending her, it'd been some sort of cruel joke. She should have seen it coming.

"My father's dead," she said flatly. "I've told you that."

"No, he's not." He pulled a folded sheet of paper from his pocket and carefully smoothed it out on his lap. It was a roster of sorts.

"See?" He pointed to a name that was underlined.

Not just any name. *Her father's name.*

"Right here," he said. "Kuroda Noguchi. That's his name, isn't it?"

Allu blinked hard. She couldn't believe it. Sure, she'd mentioned her father's name to him in passing, but this? It wasn't believable. Surely, he was mistaken.

"Where did you get this? It's a joke. I can't believe you would do such a thing." But even as she said it, she noticed the frown creep around Richmond's mouth, and knew she'd offended him. "Kuroda's a common name," she stammered, trying to convince herself. "There are many others with that same name."

"All farmers from Santa Ana, California?" Richmond raised his eyebrows. "Look. It also lists you and Robbie. Well, Robert."

This was all too much. This couldn't be right.

"Allu? What's wrong? It's him, I'm sure it's him."

She hesitated, suddenly feeling small and vulnerable. "I'm scared to believe it." But she allowed her heart to leap just a little.

***

Mama hardly threw Allu a glance as she tugged on a yellow strand of yarn, stretching it between her outstretched arms. "You can't believe everything you hear."

"Mama, I saw it with my own eyes!" Allu glared at her. "Stop knitting, and look at me!"

Sighing, Mama set her ball of yarn down and gave her a look she recognized. The truth settled in, wedging into the cracks of fear and loneliness. The cracks faith was supposed to have filled.

"You knew…" Allu couldn't believe it, even as she sputtered the words.

Her mother twisted the yarn between her two fingers, without looking up.

"Didn't you?"

She didn't answer.

"*Didn't you?*"

"Yes, Allu-chan." Mama sighed. "I knew."

"How *could* you?" Allu spit out the words. "*How could you?*" She watched her mother wrap the yarn and wanted to scream.

"There is nothing greater in this world than hope. But if anything comes close, it's fear. Fear of death, fear of loss, fear of the unknown. I couldn't bear to watch your hope rise only to be killed by fear. You already lost him once. I couldn't bear to watch you lose him again."

"And you thought that was your place to decide?" Allu tasted blood in her mouth and realized she'd been biting her lip. "What about Robbie? I suppose he knew, too."

"I told him just before he left."

Mama stood, but Allu held her hand out, stopping her from coming anywhere near her. The last thing she wanted was to be treated like a child.

"What about your big speech on hope, Ma?" She knew she shouldn't disrespect her mother, but she was upset.

"Allu-chan." Mama took another step toward her. "He could use a little hope out there."

"It's you. You can't handle seeing it, can you? And as long as you don't see it, it's okay. Well, I'm old enough to understand you like keeping me in the dark, Ma."

There was nothing to say. Robbie would have fixed this. But now it was just Allu and Mama. *Damn him.*

"You think you're old enough to know what you're doing, huh? And where did you get that list from, Allu? Where? From that nice-looking guard friend of yours?"

The words slapped Allu in the face, and she felt her cheeks burn.

"You think I didn't *know*? You think I don't see the look in your eyes or hear you singing?" Mama threw her arms up in the air. "People talk, and a mother knows her daughter's heart, even if she doesn't always trust her words. You think I deceived *you*? You're the one galloping around with the enemy. Not only the enemy, but the one who killed Johnny—and you think that I'm fine with it? I'm disappointed in you."

Allu's heart dropped to her feet. She felt as if she was about to hit the floor. It couldn't be true. It couldn't be. Not Richie. Mama was wrong. She had gotten the wrong soldier.

"No, no, no." Allu shook her head. "No. You have the wrong one. Not Richmond. Not him. You don't know him."

But Mama's face told a thousand stories, and all of them were true.

Her hands trembled, and Allu thought she might not be able to catch her breath.

"Allu-chan." Her mother's voice was soft, a thousand rooms away. "I'm sorry. I thought you knew." Mama walked toward her, and Allu collapsed into the dark safety of her arms.

Chapter Fifty-three

Camp Shelby, Mississippi

Summer, 1943

It felt good to run, even as Robbie felt the blood soaking into his socks from blisters on his heels. It felt even better to know there were people counting on him to do it.

Camp Shelby was a city entirely of its own. Thousands of tents spanned across thousands of acres of land. He couldn't help but feel small. The grinding, cranking noises of tanks driving through camp thudded through the thin walls of his tent at night, and there was a constant commotion of the organized trainings for the various companies.

He couldn't wait to write to Allu about the Women's Army Corp, the first of its kind, which was based on the other side of camp and trained more than fifty Nisei women.

Robbie also wanted to tell her how the 100th Battalion had secretly trained in Wisconsin before joining up with them—and wow, were those guys tough. And superior ball players. They even had their own team, playing throughout Wisconsin. Rumor was, many could go pro after the war. Most of them had never been off the island of Hawaii, but here they were, getting ready to ship off to Algeria.

Many men had already joined up with British allies in securing North Africa from Hitler's troops before moving on to Italy. And even though Italy had surrendered after being backed into a corner in northern Tunisia, Hitler pushed back with even more German troops, treating Italy like another conquered country.

Robbie's legs were aching. How far had they run? Five miles? Six? He couldn't keep track but was surprised his lungs were still holding out.

He found it incredible how "camp" could mean so many things. Take on so many meanings. Manzanar had had a lot of the same structure and routine, but felt like a prison camp.

Shelby was liberating. Hell, even the meals weren't half bad. He pictured Jimmy's face eating the slop his first day at camp and laughed. Jimmy hadn't had the luxury of being broken into camp food. Robbie couldn't wait to see him again. They'd have a beer and talk about the different paths they'd gone down.

And Daisy. Poor Daisy. Now looking back, she seemed the type that would have gotten roped into an unhappy marriage by obligation and fear of being impolite. Shit, she and Calvin probably had a couple of their own rug-rats running around. Biting ankles and pulling hair. He wasn't going to dwell over it.

Later after supper, Robbie pulled the picture of Papa from his pocket he'd kept. White creases had worn into the photo, making it appear Papa had a large white stripe running across his shirt. But his face was still clear. He'd shown it to a few of the vets, and they thought most likely, he was helping with some missions against the Japanese. That was where the ones with war experience and translation abilities ended up, one guy said. The irony didn't escape Robbie. He wondered if his father would recognize him, and quickly shook off the idea. How ridiculous. Of course, he'd recognize him.

"Is that a photo of your sweetheart?"

Robbie jumped and turned to see the voice came from a soldier at least a few inches shorter than him.

"No, it's a picture of my pa," Robbie said to the man, who sat beside him.

"Is he serving?" the soldier asked.

It was an innocent question, but it gave Robbie a small pang in his stomach to hear his name used in present tense.

"*Served.* World War I. The FBI took him." He put the picture back in his pocket.

The soldier's face softened. "I'm sorry. Private Sam Jones, Wyoming," he said, extending his hand.

"Private Robbie Noguchi, California. You come from an internment camp, too?"

Sam shook his head. "Heart Mountain. I was a rancher before the war."

"A Japanese American cowboy?" Robbie chuckled at the thought. He couldn't make out whether the kid was serious.

Sam's face went red.

"I didn't mean to offend you," Robbie said, regretting the comment.

"It's just you're…"

"Short?" Sam cut him off before laughing. "Well, believe it or not, I'm one of the best riders in our area."

Robbie liked him instantly. "My pa was a farmer. Not with horses or anything, but grew crops. I could see why the FBI thought he was a spy."

Sam smirked. "You scale any walls here yet?"

"Sure did," Robbie said. He could still feel it in his arms and legs from two days ago. Or, maybe it was the weight of the guns he'd carried. Ha! He wondered how Jimmy had done in training. One thing was for sure: you couldn't talk your way out of anything with the drill sergeants here.

"I made the two, four, and five-foot wall, but I'm not proud to say I'm practicing for the eight-footer."

"What did your drill sergeant think about that?" Robbie had seen a man get in soldiers' faces on many occasions for lesser reasons.

"Well, I can tell you he didn't like it much."

They both laughed.

"I'm pretty good at doing chin-ups on the eight-foot pipe, though. Not much weight to lift."

Robbie smiled. The kid weighed maybe 140 pounds soaking wet.

"The rope ladders aren't that bad, either," he said.

"Private Robert Noguchi!" a loud voice called through the barracks, interrupting them. "You got mail."

Robbie jumped up and grabbed his letter from the soldier, who moved on to the next soldier with mail. He didn't get many letters, but every so often, Allu would send updates from Manzanar. Mostly about how Ma was doing or the new groups that were forming in camp. His heart ached every time he thought of them, even knowing this was something he must do for his family. He wondered whether they'd ever make it back to the farm.

He sat on his cot and read the envelope. It wasn't from Allu. His heart nearly stopped. *Daisy?*

"I'll leave you to it," Sam said, getting up.

Robbie nodded, grateful for the solitude. The envelope was thin. He hadn't seen her or spoken with her in over a year.

He ripped the top of the envelope open and reached inside. It was a newspaper clipping, yellowed with time. He unfolded it, expecting to see an engagement picture of Daisy and Calvin. He wasn't sure why Dee would send it, but it was the only thing that made sense. Instead, he saw Jimmy's face peering back at him. But it didn't say Jimmy. It said

James. Nobody called him by his formal name.

His breath hitched at the realization it was an obituary.

I thought you would want to know. I heard you volunteered with the 442nd. I'm sorry. Dee.

He read the heading of the article.

James Hanson Dies of Wounds on French Front

James Hanson, son of...

Robbie folded it with trembling hands. He couldn't. Not Jimmy. God, no. *Not Jimmy!* It couldn't be true. No, he refused to believe it. Jimmy was, *well,* Jimmy. He was smooth with the ladies and indestructible. He was his best friend. How could he go down? No, not like that. Not the Jimmy he knew.

Tears stung his eyes. It became hard to breathe. Scream. He needed to scream! He rolled to his side to face the wall, and for the first time since he could remember, he sobbed. There were a few other soldiers there, but they respected him enough to give him space. They were brothers now.

Night was drawing near, but it didn't matter. None of it mattered.

He remembered Jimmy on the day he first met him at baseball practice as a kid. He always had that goofy smile and self-assured confidence. He could talk his way out of anything.

Anything, but death.

And now, Jimmy was a war casualty. He didn't deserve to be. He'd had a good heart.

Robbie's throat tightened. He wondered how many other friends he'd lost without even knowing they were gone.

Chapter Fifty-four

September, 1943

Allu folded the letter and examined the handwriting on the envelope. A few of the lines had been crossed out, most likely at the War Relocation Unit's discretion, but she didn't mind. In all the years she'd known him, she'd never noticed what good handwriting Robbie had—the way he curved the lines of his letters into loose loops. Carefree Robbie. Oh, how she missed him.

"Can you believe there's a women's unit?" Kiko said, breaking the silence, shaking her head in disbelief. "I've never considered joining the army before."

"Nah, I don't think I could do it," Allu said.

"Not sure I could, either, but it's nice to know we could."

"Yes," Allu agreed thoughtfully. "It *is* nice to know we could."

Many possibilities had arisen from the war. Women were working outside the home, and even on the warfront. It seemed almost anything was possible.

They sat in silence, trying to avoid the weight of the unspoken.

"Allu, I can't stand to see you this way." Kiko gave her a look of concern.

Allu realized how much she cared. Still, she felt miserable.

"Look, this war makes everything confusing. I know you're hurting over Robbie."

Allu considered whether she wanted to open the door to the conversation on her mind, but then again, how could she feel any worse?

"It's not just that," she said, folding the letter and slipping it back into the envelope. She waited for Kiko to say something, but instead, she sat quietly, waiting for Allu to elaborate. "It's Richmond, too."

She glanced at Kiko to gauge her reaction, but her eyes didn't give away how she felt. "I just can't believe he…" Her voice broke. "He killed him, Kiko. He killed Johnny. Of all the guards, why did it have to be him? I trusted him and he never told me. And I talked about Johnny to him. He knew Johnny was like a brother to me."

Kiko pursed her lips in thought. "I know, Allu, but maybe he was trying to protect you."

"Protect me? From what?"

"I don't know. Maybe the pain of knowing. Johnny didn't deserve to die, but Richmond was doing what he had been trained to do. Maybe he didn't have a choice in the matter."

Allu knew she was probably right, but she still couldn't forgive him. "You should have seen Johnny's mother after it happened. Rocking him in the dirt." Tears welled up in her eyes, remembering. "I'll never get that image out of my head."

"I know," Kiko said, wrapping an arm around her. "But I'm sure he'll never get the feeling of guilt out of his heart, no matter how much he tortures himself. It's a penance he'll carry with him."

"What is the meaning of all this pain? What is the purpose?"

Her friend shook her head. "I don't know. If we knew, we'd all live a lot differently, I'm sure. There probably wouldn't be wars over money, and land and dominance over people."

Kiko was a good friend, and she was right. It felt good to have someone know her so well who knew just what to say. Someone who was not afraid to disagree with her when she was wrong but knew her well enough to do it gracefully.

Her friendship was a beautiful thing, grown out of the ugliness of their circumstances, and Allu felt bad when she remembered how she had treated her early on in camp. Maybe, she could try harder to accept others, even at the risk of being hurt, the risk of being abandoned or possibly worse, the risk of being rejected. It was, Allu decided, one of the most important things in life.

And oddly enough, with all of the uncertainties of the world, it was something she could control.

Chapter Fifty-five

Oran, Algeria

September, 1943

Yukio's battalion had attached to the 133rd Infantry Regiment of the Red Bull 34th Infantry Division. They'd been serving in the North African campaign, securing it for the Allies, to keep it from falling into the Axis Powers' hands. Most of the men were from National Guard units in Iowa, Minnesota, and the Dakotas. Their red buffalo skull shoulder patch easily identified them as such. They were a good lot, and liked to drink wine and sing "Lili Marlene." Yukio knew every word by heart now.

The vets taught them how to identify German mines. And more importantly, how to diffuse them. There was the picket mine and the Bouncing Betty, which when tripped, would bounce to a guy's shoulders before spraying shrapnel mid-body. Teller mines were known to blow up tanks and vehicles.

The men trained, serious about their duties. This was not a war game.

They'd been diverted to Salerno, Italy, along with 190,000 Allied troops, 30,000 vehicles, and 120,000 tons of supplies.

Along with the rest of his company, Yukio threw a heavy bag on the back of a stinky mule. He'd never even ridden a horse. Who would've thought he'd be riding a mule through enemy territory? Life was full of surprises.

The rain beat down on him, cold and constant. Climbing onto the mule wasn't the hard part. The bumpy ride and the feeling of falling to your death when the mules slipped on the steep ravines was.

This particular ravine ridge he was currently riding on was a deathtrap. Mud slides dropping sharply several thousand feet into a rushing river. Yukio held onto the leather strap, reminding himself not to look down.

The soldier on the mule in front of him turned his head so Yukio could see his profile. "We need to cross that river," he told him. "There should be a bridge up ahead."

There was no chance Yukio was taking his eyes off the front of his mule. "WE NEED TO CROSS THE RIVER," he said loudly to whomever could hear him from behind. "THERE SHOULD BE A BRIDGE UP AHEAD."

But once they got around the bend, their spirits sank. The Germans had wiped out the bridges.

"Well," Yukio said to his mule, "looks like we're going to be best pals by the end of this war."

And then, a sound echoed off the ravine and a spray of ammo hit the men in front of him. The mules cried out, trying to run, while injured and healthy men alike jumped off their mounts.

"Get down!" someone shouted.

Yukio's knees hit the ground and his mule was gone. *Damn thing.* His heart pounded as the rocky hill above him showered him and his comrades with rocks and chunks of grass from another round of ammo.

"Where's it coming from?" he asked the man lying next to him.

The man crawled on his stomach to the safety of a large rock. "I think the nest is over there." He pointed.

"Aim…" Yukio's voice trailed off as he turned to the soldier next to him, realizing the man was lying in a pool of his own blood.

Yukio thought of *gisei*…sacrifice. Surrendering something of value for the sake of a higher goal. American lives—*people's* lives—were the higher goal, he reminded himself. Their country and what it stood for was at stake, as was the world. He hoped the Americans back home would know this soldier's name and that his sacrifice would be worth the result.

He raised his gun and began to shoot.

Chapter Fifty-six

October, 1943

Allu knew. Richmond had been expecting this, but was unprepared nonetheless. It had been several weeks since he'd seen her, and it didn't take a scientist to know she was avoiding him.

"I was going to tell you," he said, not knowing how to start. He should've expected to run into her by the rec hall when changing posts with another guard.

Allu raised her eyes to meet his, her face turning red.

"Look," he said. "I didn't know how."

"You didn't know *how?*" Allu was beginning to yell. "Maybe, '*hey, how's your day going? Before we become friends, you should probably know that I'm the one who shot your friend.*' That's a good start! You knew we were friends, Richmond!"

His eyebrows scrunched together. "Look, I didn't know. I was just doing my job." He knew it was the wrong thing to say as soon as the words left his mouth. "I mean…"

"*Doing your job?*"

A couple of people turned their heads to watch the commotion.

Allu didn't seem to care. "I suppose to you it was just another Jap? Right? They don't have feelings. They're hardly even human."

"That's not what I meant. I'm sorry." He placed his hand on her shoulder, and the people watching began to whisper amongst themselves.

"Don't touch me. Get your dirty hand off of me."

Richmond flinched, pulling back his hand.

"Mama was right. You're all the same."

He rubbed his temple. This had been a bad idea. He should've left her alone. Still, he cared about her. He had to explain. Help her to understand the circumstances.

"Allu, we're not all the same, just like the WRA is wrong to assume *you're* all the same. I couldn't see, damn it! The dust storm. He wouldn't move. I prayed. Damn it, I prayed he'd move away from the fence, but he didn't move. He couldn't have heard me if I'd tried."

"So that's it. You didn't even try. Shoot first, wish you tried later. You *disgust* me. How disappointed your mother would be. You're a horrible person! A good soldier and a horrible person."

And there it was.

Richmond opened his mouth to speak and shut it again. Allu was right. He quietly pulled himself up and straightened his shoulders.

She looked at him, waiting for him to plead his case. Waiting for him to swoop in and save the situation. But nothing he could say would make it right. The kid was dead, and he had killed him. He was a good soldier and a horrible person. There was nothing more to say. And he doubted she'd ever forgive him for it.

Chapter Fifty-seven

Castle Hill, Italy

October, 1943

Yukio paused briefly to bend and straighten his fingers, stiff from the cold rain. He tried not to think of the Hawaiian friends he'd lost crossing the Volturno River. Engineers had done a fine job building temporary bridges, but nothing could've prepared him for the heavy fire.

He carried the last wounded man into a relay emergency station the 100th had set up, trying not to think of the wounded he'd watched being shot down as they limped, easy targets just trying to backtrack the ridge.

Yukio watched the army medic inject the man with morphine to kill the pain before infusing him with blood plasma. He wondered whether he'd make it. He'd have to remember to tell Leinani to thank all the people back home for their donations of pints of blood. They were saving lives.

On the following day, they hiked through more rocky mountains, covered with patches of snow. His feet hurt, and he prayed he didn't have trench foot. Their mission was to drive the Nazis out of Castle Hill. The Germans liked to find the best vantage points for raining havoc on their enemy, before skirting away to another point. Not this time. This time, they were going to get them.

He spotted the old building on the ridge. The "castle" which deemed the hill, *Castle Hill*. It looked abandoned and quiet. An uneasy feeling gripped his stomach.

They advanced quietly, careful not to step on any land mines.

An officer motioned to him and Yukio nodded. Fixing his eyes in front of him, he slowly kneeled down into the cold snow.

Another soldier squatted beside him, as they worked quickly and quietly to set up their equipment with nearly frozen hands. They didn't have the sighting equipment, but all they needed was to reach the other side of the hill. Yukio remembered his training and looked everything over carefully before nodding to his partner.

Together, they fired 60mm mortars to the other side of the castle on the hill. There was a brief silence as their shells echoed in the valley.

And then the rain of artillery came.

The fighting was fierce and loud. Yukio wondered briefly how many Germans they had taken out.

Men fell, and within minutes, he watched in horror as his partner was picked off by a sniper on the hill.

He crouched lower on his stomach, loading and reloading. It was hours of loud shooting and trying to stay alive before darkness fell and all was quiet again. He both welcomed and loathed the darkness and its ability to hide the enemy.

Yukio was cold and hadn't eaten anything in over a day. But even the cold C rations had to be rationed as much as the water, and the fighting was too intense to even think about eating.

It had been quiet for over an hour. Feeling it was safe, Yukio crept down the hill into the darkness, holding his breath. Slow, ever so slowly, he told himself. He found a large rock, large enough to shield his body while he relieved himself. When he was finished, he climbed back to his post. He was so tired but forbade himself the vulnerability of sleep.

How long had it been since he'd seen his family? His heart sank. Over a year, with several deaths marked between. He tried not to think about it often, but still, when he least expected it, his family would enter his mind, disrupting his thoughts.

Leinani. Poor Leinani. Would she have been better not knowing him? His heart ached at the thought, trying not to think about their marriage that had to be postponed. And now it had been a year without her already and still, she waited. Yukio read letters from his family as often as he could. It kept his spirits up and helped remind him of the reason he was fighting.

Hitler had to be stopped. They'd heard that already in Italy, he'd shipped over 640,000 Italians to slave labor camps with hardly any food. The people had been so grateful to see the Allies there. They'd offered what little food they had, shaking their hands in the streets, despite putting their lives in danger to do so.

He'd heard soldiers say that many of the older men in these camps tried to salute the American and British soldiers, but were so weak, they nearly fell over in doing so. They hadn't asked for this Hell, and they deserved liberation.

A sickening feeling filled his stomach. A combination of fear and anger, amplified by hunger, thirst, and exhaustion. He felt alone. Helpless, despite being surrounded by brothers who had his back and would surely take a bullet for him. He longed for home. To be on Waikiki Beach, watching the sunset on rolling waves without the shrill shrieks of suffering men and screaming torpedoes filling his ears with death. A beach without barbed wire.

It had been a month in action. They'd traveled 267 miles from Salerno, nearly half of it by foot. They'd built a solid reputation as a unit as they fought beside fellow Americans of all colors, and the British as well.

Still, they'd only covered a quarter of the distance to Rome, and there was no way of knowing what lie before him and his comrades. He let out a deep breath and made his way back up the hill to his post.

Chapter Fifty-eight

Camp Shelby, Mississippi

November, 1943

Robbie placed another float in the water, thankful for the repetitive work.

The pontoon bridge was almost complete and once done, would be buoyant enough to support a deck for quick soldier and vehicle travel. He slapped another bug from his skin, slick with humidity. He couldn't get out of this place fast enough.

He was surprised at the way things were in what they called the "deep South." He'd heard of places where only white men were allowed to sit, but couldn't imagine it until he saw it first-hand. The days he was allowed a pass off the camp, he opted to make a quick run to town for food.

Placing the last piece in the water, he stood up to admire his work. They'd come far as a unit. He offered to help with the last bit so they could move on with practicing attacking strategies across a bridge. He wondered how often these bridges would need to be built overseas.

He'd heard they'd be training in the DeSoto National Forest later that winter, while the 522nd Field Artillery Battalion practiced maneuvers in Louisiana. But who knew? The military was often illusive in its plans.

"Attention!" A sergeant said, and halted Robbie's thoughts.

Within minutes, he was holding an M1 semi-automatic rifle. According to some of the vets, it could be equipped with a grenade launcher, in addition to a bayonet. Time would tell how many times he'd use the weapon. He knew the drills were important, but he wanted to get overseas and see some action. He wanted to pay them back for what they did to his friend and what they were still doing to so many others and their families. Their children.

The drills were worth the effort if it meant teaching him the means to save others like Jimmy.

Chapter Fifty-nine

December, 1943

Allu held the baby in her arms as she rocked. She hummed for a few minutes, admiring the chubby cheeks of the little girl before realizing it was a song Papa had whistled on many of their bird-watching walks.

She'd started volunteering at the Manzanar orphanage in the fall to fill her lonely afternoons while Mama was working. It was hard to imagine why the U.S. Army had ordered the orphans and foster children to be incarcerated, but she'd given up trying to figure the whole situation out.

Children's Village was a one-story building located on the northwest section of camp, near the makeshift hospital, and held over one hundred children, many of them babies. There was a total of three barracks, but unlike their own, these had running water and bathrooms.

Allu volunteered in the girl's section of the dorms and liked rocking and feeding the babies. Most of the kids, she noticed, were under seven years old. Sometimes, she stayed for arts and crafts with the older kids or would eat with them in their mess hall when Mama worked late.

Allu gently kissed the baby's cheek and wondered where she would go if the war ended. She didn't have any family. None of these kids did. This was the only family they had: the caregivers and volunteers.

She tried not to think of Richmond, though she had to admit that her heart had softened a bit with separation. The war was complicated. She'd been just a kid when it started two years ago and yet, the camp had aged her.

Several weeks back, she'd decided she'd work with children when she was older. Already, she was thinking of what she could do. There was always teaching, but there was also so much more opportunity now that the war had encouraged women to join the workforce in factories and other industries.

The baby stirred a bit before settling back into sleep.

Allu glanced at the clock. Kiko was meeting her after she was done with the newspaper club she'd joined, but right now, all that mattered was that this tiny baby knew how important and loved she was.

Chapter Sixty

Majo Hills, Italy

January thru February, 1944

Yukio gripped the hand of the soldier next to him. He couldn't see his face in the darkness, but trusted his grip. The slope was steep and snowy. Already, they'd lost a few mules' worth of supplies. The only thing preventing him from losing his footing was the soldier's hand which linked him to the next, and so forth.

Several wounded men were forced to backtrack over the steep slopes to medical relay stations with minimal emergency care. Yukio felt sorry for these men. As bad as it was, as exhausted as he was with stomach cramps and trench foot, nothing could be as bad as being severely wounded and stuck in the mountains. The medics were invaluable.

Yukio could feel the enemy. They knew they were there. The black night and steep hills had, for once, become their ally.

As he stepped in the darkness, he thought of Leinani and smiled. He'd met her on campus in Hawaii at college. How beautiful she was. She was twenty at the time, a few years younger than him. He usually didn't cut through campus to get to his class, but that day he had.

"Would you consider donating to support local farmers who are still recovering from the Depression?" a sweet voice called out to him.

He had turned to see who it was coming from.

"I am a local farmer," he said, smiling. She had to be a freshmen he'd thought. Or close to it. He'd never seen her on campus.

"Well, in that case, I'm assuming it's a yes." She grinned, grabbing her clipboard.

She was persistent, he remembered thinking, unlike any other girl he'd sought out.

"Are you a freshmen here?" he'd asked, suddenly not caring about attending his next class.

"Sophomore," she said, without looking up.

He waited for her to expand, but realized she wasn't offering any more information than needed.

"Are you always working on different causes, or do you make time for comedies, like other students?" he asked.

She considered that for a minute, tucking her pen in her pulled-up dark hair. "Sometimes." She shrugged. "I guess it depends on who's asking."

Was she sweet on him, he had wondered.

"There's one at the theater. I might just be there tonight," he said, giving her his best smile.

Her eyes sparkled.

Wouldn't you know it, later that evening, he walked into the theater with his best clothes on. He scanned the crowd, searching for her but couldn't find her anywhere. He was disappointed to say the least.

He decided to stay for the film as he had gone out of his way to get popcorn. Not even ten minutes later, there was a tap on his shoulder.

"Excuse me, sir," came the familiar sweet voice. "Are you looking for anyone to fill that seat? There's quite a line waiting to get in."

He looked up and saw she had on a name tag!

"Do you work here?" he asked.

"Yes," she replied simply. "Does that bother you?"

He shook his head, trying to play it casual. "Only if you refuse to sit with me."

Yukio sighed, remembering. He missed her. They'd been dating ever since.

Almost out. The mountains were overbearing in the distance, even in the darkness. Rapido Valley was just ahead. They had to make it through the most guarded line in the Nazi operation: the Gustav Line in Monte Cassino.

***

The enemy line was said to be over two hundred miles long, guarded by several 75mm Panther guns, embedded in the concrete of steel shelters. And above it all, watching and waiting atop a 1,300 foot mountain, was the Benedictine Abbey.

Their boots were weighted down not only with exhaustion, but with thick mud after the Germans had dammed up the Rapido and flooded the bank. Tanks and transport vehicles had required the time-consuming job of laying steel matting down for support. The Engineer Corp cleared the trees away, providing a field of shooting for the Nazis as they watched from the advantageous height of the Abbey.

Yukio's comrades crawled slowly and steadily in the mud, praying to avoid tripping up any mines or getting wrapped up in the barbed wire edging the river. It was just before midnight, making it difficult to feel for mines in the dark. Mortar and machine gun fire rained upon them, flashing brief moments of light…long enough to see men grow still.

By morning, Yukio could see just how many of their men had been killed and wounded as they lay lifeless in the mud along the river. Anytime a wounded soldier would move, the enemy would snipe the life out of them, leaving them no option but to lay and wait.

Yukio drew in a deep breath and climbed into the flowing water. Instantly, his breath left his lungs as an icy chill swept his body. He held his arms high above the water. He had to keep his back pack and gun from freezing. He could see the smoke from fellow men, an effort to provide cover for their crossing, but the wind kept shifting the smoke, and enemy fire took out many soldiers.

"Pull back!" The orders were passed along the line.

Another failed attempt at crossing the Rapido.

Chapter Sixty-one

April, 1944

"This your first time on a ship this size?" Sam asked, leaning against the railing.

"It is," Robbie said.

They gazed at the land, watching the buildings shrink in size, a cool breeze blowing in their faces. They'd boarded the troop transport at Hampton Roads from a staging area at Camp Patrick Henry in Virginia, and now, here they were, finally going overseas to fight.

"Liberty Ships," Sam said, adjusting his hat that kept shifting in the breeze. "I sure hope so."

Robbie glanced at him. "Me, too. I'd hate to see this world if Hitler or the Imperial Army take over."

Both were silent for a few moments.

Robbie had heard they were heading to Italy to join the 100th. He couldn't wait to meet up with them. They had seen so much and done so much for both the war effort and for the Nisei also. His mind shifted to Jimmy and he wondered what he'd seen. Poor Jimmy, who would always remain a twenty-year-old mischief-maker in his mind.

"I hear we're meeting up with another convoy."

Robbie was grateful Sam interrupted his thoughts.

"That'll be a sight to see, if it's anything near the size of this ship," Robbie said. It was the largest ship he'd ever seen. Even bigger than some of the ships that he'd seen at the ports in California with his father.

Sam made a heaving noise.

Robbie turned his attention from the horizon and found his friend bent over the railing. Despite himself, he began to laugh. "Not so much a sailor then?"

Sam held one arm up to keep Robbie back, while holding his hat with the other.

Over the next several hours, several men from the ship found they couldn't handle the waters or the constant zig-zagging as they crossed the Atlantic. Robbie figured it was a small price to pay to avoid being hit by German submarines, but then again, he wasn't one of the seasick ones.

Over the course of their route, they met up with other convoys of United States ships about four to five times until hundreds of U.S. ships covered the waters as far as the eye could see. Rumor had it, they were preparing for a landing at Normandy Beach in France. The most talked about operation in the war.

At a certain point, Robbie went back out to the deck in time to watch many of the ships veer off their route. Those ships were headed to England, while his was headed through the Straits of Gibraltar. Just watching those ships and the sheer mass of them, gave him pride. He finally felt he was part of something bigger than himself.

***

They finally arrived in Italy. Ten officers and 151 men. Robbie thought it seemed like just yesterday he'd entered Camp Shelby. He'd never been out of the states before, and in Italy, everything was historically old. Hell, there were bridges older than the entire U.S.

The men from the 100th welcomed them, even if they shot barbs at their youth and mainland mentality, having been raised in the pop culture of America. Robbie noticed most of them were in their thirties. Many were college graduates or had families of their own back home. They had a special bond and a pride about them. They'd been fighting since the beginning of this damn war, had seen their homes destroyed and lost friends firsthand. If not in Hawaii, then out there on the field.

Many of them were recently back from crossing the Rapido, having lost many men.

"God willing," one of them told their unit, "your tour in Naples won't be anything like what we saw at Castle Hill."

By the looks on their faces, Robbie could see even they doubted it.

Chapter Sixty-two

Civitavecchia, Italy

June, 1944

Yukio adjusted his gun on his shoulder. Every part of his body ached. He needed this rest stop and judging the other men, they did, too. Most of the 100th had entered camp already, but he had chosen to stay back and help with the wounded.

The few men standing around clapped for them when they entered camp. The 442nd. They were a young bunch. Much younger than most of their 100th Battalion. For the first time, he allowed tears to enter his eyes. He was exhausted and couldn't help himself.

Later that evening after perhaps the best sleep he'd had overseas, Yukio found himself a good ol' crap shoot game. Several of the men from his battalion were there, along with some much younger faces, he assumed to be from the 442nd.

"You buying in?" one of the young ones asked. He looked too polished to have seen much fighting.

"Yes, sir," Yukio said, pulling a couple of dollars from his pocket. "You with the 4-4-2?"

The Army had been sending in replacements, a steady stream, along with the 232nd Engineer Company and the 522nd Field Artillery Battalion.

"The one and only," the young man confirmed, taking his money. He squatted down and threw the money in the pile of dollars in the dirt in front of the circle of men. "So, you must be a Budda-head?"

Yukio eyed the young man and for a moment, all was quiet. He could feel the tension and wondered whether it was a good idea to jump into a game like this with men he didn't really know. And then, the young man who took the money, laughed. "And I'm a kotonk, right?"

Yukio began to chuckle.

Soon, everyone around the circle was laughing. It was a common thing for the new, young soldiers from the Mainland to be called kotonks and the islanders Budda-heads, names they made up when united at Camp Shelby.

"Empty-headed like a coconut hitting the ground." Yukio smirked. These men, he knew, were a bit unsophisticated and arrogant with youth. Give them time in war and life.

"That it?" the young man asked. "No one else wants to show their skill?"

A few more men threw in money and the game got started. The soldier to his right rolled the dice in the dirt.

A few rolls in, the young man spoke up, lighting a cigarette. "I'm just joking with you, you know."

"What do you mean?" Yukio asked. He hoped he was okay to play.

"About calling you a Budda-head." He pulled the cigarette from his mouth and exhaled a cloud of smoke.

Yukio was used to the smoking. It was one of the few luxuries they had overseas, besides the occasional drink.

"All us guys really respect your battalion. How long you in for?"

Yukio smiled. "Not much longer. I had one year left before Pearl Harbor was bombed."

The men were silent, and the young man shook his head.

"I can't imagine what it was like to watch your home be destroyed like that," he said.

"You ever been to Oahu?" Yukio asked.

The young soldier shook his head.

"It's paradise on earth. There are beaches as long as you can see. Nothing but soft sand that slides into teal waters. The hills are green and lush with tropical flowers so thick, you can smell them before you even see them. And the women—" Yukio grinned.

Then, a dull ache settled into his heart and he wondered when he would ever see his home again.

"Sounds beautiful," the young soldier said, his cigarette dangling from his lips. "You born there?"

"Yes," Yukio said. "My grandparents went there to work the fields and start a new life." He debated whether to mention Leinani, but decided against it. Tonight was a night he didn't want to worry about his future. *Their* future. He wanted to forget about the war as much as he could and what might come of it. "I'm a teacher there. You?"

"I'm a California boy, born and raised." He stubbed the butt of his cigarette into the dirt and extended his hand. "Private Robbie Noguchi."

"Pleased to meet you," Yukio said, shaking the young 442's hand. "Sergeant Yukio Takahashi. You have a big family there?" Something shifted on the young soldier's face. Maybe he shouldn't have asked.

"A mother and sister," Private Robbie said, his face softening. "They're in Camp Manzanar."

Yukio noticed the young soldier didn't mention a father and didn't know what to say. He'd never experienced camp, nor had his family, although many other Japanese American Hawaiians had been sent to the Honouliuli Internment Camp, otherwise known as Hells Valley. He suddenly felt bad for judging him.

"I'm sorry," he said. "It's not right how they've handled things."

"Not your fault," the young soldier said. "And we're fixing it one battle at a time."

"Yes," Yukio said in agreement. "We are."

"You want a drink after the game?" Private Robbie asked. "One of the 4-4-2s got some vino when he was out to town with his leave pass. Believe me, there's plenty to go around."

"That sounds good," Yukio said. It had been too long since he'd had a good drink.

The game didn't last much longer than an hour and much to Yukio's surprise, he lost his money to one of the young soldiers from the 442nd, but he didn't mind. He felt sympathetic for these men. So young. Not that he was much older, but in war years, he felt much older. These guys were fresh out of high school. He wondered how many of them would make it. Then quickly brushed the thought aside.

"You have to be careful to watch for the Bouncing Bettys," he told the young group who accompanied Private Robbie later that evening. "They'll get you out of nowhere. They aren't your average mine. They're bouncing mines. One-hundred percent German. Step on one, and it'll launch into the air before it detonates, spraying shrapnel in every direction." He had the young soldiers' attention and no one interrupted. "The worst part of these is they don't immediately kill you. The Nazis designed them so they might slice off your hand or lodge shrapnel into your foot or stomach, but they will give you serious injury and a slow death."

The young soldier sighed. "I'm just appreciative you got through the Anzio Beach head."

"Well," Yukio said, "we're in this together now. Now that we're attaching to your unit, I thought it my responsibility to tell you how it is.

Try to bring as many of us back as possible."

There was a pause in the conversation as the men reflected and drank their glasses of wine. Yukio wondered if this would be his last.

"Thank you," Private Robbie said. "*Salut* to the 100ᵗʰ Battalion for paving the way for us!" He raised his glass and all of the other men did so in uniform.

Men that had become his brothers. Yukio raised his glass with them and nodded his thanks. Wine had never tasted so good.

Chapter Sixty-three

Castellina Marittina, Pisa, Italy

July, 1944

Robbie didn't realize he'd been holding his breath until it all came out at once. Pressing his body against the ground, there was nowhere to hide from the rain of German bullets and nothing to block out the explosive sounds screaming of death in his ears. The hill was swarming with the enemy.

He tasted dirt and had to piss. How long had they been there without moving? Half an hour? An hour? Two? They'd been crawling, gaining ground by inches. Robbie's muscles burned.

Just a few days ago, they had taken Belvedere and Cecina before approaching the Arno River, driving the enemy north. Breaking the German defensive line in the mountains would be rough and slow, considering the Nazis had blown out most of the bridges and roads, but Robbie would be damned if he would go down on a hill in the middle of nowhere with piss on his pants.

Movement from a tree to his left caught his trained eye. A machine-gun nest. The caves and trees were filled with them.

Fixating on the branches, he quietly motioned to the men who flanked him. He couldn't wait to get out of this rugged terrain. The enemy was nowhere. The enemy was everywhere.

All at once, fire exploded in a loud boom in front of them, flooding his face with heat. The sound of mortar shells and German burp guns coincided with puffs of dust popping up around him, and men falling to the dirt.

Everywhere Robbie looked, both trees and grass were red with blood. There was no telling how many of his friends were alive.

There was no time to check the faces of the fallen. He had to move.

Chapter Sixty-four

August, 1944

Allu wiped her forehead as she sat beside Mama at the table. It was a hot day in the desert.

Mama got up from the table. "Drink something," she said. "This heat isn't good for you." She unscrewed the lid from the jar of water and poured her a small glass. "Another letter came today."

"From Robbie?" Allu looked forward to reading about his adventures and tried to imagine the scenery. "A postcard?" she asked hopefully.

"Not this time," Mama said, shaking her head. "A letter."

"Have you opened it?" Allu was sure she'd waited for her but asked just the same. It had become their ritual to wait until after supper to read Robbie's letters—a small light in the endless gray days. She couldn't bear to talk to Richmond and avoided supper at the mess hall when he was working nearby.

"Of course not." Mama walked to the side table Robbie had made her before leaving and pulled an envelope out of the drawer before joining Allu at the table.

"It's your turn," she said, sliding the envelope across the table.

Carefully, Allu slid the paper from the envelope and let out a deep sigh to brace herself before reading aloud.

July 24, 1944

Dear Mama,

One-thousand, two-hundred and seventy-two of our men have been lost within a forty-mile stretch. Sons. Brothers. Fathers. We've fought hard and welcome rest, as we are stationed to guard the north side of the Arno River while bridges are being built.

I was fortunate enough during a day of rest to visit Rome. Hitler instructed his troops to leave everything intact when they pushed out the civilians. It's hard to believe, after what they've done to most other structures around here. Many of their lookouts are in ancient monasteries without any regard to the destruction of ancient texts and architecture.

Anyway, the Red Cross gave us tours of things I never thought I'd see in my lifetime—the Colosseum and catacombs, to name a few. The food is good (I'm grateful to never eat a Manzanar hot dog dish again), although there's little meat and poor refrigeration. Don't worry, Ma, none of the meals compare to yours.

After many days of fighting, we also got to rest awhile in Vada, off the coast of Pisa. Tell Allu there were chickens everywhere! We made homemade soups from tomatoes we picked off the vines, and bouillon cubes from our army rations. Who knew I could cook?

It was nice seeing the beach. One of the men even tossed a grenade in the water as a means of "fishing." We're soon to be reassigned to the 85th Infantry Division, and will continue to move along the Arno. God willing, we'll drive the Nazis out for good once we get past the Gothic Line. I'll be thankful for flat land on the other side of the mountains in the Po Valley.

I hope this letter finds you well, and I hope I've brought honor to our family name. I'll write again soon.

Love,
Robbie

"Of course he makes our family proud." Mama sniffed.

Allu couldn't bear to look at her, or she might break down completely. Instead, she tucked the letter back in its envelope and placed it by his picture on the shelf. She had to get away. Get out.

"I'm going to walk around camp," she said.

Mama nodded, and sat motionless as she left the barrack.

***

A nice, elderly gentleman directed him to the rec hall where most of the young teenagers liked to visit, or so he said. He'd seemed to recognize the girl's picture. It had been a long train ride and now the anticipation made him both excited and nervous.

He watched her for a while, just to be sure. There were so many things he wanted to say. He needed to help her understand. There weren't many things that scared him in this life, but meeting her now was one of them.

He noticed her face was that of a young woman's, not a little girl's. Had her hair always been that long when it was down? She'd hardly ever wore it down. She was beautiful and looked so much older when she smiled. Not the little girl he'd been forced to leave behind.

Sadness filled his heart at the realization she wouldn't ever be that young again.

Forcing the thought from his mind, he staggered forward.

The girl glanced up, and his heart nearly exploded. He gripped himself, his left leg nearly dead weight. Her eyes were undeniable.

"May I help you?" the other girl next to her asked.

"Yes," he said.

The girl's head jerked up at the sound of his voice, a look of disbelief across her face and for a moment, she stood there.

"Papa!"

Allu. His dear sweet Allu.

She pulled him into her arms, nearly knocking him over.

He stroked her hair the way he used to do, as if the past couple of years hadn't separated them.

"I thought you were gone forever." She clutched him tighter, as if he might suddenly disappear. "How did you find us?"

"A little detective work." Papa chuckled between sobs.

She stood back at arm's length to have a look at him, unable to stop laughing. He was finally home.

***

Mama's eyes welled with tears as she and Allu sat quietly on each side of Papa, listening as he told them what had happened to him on that fateful day the FBI took him away.

Crevices disrupted the smooth, strong face Allu remembered, and his hair had turned gray. Regardless, his embrace was as recognizable as the day he had left. He wrapped his arm around her and held Mama's hand. Mama glued her eyes to him, as if at any moment he could be ripped away again.

As a Japanese-speaking World War I vet, he explained, he had been an asset to the government. He'd been sent to Camp Savage in Minnesota to help interpret Japanese messages for the Military Intelligence Service. He had been responsible for many things, such as interpreting diaries of dead Japanese soldiers, along with documents and messages. He had instructed the linguists in *heigo*, terms used by the Imperial Japanese Army and Navy for weapon systems and military organization.

"The linguists are helping to win this war," Papa said, a sense of pride in his voice. "The Imperial Japanese Army doesn't encrypt their radio messages. Their troops are so isolated, many of them don't even know they are losing the war."

They listened to him speak of the men he had bunked with, who had moved on to continue their services at Fort Snelling. He spoke of snow so cold, it brought tingling to your fingers until they no longer felt a part of your body.

Someday, Allu wanted to see it.

He grew silent when they told him of Robbie, but didn't look surprised. Allu pulled out the slides Robbie had given her so many months before, along with an early letter he'd sent in hopes of Papa's return.

April 20, 1944

Hampton Roads, VA

My dearest father,

As I write this, I admire the moon's reliability. It's the same old moon I've stared at endless times in camp, indifferently unaware that everything beneath it has changed. I'm liberated. Empowered. Transformed by a uniform that represents possibility. And for the first time in my life, I feel the pull of the ocean calling my name.

As part of the 442ⁿᵈ Battalion, I'm set to ship out May 1ˢᵗ to join the 100ᵗʰ Infantry Battalion just outside of Rome. They're a tough lot, mostly comprised of the Hawaiian National Guard. They've seen their families killed and their homes destroyed by the Pearl Harbor bombing. Having the highest casualty rate, they are in need of replacements for reasons I don't care to think about. It will be a chance to test my knowledge, skill, and strength on the battlefield, and God willing, I'm ready.

The only regrets I have are those beyond my control. I regret the forces that separated our family and left me to raise a young girl when I myself still had much growing to do. I regret hurting Allu and Ma, though I did the best I could to replace you in the most loving way I knew how. And most of all, I regret that I may not live to ever see you again. A fear that only a fellow soldier could understand.

Despite these things, I am proud of what I've become, and you can be proud of the family you've raised. As you will find out, Allu has turned into a fine young woman with a strong streak of independence and a mind that will change the world. If I have failed you in any way, know that it is not in the way our family has persevered through the hostility of this war. I am forever indebted to you for the way you have raised us and the love you have given us.

I will love you always.

Yours,
Robbie

Papa shook his head slowly.

Allu wished she could offer him a comfortable bed, at the very least. He deserved better. So much better. He decided to use Robbie's, and that seemed to be good enough for him.

He was home! Things were going to be okay, and soon the war would be over and they could go back to the way things had been before.

***

The next day, Papa presented Allu with a new sketchbook. His hands shook slightly when he handed it to her, a result of nerves. What kind of pressure was he under, she wondered, but knew it was classified and thought it better not to ask.

"Open it," he said, encouraging her with his smile.

Allu carefully lifted the cover and found a sketch of a bright red bird perched on a branch.

"Northern Cardinal," he said. "You should hear them sing. And they sing during the coldest days I've ever experienced."

Allu smiled, admiring the bird. "You drew this?" she asked.

Papa laughed. "I did, with a little help from one of the fellow linguists who was an art instructor before the war."

She flipped the page.

"Clay-colored sparrow," Papa said. "These little ones typically form flocks with other types of sparrows, different from their own."

Looking through the sketchbook, it felt like nothing had changed. Papa was older, but they'd all grown older. Wars matured people more than peace and they'd all experienced lifetimes of what some never would.

"This part," Papa said, flipping to the blank pages, "is for you."

"Thank you, Papa," she said, a tear trickling down her cheek. "I'm sorry."

"About what, Allu-chan?" he asked, his face concerned.

She sniffed. "About losing hope. I didn't think you were coming back."

Papa wrapped his arm around her and leaned in, giving her a kiss on her head. "My dear Allu-chan, I carried enough hope for all of us."

Chapter Sixty-five

Vosges Mountains, Bruyeres, France

October, 1944

Exhaustion had overtaken Robbie's body, but he refused to break. Even as his eyes played tricks on him. Tree branches moved in the wind, evoking a heart-racing adrenaline, and his hand never left his gun. Two hours of sleep a night, paired with dense fog and heavy rain, was the Devil laughing in his face, and gunfire and explosives were crickets in the night. His feet ached with trench foot and cold from water-filled foxholes. It seemed like both yesterday and a lifetime ago since he had landed in Marseilles. Three months of action, and so many friends lost.

Facing Hitler's last barrier between the Allied Forces and Germany scared the hell out of all of them, though they would never lead on to it. Instead, they trudged onward, trying not to wonder how many of them would be picked off by snipers hiding in trees, or grenades falling upon them as unexpectedly as shooting stars. And yet, the 36th Infantry Division Command had made it four hundred miles North of Marseilles since May, with pressure to push quickly towards Germany. They couldn't stop now.

Robbie had started a journal of those he owed his life to, but had lost count. Many of them were no longer there to thank. Sometimes, he would list an entire unit. The 232nd Engineers he had listed three times already, as they had dismantled roadblocks and cleared trees and mine fields, facing the threat of death before the rest.

The enemy was everywhere. The enemy was the terrain. The enemy was the wind and freezing temperatures unlike anything Robbie had ever experienced. The enemy was their own self-doubts and sleepless paranoia. The black of night threatened to swallow them whole and lingered into the shortened days. They were in a race against winter.

Sometimes, Robbie could hear the Germans speaking, so close he could have touched them. They shared the same stretch of air between them, ghostly voices without faces, lit only by explosive light and haunting screams.

And God seemed just out of reach.

Chapter Sixty-six

October, 1944

The war had changed Papa in a way Allu couldn't explain. His eyes had lost that sparkle which had once held the moon and stars. The war had stolen something from him…from all of them. But Allu chose to smile and shower him with the beauty of this desert camp. His body was slower and worn with time and experience, but the warmth of his smile was the same.

Crops started springing up everywhere, and the internees were allowed more freedoms. Though the government owned much of the farming profits for what they deemed "camp upkeep," being able to work did more for these families than money ever could have. It was not uncommon to have pigs and chickens squawking about. It brought life to Papa's soul and gave the men self-worth once again.

They had created something diverse and special, a community of sorts, among the conformity society desired. And every night, Allu and her parents came together as a family to read or talk about the day. Because for the first time in years, they had things to talk about. And Robbie was there in spirit, because of the letters he wrote.

Papa approached Allu one day while they tended the garden. "I hear there might be a special young man at camp," he said.

His words surprised her. Mama must have mentioned it.

"Are you upset with me? I never meant to cause our family shame." Allu looked to her father for reassurance, and he smiled.

"Only if you give up your friendship. If that happens, you let the war win."

"I don't know how to forgive him." Allu propped herself up on her heels and set down her tool.

"You know, as a soldier, you sometimes do things you later regret."

Callie J. Trautmiller

There was pain in his voice, and she wondered what he'd gone through. What he'd seen.

"Unimaginable things that seem logical at the time. Wars feed on the souls of men and sometimes turn them into people they're not."

She shook her head, understanding. There were times she felt detached from her body. From this life. Like she had become something she wasn't, but something the war wanted her to be.

"Go talk to him, Allu. Life is too precious to hold onto hurt and anger. Pride will eat at your insides and leave room for bitterness to thrive."

She knew he was right. Somehow, Papa could always try to make sense of it all. Even if she may not ever quite understand. But how could she ever forgive Richmond?

Chapter Sixty-seven

Belmont, France

October, 1944

Robbie adjusted the weight of the BAR. The damn thing had to be at least eighteen, maybe twenty pounds, even with the stock off. But the twenty-round magazine had saved him more than once, and it made him feel a hell of a lot safer than his regular eight-round clip rifle.

The hill was crawling with Germans. He could feel it. From where he was, if he crept to the ridge, he could see the town of Bruyeres in the distance. The T-Patch men—a group made of mostly Texans, but a few from Oklahoma as well—were positioned within fifty miles of the German border. Despite what the general had said, Robbie knew something was off. The light Nazi resistance couldn't last for long. Especially after being pushed four hundred miles in just six weeks.

Robbie gave his chess piece a squeeze for good luck and tugged on the shirt of the private flanking him. The kid's shadow nodded in the dark. Sam Jones, from the Heart Mountain War Relocation Center in Wyoming. They'd been through a lifetime of pain together in the few months they'd known each other.

Sam crawled on his stomach, his breath creating pillows of white as a trail for Robbie to follow. The wetness of the frosted ground seeped through his clothes and chilled his body. They were lucky to gain a few inches within a good half hour. And then, Sam stopped.

Robbie held his breath, the beating of his heart growing louder.

And then, he heard it: whispers. *Their men or Germans?*

He waited in the darkness, and the whispering stopped. *Shit.* Had they heard them? His legs were in an awkward position, making his muscles burn, but he didn't dare move. Footsteps grew closer and closer, coming from above them. Sam was almost invisible…he could've been a fallen tree. The movement stopped and then a loud voice was speaking in German.

He nudged Sam's foot and gestured ahead.

Sam nodded.

Slowly, Robbie stood to a crouching position and pulled the pin before throwing a hand grenade.

A man yelled some kind of warning to his men in German, but it was too late. Trees exploded with fire, and men swarmed like wasps from a hive.

In the light, Robbie could see the first man was not a man at all, but a young boy. Shit, he couldn't have been much older than sixteen. The boy set his eyes on Robbie in a moment of confusion before raising his gun toward Sam.

Robbie panicked. Where the hell was his gun? He frantically felt the ground beside him as a loud shot went off.

Sam.

"Sam!" he cried out to his buddy, but the shooting made it too loud to hear. The silhouette of the Nazi boy dropped to the ground, lifeless. Sam was safe.

Another set of parents would grieve, but Sam and Robbie's would not be among them today.

***

They were resting in Biffontaine, a small French town they'd liberated from the Germans.

Allu would love it here. They all would.

There were rolling hills of green pasture and fertile, black soil. Farms spotted the French countryside, many of them lacking the familiar machinery and tractors from back home, but instead, had an abundance of large, sturdy workhorses.

"This place reminds me of Wyoming," Sam said, biting off a chunk of carrot.

Robbie still felt bad about taking it from a farm they'd come across, but even raw root vegetables were too enticing to pass up when your rations were low.

"You know," Robbie said with a chuckle, "Nazi soldiers always think we're Imperial Army. Did you see the shock on the soldiers' faces when they saw us? They thought we were Imperial and we'd turned on them!"

"Sure did." Sam took another bite of carrot. "The guys like tricking the POWs into thinking we're Imperial soldiers who've turned and joined the Americans."

Robbie shook his head. "Not entirely anyone's fault with the language barrier. Let them think what they want."

"Imagine how confused they'd be if I threw on my cowboy hat!" Sam tossed the leafy top of his carrot into the grass.

Robbie couldn't picture Sam in a cowboy hat and shook his head. "I think that'd confuse all of us!" It sure felt good to laugh again.

"You know any Japanese?" Sam asked.

Robbie thought about it for a moment. "Sakana. Gohan…"

"Really?" Sam interrupted. "Fish? Rice? I think my pops speaks more than that, and he's white." He adjusted his hat.

"And here I thought Jones was a Japanese name." Robbie smirked. "Ma speaks Japanese, but always insists we speak English. Little difference in classifying us as American, eh?"

Sam shook his head. "I'm just glad we get to fight. You know what they did with the no-no boys from the loyalty questionnaire?"

"Yeah, we had a few go to Tule Lake Camp. I heard some of them even got shipped off to Japan."

"Crazy, isn't it? I don't even know of any family in Japan."

"Me, neither," Robbie said, agreeing. "But imagine the look on their faces at the sight of a cowboy like you showing up." He thought of the picture he'd seen of Sam in his big ol' western hat and boots. "A regular Japanese American cowboy."

"Well, they ain't seen nothing yet."

Robbie laughed. "You know, when I was in Camp Shelby in Mississippi, sometimes we'd leave camp and go to town." He shook his head. "I didn't feel like I belonged anywhere. You could only sit up front on the bus if you were white. I sat in the back with everyone else, even though some drivers insisted we sit up front because we were in the army. It isn't right."

"That bad there, huh? I don't know if any of my classmates even noticed I wasn't white until the war began. Newspapers did that. Seemed like everywhere I went, someone was reading a paper. It might as well have been written about my family. We were the only Japanese Americans in town."

"Will you go back to Wyoming when the war's over?" Robbie wasn't sure where the hell he and his family would end up. They'd lost everything. They hadn't been as fortunate as some of the guys who'd had neighbors willing to store their things. The thought both enraged and saddened him.

"Sure will," Sam said thoughtfully. "Probably take over the family ranch. It's in my father's name." He glanced over, noticing the troubled look on Robbie's face. "Sorry. Sometimes I forget how lucky I am. Did you lose your land?"

"Can't lose what you never had."

"Well, I'll tell you one thing. I'm sure glad to reunite with the 100th," Sam said, changing the subject.

They'd captured the ridge above Belmont, gaining security for the crossroads at Bruyere, and drove the Germans off. It had taken five days to cross two hills and was some of the fiercest fighting Robbie had seen.

"Completely isolated and surrounded by Germans. Can you believe the 100th held Biffontaine so long? They're a tough lot."

"Sure are," Sam said thoughtfully. "But then again, so are we."

For a few minutes, they were quiet, taking in the views.

"Someday, I'd like to come back and see this place without the blood and shooting," Sam said, breaking the silence.

Robbie nodded, but not entirely sure he ever wanted to be reminded of this place again. Home never looked so good.

"I just hope someday I can get the soldiers' faces out of my head." Robbie lit a cigarette and leaned against a fence post. Their faces haunted him at night. Many of them, young teenage boys forced to fight for the Nazi Reich. There was a veil of death that had stolen the expressions right off their faces. Before the war, he'd never seen a man die, but now, hundreds of faces haunted him and woke him during the night in a sheer of sweaty panic.

The sad part was, he knew the faces would soon be joined by others.

Chapter Sixty-eight

Being called a Jap-lover didn't sting like it used to. Hell, he'd been called worse by his father. Besides, Richmond couldn't say he really had any friends at camp, anyway. He just had to bide his time until the war was over. Although he'd be lying to say he hadn't been jealous when the 442nd Infantry Regiment had been recruited from camp and he'd had to watch them leave while he stayed. Now, the most he participated in the war effort was reading the headlines when alone in the orchard, which is what he meant to do now.

"What will you do after the war?" a voice asked hesitantly, startling him.

Allu hadn't spoken to him in weeks. A pang of regret crept into his stomach.

"Probably re-enlist." He turned around to face her. "Not much to go home to, and I'm told I'm a good soldier. Not much good at anything else."

She winced. "I didn't mean that. I came to say I'm sorry."

It felt good to hear her voice. He should be the one who needed to apologize. "Allu," he began, his voice strained as he held a world of turmoil in the lines above his eyes. "If I could take back the day Johnny was shot, believe me, I would in a heartbeat."

It hurt his insides to say his name out loud.

Her face softened as she sat beside him, her eyes warm. "In the early days at camp, I dreamed of all the things I'd do when I got out: go to the ocean, track down some good authentic food." She laughed. "There's a high probability I'll never eat a hot dog again."

Richmond laughed, his shoulders dropping. "Amen to that. Food in our hall isn't much better. They should make it a personal requirement that all officers know how to cook *before* taking the position." Richmond shook his head. "So, what's it like?"

"What's *what* like?" she asked.

"The ocean. I've never seen it."

She raised her eyebrows, like she couldn't believe she had seen anything Richmond hadn't.

"Well, you know the feeling you get when you look out over the desert?" Allu paused until Richmond nodded in agreement. "There's nothing but vast sand for miles. It seems to hold all the possibilities in the world, but also brings a fear of your own limitations with it? That's how seeing the ocean feels. It's glorious and commands respect. It makes you feel small and grateful for being allowed to appreciate its waves."

Richmond understood. He'd felt the same way when looking out at the mountains, whether for the first time or the hundredth. It made him feel small and trivial in their presence. There was something unworldly about them.

"I think I'll add it to my list," he said thoughtfully. "What are your plans for *after* you visit the ocean and eat authentic food? Then what?"

Allu shrugged, her eyebrows pulling together in uncertainty. "Then, I have absolutely no idea. Quite frankly, the thought scares me."

"You know," he said, "there are plenty of art schools looking for female students."

Allu laughed, and he gave her a funny look.

What was so funny?

"You sound so much like my papa. I never could imagine that a white soldier would remind me of my father. Did I tell you he's back?" Her eyes sparkled, as though just remembering she hadn't told Richmond yet. He noticed again, almost like the first time, how beautiful she was.

He smiled. "That's great, Allu."

She caught his glance, and for just a moment, their eyes met.

He turned, suddenly feeling foolish. But not without seeing her cheeks grow pink.

Chapter Sixty-nine

"Suicide Hill," Domaniale de Champ Woods, France

October, 1944

The T-Patch men of the Lonestar Division had become the Lost Battalion. Robbie's comrades owed it to them to help find them. Being a part of the 36th Infantry Division, the battalion Robbie marched with had reached Marseilles before the rest had left Italy. They had been welcomed into France with heavy fire ashore Blue Beach. The T-Patch men had fought for security of the port, and by the time the 442nd had reached it, there hadn't been a trace of Germans left there.

The march was slow, but deliberate. The 232nd Engineer Combat Company had the pain-staking job of turning rough mountain trails into roads suitable for tanks. Hell, the men could hardly even walk on the rocky, steep trails before the engineer team got to them. The trails were winding, rising as high as a thousand feet up the mountain. This required the engineers to cut, split, and place logs over the slippery mud, all the while being shot at, like the rest of them.

The T-Patch men could be anywhere in the woods. All communications had been lost. All Robbie knew was that they'd been outflanked and surrounded by Germans, taking on fire from every side, suffering heavy casualties.

Robbie admitted he wished he didn't want the much-needed rest the general had promised them. He'd do anything for these guys, as they'd do anything for him and his comrades. He didn't need the army handbook to remind him they were family. No man would be left behind.

The woods were dark in the middle of the day. A forest of ominous pines and slippery slopes of sticky mud stuck to the bottoms of his boots and made Robbie's legs feel much heavier. But what he gained in the weight of his legs, he lost in the weight of the big equipment, now useless for scoping in the dense fog. Instead, the men carried bayonets and pistols. Killing had made casual, and death intimate. Already, random land wires had finished off a tank with a loud explosion. Most of the tanks couldn't handle the greasy hillsides and fallen trees.

All was quiet, except for the occasional thought that accidentally slipped from his comrades' lips.

"I wonder how many men strong the German line is."

"We've got to get to those men."

"I wonder when supplies are coming."

"I wonder if I'll live through this…"

The Nazis were waiting for them, lurking behind trees, in nests, in caves. They were ruthless and would stop at nothing.

And as Robbie and his comrades pushed closer to Germany, the deeper they marched into the Nazi Reich and the greater the devastation.

An uneasiness grew with each step he took, with every soldier fallen beside him. They were pushing further into the pits of Hell and he knew the devil was waiting.

Chapter Seventy

Yukio heard a snap, jerking his head to the sound, but everything was black. Lifeless. Every sound heightened by his inability to see. There was no way to know just how close the Nazis were.

He shuddered. Suicide Hill.

The woods were eerie. A thick darkness entangled them, pressing down on their shoulders with cold rain. Were the Germans encircling them now?

Find the Texans and get the hell out. It had become their mantra.

A loud shot, followed repeatedly by several other shots, echoed off the hills in the distance. Were the Germans shooting at the Texans? Yukio hoped they weren't too late.

The 442nd had been called, their promised forty-eight hour rest canceled. They needed all the men they could get. And now Yukio and the 100th Battalion were joining them in the Domaniale de Champ Forest.

A flash of light lit up the pines, followed by the thud of trees hitting the ground, their needles hissing in the heat. It was all so surreal, and for a moment, Yukio was mesmerized by the fire.

"Get down!" a voice yelled.

Yukio fell to his knees and dared not look at the limp bodies beside him, which had been so full of life just moments before.

***

"Sam!" Robbie screamed. He watched his fellow private drop to his knees as the sound of a bullet hit the tree behind him.

Everywhere, soldiers fell like flies. *Bloody flies.*

Pull yourself together. You're a soldier and a damn good one. It took him a second to release the shock that always came with the first heavy fire.

Robbie grabbed his Colt .45 and pointed it at the figure running toward him, waiting until he could see his Nazi uniform.

He pulled the trigger and didn't stop to watch him fall.

"Robbie."

He could hardly hear the voice through the ringing in his ears. "Robbie!"

Sam flanked him on the right, waving him forward and pointing uphill. Sniper nest.

Robbie nodded, grabbing a tree for support as he half-pulled, half-climbed his way up through the mud. He was surrounded by his brothers. They were everywhere, protecting him as he protected them.

The hill was crawling with soldiers from both sides. Sam was ahead of him and easy to identify, inches shorter than the rest. But Sam lost his footing, slid to his knee awkwardly, and glanced back long enough to flash Robbie a *here-goes-nothing* smile before disappearing over the ravine.

This was what they'd volunteered for. Robbie followed him, not knowing what he'd find on the other side.

***

Yukio inched forward. Sticky mud clung to his pants, enveloping him in a wet coldness. Shots fired, hitting trees all around him.

Tanks were useless against the terrain of slippery hillsides. Here it was man on man.

He lifted his head, peering through the fog. Slow, ever so slowly. He slid his right knee forward, digging it into the hill, and then his left.

More shots rang out above him. *German shots.* The nest was up there. Yukio felt his pockets for any hand grenades, knowing he'd run out.

The Germans' silhouettes were barely visible. Trees or men? He'd prided himself on his good eyesight, but never had he been more aware of it than now.

One moved. *Men.*

Their backs were to him. Four, maybe five men.

Yukio twisted to his right, taking cover beneath some thick brush.

Loud explosions filled the air. He could see brief flashes of light, but now lost his sense of sound.

He crawled on his knees, only stopping between shots, during pauses of silence. *Had it been hours or minutes?*

222

Time melted into oblivion, measured only by distance. Inches until ten yards.

Something rustled to his lower left.

He jerked his head to find a young 442nd Nisei soldier. Couldn't have been more than nineteen, maybe twenty years old, but it was hard to tell with the mud and blood on his face.

He glanced quickly to the Nazis on the hill.

Someone yelled something in German, and the silhouettes moved, enough for Yukio to see they'd turned toward the Nisei soldier.

Without thinking, he jumped from the safety of his position.

Chapter Seventy-one

Someone shoved Robbie, jarring him backward down the slope of the hill.

His gun. Where was his gun?

He grabbed an outstretched tree limb and pulled himself up, planting his foot into the hill. His face was dripping. Rain? He wiped his forehead.

No, blood.

He patted his chest but didn't find any wounds. A soldier lay lifeless beside him. The blood belonged to that man. A hundredth, by his uniform. He'd saved Robbie's life.

He moved quickly to the soldier under a rain of bullets. The man's chest moved slowly, his breathing labored. *What do you say to a man who's dying?* A man who'd saved his life? Robbie thought for a moment and did what felt right.

He knew this man. Damn it, he knew him. A sickening feeling gripped him, and he thought he might faint.

"Yukio, damn it," he tried fighting the tears so as not to discourage Yukio. "Why, Yukio? Why?"

Yukio blinked, then smiled as recognition dawned in his eyes. "You owe me one," he said weakly.

A shot fired nearby but didn't seem as important as this moment.

The man sucked in a deep breath. It was his last.

A shriek sounded from Robbie's right. *Sam. Where the hell was Sam?*

"Thank you, brother," Robbie whispered through his tears. "Thank you." He gently closed the lids of Yukio Takahashi, the bravest soldier he'd ever known, who had died saving him.

A shrouded figure lay in the underbrush just off the trail. The shrieking was coming from him.

Sam!

Robbie crawled frantically to Sam's body as he lay rocking back and forth in shock.

224

"Where are you hit?" Robbie cried, turning Sam over. "Sam!" He shook him.

"My arm," Sam moaned, rocking.

Robbie turned him to the side. His uniform was wet with dark blood as his arm hung limply from his shoulder.

"It's okay, it's okay. We'll fix you up. You'll be okay."

"No," he said meekly. "We have to save them, Robbie." He sat up, bracing the weight of his body on his good arm. "The Lost Battalion. We have to save them."

He'd lose his arm. He needed a medic.

Sam propped himself up and grabbed the gun with his left hand. "Cowboys can shoot with either," he said, wincing.

They were pinned down. Everywhere around him, men wailed out, covered in blood as medics frantically crawled to get to them, risking their own lives to pull them to safety with the little bit of supplies they had left.

"Let's do this," Sam said confidently.

There wasn't any other choice. Robbie drew in a deep breath and nodded.

They climbed the hill toward the machine gun nest as heavy fire rained down. If they wanted a good fight, they'd picked the right guys. Robbie and Sam would make them pay for what they'd done.

They paused when they reached a thick trunk of pine, catching their breath. Sam's face was pale, and Robbie wondered how much blood he'd lost.

"Promise me," he said to Sam, wanting to take his mind off his dangling arm, "you'll teach me to ride horses when the war is over."

Sam chuckled, wincing with pain. "Promise."

And in that moment, he saw Jimmy in him. He saw all the guys.

Robbie patted his pocket, feeling the familiarity of the chess piece. He felt better knowing he had a piece of home with him, even in this mess of a place. He couldn't wait to share his stories with Allu. To tell her about the glimpses of beauty he saw in the countryside by day. The architecture of the cathedrals. How much she'd love to sketch the many houses among the hillsides. Sometimes, during quiet moments, he could almost imagine their charm before they had been reduced to shambles.

Someday, he hoped, she'd make it here. After they won the war and things returned to a new kind of normal. When the buildings were rebuilt and the grasses had regrown. When flowers speckled across the ravines and the evil was cleared from the beauty of the landscape. Hell, maybe he and Sam would be one of the lucky few to make it back and join her. He smiled at the thought.

Sam looked over at him. "Ready for this?"

Robbie thought of Jimmy and Yukio, and nodded. "Let's go find those Texans."

They snuck out from the tree and charged the nest, Robbie knowing they might not make it to the other side of the mountain.

Chapter Seventy-two

November, 1944

A llu cursed at the pink mess of yarn in her lap.

Mama had insisted that at fifteen, she become a proper lady and learn to knit. Allu had reminded her there were some women fighting on the battlefield and that knitting wouldn't save the world. But it was important to Mama, and she acted as if their very family heritage depended upon Allu's ability to learn to sew, knit, and prepare Japanese dishes from years past.

It was a tall order and a lot of pressure, but when Ma's mind was made up, there was no arguing with her. She was determined to make a lady out of Allu and fix Robbie up with a nice Japanese American girl after the war ended. They had secret plans for Kiko to fill this ambition. There was, after all, a good eight-year difference between Mama and Papa.

A tapping on the door startled Allu. She and Kiko had plans to visit the gardens so she could finish her book of portraits before the incoming summer sun became too hot. Relieved, she tossed the ball of knots to the floor.

Two soldiers in uniform stood in the doorway, their hats in their hands as they asked if Papa was there. One shuffled uncomfortably, a bead of sweat trickling down his face.

Allu's breath hitched, and she wondered if she could ever get used to talking to soldiers in uniform. Well, besides Richmond, that was. How silly. She felt like the little girl from the farm, that day they came to take her father away. Were they taking him in for questioning? Could they do that? He'd paid his price. He'd done his job. Did they know how old he was? He wasn't the young farmer they had taken three years ago…he'd aged decades since then. His cane was proof of that.

"You can't take him," Allu cried.

The two men exchanged glances. "We're here on behalf of the United States Army."

"No! No! No!"

Allu jerked around as Mama's knees hit the floor. When she looked at the officers, their faces told a thousand stories, and for the first time, Allu realized she was being regarded with respect. Officers had never taken their hats off for them.

And then, it hit her.

Time stopped, and she noticed every detail, from the silver buttons on the soldier's shirt to the feeling of splintered wood beneath her feet. Nerves jumped chaotically from under her skin, and she felt as if she were suffocating.

She turned to Papa, who would know what to do, but his face was torn between comforting Mama and greeting the soldiers.

Eventually, he hobbled over to the doorway, his cane tapping irregularly against the wood floorboards.

"I'm sorry, sir..." the soldier began.

Allu didn't want to stay to listen to anything else the man had to say. Her heart caught in her throat and she knew she'd never see her brother again.

Chapter Seventy-three

Oahu, Hawaii

*G*iri. *Meiyo. Gisei.* Duty. Honor. Sacrifice.

The words sang out through Yukio's letters. His grandson, who had brought so much honor to his family, and so much joy to their lives, was gone. The old man held the bundle of letters with shaking hands.

Go For Broke; Remember Pearl Harbor.

"We'll never forget, Yukio-Chan. We'll never forget."

***

On the other side of the island, Leinani clutched the wedding dress she'd never wear. The war had stolen the future she'd imagined from her. The happily-ever-after, with her visions of a life with the man she fell in love with so many years before on that sunny day in the college courtyard. Visions of a joint life filled with making memories with the kids they'd raise on the island. With Yukio, who was so patient and kind. So good with kids.

All of it was gone now.

The war was over and many celebrated. But among those celebrating, there were many who mourned. She couldn't stop the tears that streamed down her face.

Chapter Seventy-four

Kiko sobbed, which made Allu cry even more. Her brother was gone. It couldn't be true. She couldn't imagine her life without seeing his smile. His teasing barbs. How many years were ahead of her without seeing him? Forty? Seventy?

The thought was unbearable.

Kiko held her and together they grieved, tears dripping onto Robbie's last journal entry.

Cold dark nights and thick fog force us to hold onto the soldier's shirt in front of us. Trees explode, splintering into the forest but snow continues to fall. Fir trees block rainfalls of shells but hide snipers. The forest floors of these valleys are carpeted with dense underbrush, and every bush must be carefully investigated before we are allowed to pass.

We become more hesitant with each step deeper into enemy territory, and there are times I can't bring myself to leave my foxhole. These are the times I think of myself as a kid. Think of the tree forts I used to build. And for a moment, I close my eyes and pretend I'm naïve again.

And a blink later, I'm in senior high, during a time when my batting average and hair was all I worried about. Then, I think of Jimmy and the times we used to have, and I wonder where he is out here. I don't feel so alone knowing there's someone else from Santa Ana so far away from home, just like me. It gives me the strength to push out into the showers of shrapnel that rains upon us.

Driving forward, we fire from the hip as we launch grenades.

Despite not wanting to, Allu had listened as the soldiers explained about how Robbie had gone missing somewhere in the mountains of

France. The last recount of him was of Robbie pulling a fellow soldier from enemy fire. That was just like Robbie, always protective, typically the last one to move on, making sure everyone else was accounted for first. He wouldn't leave until a job was done. He had probably had a smirk on his face until the end, cracking some joke to lighten the mood with the wounded.

The soldiers had presented their family with a wooden box with Robbie's personal belongings from their camp: a king chess piece, a journal, and a letter dated December 15, 1941 from the University of California, Berkeley, offering a partial scholarship to play baseball for the Golden Bears.

All this time, and no one had ever known just how much he'd given up when Pearl Harbor was bombed that day. And yet, he had never complained. He'd kept a smile on his face.

Papa had stared at the letter for some time, and then broke down, shaking his head. "Sure could play ball, couldn't he?" He smiled at some distant memory. "Nothing like it."

They framed the letter by the door, a tribute to a life of potential gone without apology.

That was the last day Allu checked the mail. There was nothing left to wait for anymore.

They received one more letter before the camp closed. It came weeks after Robbie's death. Allu tucked it in her box of her most treasured things, shedding more tears as she did so. She couldn't bear to read it, not now. Not yet.

Chapter Seventy-five

September, 1945

With the war at an end, and the camp near closing, it was time for Allu to say good-bye to Kiko. She had made joy possible during the several years at camp. Without knowing where they were going to live, it was impossible to keep track of each other, but they both knew if it was meant to be, they would someday meet up again.

Allu had heard of the stories told by newspapers of soldiers who witnessed horrors beyond imagination when entering concentration camps found in Germany. The people were walking skeletons, more dead than alive: women, children, and elderly men, tortured and starved, left to die. It was the 522nd Field Artillery Battalion, part of the 442,nd who had shot the locks off the gates and had liberated captives in one of the worst camps, Dachau, though the newspapers didn't mention that very often. Nisei soldiers also knew captivity. It seemed the world had suffered at the hands of the devil.

Papa had discovered that Robbie's friend, Jimmy, had died his first year out as a soldier in France somewhere. As had the banker's son. And it was then her family understood that war was bigger than proving themselves. Bigger than baseball competitions and the separations of wealth. Pain was universal and gave them all a commonality.

But so was healing, love, and forgiveness.

Many families stayed at camp as long as possible. Some had become too old to travel, while others were fearful of the unknown after being encamped for the past four years. Papa decided to move the family out of California and into the Midwest, at the invitation of a fellow farmer from Fort Snelling who had land he intended to rent out.

Allu imagined what snow must be like. A fresh start in a new place.

As Mama and Papa packed up the remnants of their life, Allu went in search of Richmond to say good-bye. She found him staring at the mountains.

"So." She sat on the bench beside him. "This is it."

He smiled, meeting her eyes for a moment before looking away. "This is it."

"When do you go home?" she asked.

"We're sticking around for a while, you know, to clean things up. As much as possible."

"Good luck." She smirked.

"Here," he said, digging out a piece of paper from his pocket. "Here's my address. I'll be heading home at some point, just after I check out the ocean." He frowned slightly, before returning his focus to the horizon.

She hoped the ocean spoke to his heart louder than the mountains, and maybe in time, it could even help him forgive himself.

"I hear there are some great art schools in the Midwest," she mentioned casually. "I may even check them out."

"Well, don't get so focused on boys that you forget to write an old friend." Richmond gently elbowed her side and grinned.

"I think I'll just focus on my artwork."

If only he knew what he meant to her. Maybe someday he would.

Chapter Seventy-six

November, 1945

Richmond couldn't pull his eyes from the window. From the beauty of the kudzu, even as it invaded the tall trees, creating curtain-like filters for the occasional streak of sunlight. It was supposed to be the human "fix" to the Dust Bowl, but at a growth rate of a foot a day, like most things humans tried to control, it had a natural mind of its own and was now eating up the forests in the south.

Just around the corner and up the road a few miles, was his hometown. The bus was quiet, despite the entourage of families and well-wishers who waited to greet them home from their war duties.

He was nervous. Nervous to be home. Nervous to see how the war had changed the people he knew. Nervous to see who hadn't come home and never would. Even as the bus drove this familiar stretch of road, it felt unfamiliar in a way he couldn't explain.

The bus rounded the corner. The sides of the road were crowded with several hundred faces, peering their way. When they saw the bus, the crowd held signs and cheered. Women pulled handkerchiefs to their faces, patting at their eyes. Grown men broke down. Richmond doubted his father was among them.

He drew in a deep breath as the bus screeched to a halt. He waited patiently and watched the other soldiers as they stepped off and were lost in the swarm of the crowd. His stomach tightened.

Richmond slung his bag over his shoulder and sucked in another deep breath before exhaling.

"This is it, son," the bus driver said to him. "You're home."

He stepped into the crowd and put on a smile.

"Richmond?"

He thought he heard his name. Looking around, he couldn't tell where it was coming from.

"Richmond!"

It was his mother's voice.

"Mom!" He frantically looked around until he spotted her a few feet away, waving her arm in the air, a bright red handkerchief in her hand.

"Mom!" He made his way to her, sliding between several groups of people, many of them embracing.

When he reached his mother, he pulled her up into his arms and swung her around as she cried. He set her down and regarded her, beautiful as ever, even with the fine lines etched around her face. She wore minimal makeup but had on red lipstick for what he reasoned she thought was a special occasion. And special occasion it was.

"You're home," she cried. "You're finally home."

Just then, he noticed his father as he stood a slight distance away. He stood straight and tall, but his shoulders didn't seem as broad as Richmond remembered. He stepped forward and for a moment, Richmond thought his eyes gleamed.

"Son," he said, tipping his hat.

They regarded each other, unsure of what to do next, where they stood with each other. They hadn't separated on good terms. Although, Richmond couldn't remember a time they had ever been on good terms.

And then, without warning, his father pulled him into an embrace.

Richmond had never been this close to his father before. He smelled different. What was it about him that had changed? The war changed people, yes, but something else. His father had seen war before.

His mother looked at his father, and her eyes held something he'd never seen in them before—pride. And love, too.

"Three years," his father acknowledged. "Three years sober."

He could hardly believe it. It must be a joke. But Richmond knew better. His father didn't joke.

And then, for the first time since the war had started, Richmond cried like a baby.

There was power in war, but people often underestimated the power in decision.

Chapter Seventy-seven

1992

Forty-seven years later.

Allu stood at the podium and took in everything: the smell of the freshly-blossomed apple trees with their sweet scent and promise of ripe fruit, a scent that will forever remind her of the place. The blueness of the expansive sky and the prominent mountains, timeless and unchanging. The dryness of the dust as particles floated in the wind, leaving its remnants on her clothes and in her hair.

Manzanar looked different after the ugly buildings had been reduced to mere memory, but yet, there was a sameness to it as well, as if it could have been yesterday that she had stood here as a teenager. Maybe it was due to the familiarity of several of the people in the crowd that had been here so many years ago in internment, now there to dedicate this memorial.

She scanned the faces. Some were weary, some had tears. But all ready. Ready to listen. Ready to hear her story. *Robbie's story. Jimmy's story.* A story intertwined with or reminiscent of their own, maybe. She took a deep breath.

"It was my teacher, Miss Rose, who turned my father in on account of aiding the enemy," she began, her voice clear. "She told officials she'd seen him speaking with Japanese men in uniform while fishing, and it was enough suspicion for her to assume he was working with the enemy. The men in uniform were crew-captains on a freight boat who'd simply asked my father how fishing was going."

Allu continued, "You see, hatred is a hungry animal fed with the souls of the men who serve it. Men who feed it fear. War takes from everyone, refusing to limit itself to one's skin color or social status or financial position. It is all-encompassing, and moves about the world like the wind, touching down where it wants. It takes more from some than others, but takes some from everyone.

"Pain is universal. But so is love. And forgiveness. And kindness."

She took a deep breath as she clutched the king Chess piece and pulled out the last letter she'd received from Robbie after learning of his death. Putting on her glasses, she began to read aloud.

Dearest family,

We have served America proud, as we have liberated not only several French and Italian towns, but the Lost Battalion as well. We have proven ourselves as soldiers worthy of our uniform. I welcome our orders to attend the Maritime Alps and the French Riviera, where I'm told, merry times and rest await.

It is almost as if a man's brain shuts off during times of heightened threat, leaving his heart and instincts to take over. But as the brutal fighting sleeps, I have time to write and think about the things we have encountered. And I am grateful to have a reason to fight.

When I come home, we'll all go out and watch a game and try to make some semblance of the way things used to be. And tell Allu, I look forward to beating her in chess.

Yours always,
Robbie

Pausing, Allu wiped her nose with a kerchief. A silent wind whispered through the desert, reminding her of so many nights years ago. She folded the letter carefully and placed it next to a Congressional Medal of Honor and a Purple Heart, which Robbie would never see.

"The 442nd Regimental combat team, consisting of the 100th Battalion, were the most decorated American Unit in World War II. But at great price, as they also carried the highest percentage of casualties and deaths. My brother was among some of your brothers and fathers, uncles and friends.

"And now I stand before you today, in a place of special meaning. A place that represents a silent culture exemplified by resilience, love, and forgiveness. Today, we dedicate this memorial not only to those who survived the war, but to those who managed to pick up the pieces, fearless of the unknown and unashamed to be different. I am here to remind you to be careful which opinions you give power to. I'll leave you with these final words spoken by President Truman: '*You fought not only the enemy, but you fought prejudice…and you won.'"*

Applause filled the silence of the desert as Allu searched the crowd. Her eyes fell upon the familiar face of one of her family's closest friends: Sam Jones. She owed part of herself to him and would be eternally grateful for the kindness he had showed her family after the war, when things fell through with moving to the Midwest. He treated Papa as his own father, and together, they had healed on that ranch of his. Papa worked the crops, and the Jones family had given them a place to call home when they hadn't known where home was or what it had looked like other than with each other. Sam told of Robbie's courage and humor. About Sam's promise to teach him to ride horse. They all laughed at the thought of Robbie riding. Unless there were female spectators, it wouldn't have been his thing.

Sam smiled at her and nodded with the pride of a hero, his cowboy hat resting in his lap.

Then, Allu found the eyes of her old friend, Richmond, who had been the first to be seated in the front row. Time had allowed him the forgiveness he'd needed to find in himself. And though time had left its traces upon his face, his eyes were the same clear blue of yesterday. Eyes now reflected in those of their grandchild, who sat upon his lap. A child who someday would refuse their history be buried in the pages of a forgotten textbook. She'd found a love with Richmond akin to her parents' love for one another.

A woman walked over to Allu as she descended the steps from the stage, her body slower and stiffer with age. The woman didn't have to say a word, her sentiment was in the warmth of her brown eyes as she regarded Allu and embraced her.

"Kiko, you came," Allu said.

"Nothing could've prevented me from being here." Kiko offered her smile.

Allu laughed. "I believe it."

Her persistence had been one of the things that Allu had learned to love. Kiko had saved her all those years ago. They all had. They'd offered her love and acceptance and above all, hope.

And they'd won. Robbie would've been proud.

Author's Note

PEARL HARBOR ATTACK & EXECUTIVE ORDER 9066

When Japanese planes attacked Pearl Harbor December 7, 1941, it set much of the world at war. In Oahu, a November war alert had just been lifted, making the early-morning attack that much more of a surprise. Japanese planes first attacked the airfields, where most aircrafts were parked wing-tip to wing-tip. Next, Japanese bomber planes moved on to Pearl Harbor, where twenty-one vessels were sunk or damaged. All but one were in port that morning. By the time the second wave of Japanese planes attacked, Americans downed twenty enemy aircraft and sunk a midget submarine.

Of the twenty-one U.S. vessels sunk or damaged, all but three were repaired, and rejoined the fleet. The *U.S.S. Utah, Oklahoma* and *Arizona* would be the final resting place for many of their crewmen. The *U.S.S. West Virginia*, which sank upright after being hit by nine torpedoes, was repaired and sailed to Tokyo Bay in 1945 to witness Japan's surrender. Over 3,500 people were dead or wounded in the Pearl Harbor attack and the effects can be seen to this day as fuel continues to seep from the wreckage.

President Franklin D. Roosevelt declared war on Japan the day following the attack and the United States joined in fighting against both the Japanese Imperial Army and the Nazi Regime. Fear rose to a heightened level, most notably in California where many held the sentiment that Japanese immigrants were taking over their jobs in the agricultural sector and were now aiding the enemy.

Executive Order 9066 was signed February 1942, authorizing the establishment of military zones on the west coast and the relocation of 110,000 men, women, and children of Japanese ancestry. With only a week's notice, most of these families were forced to sell their belongings at a drastic loss, allowing for only what they could carry, and were divided into ten relocation centers/internment camps primarily in deserted areas such as swampland, deserts, or abandoned fairgrounds and racetracks. Two-thirds of these internees were American citizens by birth and most had never been to Japan.

Though most Japanese Americans were not allowed to initially fight in the war, the National Guard Hawaiian Nisei (those born in the U.S. whose parents were Japanese immigrants) already in the U.S. Army were allowed to continue their services, forming the 100th Battalion. Not knowing where to place them, they became the most trained unit in the military until finally being deployed to fight against the Nazi Regime. Their loyalty and courage was undeniable, and they were a successful unit. Based on their efforts, the military asked for Nisei volunteers from internment camps in the formation of the 442nd Regimental Combat, which would join the 100th Battalion.

The 442nd Regimental Combat Team became the most decorated unit in the history of the United States Military, with at least twenty-one Medals of Honor, 560 Silver Stars, 4,000 Bronze Medals and 9,486 Purple Hearts. The 100th Battalion has the nickname "The Purple Heart Battalion."

The government recognized the success of their war efforts. President Truman commended the 442nd Regiment, which included the 100th, with a Presidential Citation saying,

"It is a very great pleasure to me today to be able to put the seventh regimental citation on your banners... You are now on your way home. You fought not only the enemy, but you fought prejudice-and you have won. Keep up that fight, and we will continue to win-to make this great Republic stand for just what the Constitution says it stands for: the welfare of all the people all the time."

In 1988, President Reagan and the Senate awarded internees with a $20,000 per person apology and the Manzanar National Historic Site opened on March 3, 1992.

Acknowledgements

This novel couldn't have been what it is without the encouragement from several friends and family. There are too many to thank here! Special thanks to my very first editors: Jada, Jaelyn and Sterling for your honesty and enthusiasm! Thank you to my husband Freddy for always inspiring me to go after my goals, regardless of how daunting they may seem.

To my parents and brother for cheerleading this project and to my Uncle Gary ("Woody") Widgren, for gifting me with a scrapbook of World War II articles of deployment and unfortunately, obituaries, from several local men who served, allowing me to gain insight into their stories and also, Kent Smith for lending me original World War II newspapers for my reference.

To my new friends whom offered their expertise and personal stories in the research of this novel: Franci & Zeke Jeche, your story is an inspiration and your knowledge was invaluable and to my aunt Judy Anderson for enthusiastically connecting me with them; Jayne Hirata, Lloyd Kitoaka and the 100th Battalion Veteran's Club in Honolulu for your hospitality, you have been such a great resource in the telling of this story; Juanita Allen, Claire Mitani and the 442nd Veteran's Club/ Sons & Daughters of the 442nd for sharing your clubhouse memorabilia and information. To Allyson Nakamoto, Betsy Young, Jane Kurahara & Ken Yoshida of the Japanese Cultural Center of Hawaii for your dedication to beautifully preserving the memory of the World War II Nisei experience and your willingness to share your knowledge with me. Mahalo for your support!

Thank you to A.L. Mundt for your meticulous developmental editing. You pushed me to make this novel so much better. Thank you to Katy Brunette and Sunny Fassbender, for your creativity on the wonderful layout and design. You made my novel come alive. Also,

I am grateful to Brittiany Koren who far exceeds the role of editor and publisher! I can never thank you enough for blessing me with the opportunity to launch this project... I prayed for an editor who would be as passionate about this manuscript as I am, and I hit the jackpot with you! Also, thank you to Packerland Websites for all of your creative and technical support.

And thank you to all my readers. I hope you enjoyed reading this novel as much as I enjoyed writing it. If you'd like to leave a review on the site where you purchased the book, I'd appreciate it so much.

Above all, praise to God who makes *ALL* things possible. Even writing a novel.

About the Author

Callie J. Trautmiller resides in Wisconsin with her husband, their three children, and their dog. Both of her grandfathers served in World War II and inspired her research and writing for *Becoming American,* her first novel. Find Callie on social media at: Callie J. Trautmiller or at her website: CallieTrautmiller.com.

CPSIA information can be obtained
at www.ICGtesting.com
Printed in the USA
BVHW030037050322
630726BV00002B/121